GOOD
PEOPLE

ALSO BY MARCUS SAKEY

The Blade Itself
At the City's Edge

GOOD

MARCUS
SAKEY

PEOPLE

A NOVEL

DUTTON

DUTTON
Published by Penguin Group (USA) Inc.
375 Hudson Street, New York, New York 10014, U.S.A.
Penguin Group (Canada), 90 Eglinton Avenue East, Suite 700, Toronto, Ontario M4P 2Y3, Canada
(a division of Pearson Penguin Canada Inc.); Penguin Books Ltd, 80 Strand, London WC2R 0RL,
England; Penguin Ireland, 25 St Stephen's Green, Dublin 2, Ireland (a division of Penguin Books Ltd);
Penguin Group (Australia), 250 Camberwell Road, Camberwell, Victoria 3124, Australia (a division
of Pearson Australia Group Pty Ltd); Penguin Books India Pvt Ltd, 11 Community Centre, Panchsheel
Park, New Delhi – 110 017, India; Penguin Group (NZ), 67 Apollo Drive, Rosedale, North Shore
0632, New Zealand (a division of Pearson New Zealand Ltd); Penguin Books (South Africa) (Pty) Ltd,
24 Sturdee Avenue, Rosebank, Johannesburg 2196, South Africa

Penguin Books Ltd, Registered Offices: 80 Strand, London WC2R 0RL, England

Published by Dutton, a member of Penguin Group (USA) Inc.

First printing, September 2008
10 9 8 7 6 5 4 3 2 1

 REGISTERED TRADEMARK—MARCA REGISTRADA

LIBRARY OF CONGRESS CATALOGING-IN-PUBLICATION DATA

Sakey, Marcus.
    Good people: a novel / by Marcus Sakey.
        p. cm.
    ISBN 978-0-525-95084-4
    I. Title.
    PS3619.A4G66   2008
813'.6—dc22   2008007701

Printed in the United States of America
Set in Sabon
Designed by Leonard Telesca

For g.g., who has the best laugh on the planet

GOOD
PEOPLE

APRIL 24,

2006

THE SMILE WAS FAMOUS. Jack Witkowski wasn't particularly a fan, but he'd seen those teeth plenty of times. They shone in the huddle of supermarket checkout lines, gleamed on the cover of a hundred magazines. After a while it was natural to think of the smile as separate from the man, and watching him stop on the club steps to throw it at a gawking chick with a camera phone only reinforced the idea. One minute the guy was just a guy—good-looking and well dressed, sure, but just a guy, and even a little on the short side—then that spotlight smile hit, raw wattage that announced you were in the presence of a Star.

Jack gazed through the windshield, forefinger tapping absently against his shoulder-slung .45. Nines might be the gun du jour, but you couldn't beat a .45 for stopping power. "One more time."

Bobby said, "Marshall lets us in. We take the service steps up. Put on the masks. Be careful not to use names. Will and Marshall tie them. I get the money. We go back out the way we came, head for the Chrysler. If anything goes wrong, we split, meet up later." His knuckles were white on the steering wheel.

Jack squinted at that, wondered again if involving his younger brother had been a good idea. "That's right," he said, keeping his voice casual. "Remember, go in hard. These are spoiled kids. Get your pistol right in their face, yell at them. Anybody gives shit, crack them with the gun, and don't hold back. It'll just make everybody else step quicker. In and out in five."

Bobby nodded. "What about that one?" The man he gestured to was taller than the Star and his entourage, built thick through the shoulders and neck. He carried a black briefcase in his left hand and kept his right open against his stomach, fingers just inside the jacket.

"That's the bodyguard," Will Tuttle said from the back, his tone smooth as a jazz radio announcer. He'd once said he'd done some voice-over work back when he was in L.A., that he'd been the voice of a dancing soap bubble in a commercial for toilet cleanser. Easy work; two grand for a morning spent repeating *We scrub so you don't have to*. "Don't worry your pretty head, son. Let the real bad guys handle him."

"Fuck you."

Will chuckled. "What's the matter," he said, drawing Carltons from his suit jacket and tapping the soft pack to pop a cigarette loose. "I hurt your wittle feelings?"

"Enough." Jack stared in the rearview mirror. "Don't light that thing."

Will tucked the cigarette behind his ear. "Victory smoke."

Across the street, one of his entourage patted the Star on the shoulder, hooked a thumb in a *let's go* gesture. The Star nodded, threw one last smile-and-wave, then stepped through the doors. His friends followed, one of them pausing long enough to pluck a stunning brunette from the line, the girl grinning over her shoulder at her squealing friends. Movie people. Shit. The bodyguard went last, stopping at the top of the steps to scan the street. Jack stared back, just another Chicago yokel awed by American Royalty. After a moment, the man went inside, the door swinging shut to muffle thumping beats.

"Go ahead," Jack said, and Bobby put the stolen Ford into drive, sliding past the line of boys in shiny shirts and girls with spray-tan shoulders. They fell in behind a taxi to the end of the block, turned right, then left, and pulled into an unattended pay lot they'd scoped earlier. Bobby twisted the key to kill the engine, but cranked it the wrong way at first, the engine grinding.

"Jesus Christ," Will said. "What're you, fourteen?"

"I said *enough*." Jack pulled up the sleeve of his suit, glanced at his watch. They sat in silence, listening to the ticking of the engine, the sound of revelry through the windows. River North, clubland, lah-dee-fucking-dah.

"He look short to you?" Bobby not needing to say the name.

"They all are," Will said. "Tom Cruise is five-seven. Al Pacino, too."

"Pacino? Bullshit."

"Emilio Estevez. Robert Downey Jr."

"I like that guy," Bobby said. "He's a great actor."

"Don't change his height."

Jack let them talk, taking steady breaths, waiting for the rush to hit.

"Funny," Bobby said, "it's like the pope is visiting. All week I been hearing where he was spotted. Saw an article in the *Red Eye* on his favorite restaurants. He's just here to work, right? Film a movie. But where he eats is news. Kind've feel sorry for him."

"Yeah," Will said, "poor famous millionaire, neck-deep in pussy makes the skanks you date look like schnauzers."

"Will," Jack said, "go stand on the corner, scope for cops, would you?"

"What the hell? Why?"

"Because I said so."

Will sighed. "Whatever." He popped the door, the street noise suddenly louder. "Amateur," he muttered as he got out.

"Screw you." Bobby said it quietly.

They sat, Jack letting the tension dissipate. He cracked gloved knuckles. After a minute, he said, "You okay?"

Bobby looked over, face pale and eyes all pupil. "I can't do this."

"Sure you can. Easiest thing in the world."

"Jack—"

"You can." He smiled. "Look, I know where you are. First time I stuck somebody up, I had the shakes like you wouldn't believe. Almost dropped my gun."

"Serious? You?"

"Sure. Part of the job. Why do you think Will's being such a dick? Everybody gets the shakes."

"Marshall too?"

Jack shrugged. "I don't know." He smiled, reached out to put a hand on his brother's shoulder. "This is heavier than what you're used to, I get that. But try and concentrate on the score. In fifteen minutes, you'll be a whole lot richer."

"But—"

"If I thought we could do this with three, I would. I need you, bro."

Bobby nodded, took a deep breath, let it out slow. He rolled his head side to side, then said, "Okay."

Jack felt that old flush of warmth. "It'll be fun. You'll see. The Brothers Witkowski, rolling hard. Just follow my lead, it'll be over before you know it." He punched Bobby's bicep. "Besides, you're a bad man."

"Right," Bobby said. He took another breath, then drew a chrome-over-black Smith and racked it. "I'm a bad, bad man."

They got out of the car, leaving the keys in the ignition. The evening air was alive with the noise of a dozen clubs, the honk of taxis, and the laughter of girls. Rich cocoa tickled Jack's nose from the Blommer Chocolate Company a mile away.

"You ladies ready?" Will rocked his weight from one foot to another.

"Let's roll."

They started east, pace easy. Just businessmen, conventioneers maybe, on a weekend away from the wife. Out to check the scene, have a couple of cocktails, try to bang girls their daughters' age before catching a morning flight back to boredom. Jack put himself between the other two, kept his eyes alert. They jaywalked across Erie, then cut down the alley. Broken glass crunched under Jack's heels.

As they fell into shadow, he drew his pistol and unsnapped the safety.

*   *   *

INSIDE THE CLUB, Marshall Richards waited till the bartendress in the belly shirt looked away. Then he took the thick-bottomed rocks glass and poured the whiskey on the floor. He smacked the glass down with a wince just as she turned back. She shouted, "Another?"

"Sure." He put an elbow on the edge, then made a show of slipping and catching himself. Marshall smiled at her, mouthed *Oops* over the pounding music. She shook her head as she refilled him, raising her arm to stretch a rope of amber between bottle and glass, a neat trick. Then she snagged a twenty from the stack of cash he'd laid out and turned away.

He took the drink and spun on his stool, careful to keep his shoes off the ground. He'd poured about nine whiskeys there, and the puddle was growing sizable. The drunk act probably didn't matter, but life had a wicked arm for curves. A smart hitter respected the plate.

The VIP lounge sat off the main floor, guarded by a bouncer with a shaved head. Gauzy green curtains puffed and swelled with the motion of air, like the room was breathing. Beyond them a mob of moneyed twenty-somethings danced beneath a frenzy of lasers, visible only as writhing silhouettes. It reminded Marshall of something out of a Bosch painting, a vision of a sweating hell. It was early yet, not even midnight, and the lounge had only a handful of Very Important People: a group nursing the bottle of thirty-dollar vodka they'd dropped two hundred on; a sugar daddy playing garter games with his stripper girlfriend; two lipstick lesbians comped in to add a whiff of the forbidden; and, at the end of the bar, two black guys. His marks.

The boss was dark-skinned and stylish, with a precise mustache, a gold Rolex dangling from French cuffs, and a tailored Armani suit. The other, straining against a Sean John tracksuit, was clearly muscle. Armani drank seltzer. The other didn't drink at all. Marshall smiled to himself, then spilled his whiskey and ordered another.

The bartendress had just finished pouring it when Boss Man's cell phone beeped. Marshall cradled his chin in his hands and stared forward, pretending to be lost in a liquor dream. From the corner of his eye, he saw the guy open the phone and scan the screen. His fingers punched keys quickly, replying to the text message. Then he dropped a fifty on the bar and slid off the stool. His bodyguard fell in behind him.

Marshall counted to thirty, then collected his change, folded it, and tucked it in his pocket. Took his whiskey in one hand and staggered for the stairs. The bouncer yawned, looked away.

The dance floor vibrated, the bass line throbbing through his belly, a remix of Fergie singing about being so delicious, how she was so tasty tasty laced with lacy. Bodies mobbed the space, smelling of cologne and desire. He looked at the open staircase over the floor, thick-cut glass that glowed with the sheen of lasers. Boss Man and his bodyguard were halfway up. Perfect.

Shielding the drink with his body, Marshall cut to the back wall. It was painted black, and couples huddled there, the women flush with power, men leaning into them, trying to close the deal. He moved beside a door marked "Private" in white letters. Turned, did an easy scan. No one paid him any mind as he pushed through the door.

The hallway on the other side was drab and overlit. He walked past an open door where men spoke Spanish, turning his face away and walking with purpose. Not like a couple of illegals were going to challenge a man who walked like he belonged. There was a corner at the end of the hallway, and beside it the servers' steps to the private rooms. He stopped long enough to throw the whiskey down, that sweet burn. He liked one before a job. Then he palmed the glass and turned the corner.

The bouncer sat on a stool, beefy arms crossed. He came off his perch when he spotted Marshall. "This ain't the bathrooms, mate."

Marshall took a step, then another, slower. He raised his left hand and put on a confused expression, looked over his shoulder like he was lost. As he spun back, he hurled the heavy rocks glass in an overhand fastball, leg winding up and then down, arm cracking like a whip, form perfect. Once upon a time, he'd been All State.

The glass didn't so much strike the bouncer's forehead as explode against it, spraying sparkling shards in all directions, the noise lost against the raging beats through the walls, the bouncer flinging his hands up to his eyes, fluids pouring between his fingers and a horrified moan jerked from his lips.

Marshall stepped forward, drove his fist into the man's solar plexus to double him over, then hammered an elbow against the back of his neck to drop him. He straightened, shook out his hands, and pushed the release bar to open the back door.

Jack smiled as he stepped over the bouncer. He passed Marshall the .22, and the four of them started for the stairs.

THE BRUNETTE BLUSHED A LITTLE, her eyes throwing a challenge at the blonde, and then she leaned forward and touched her lips to the other woman's. The boy kneeling on the cushions tipped up a bottle of champagne, then wiped his mouth with the back of his hand and said, "Use your tongues."

Children. Undisciplined, foolish, and entitled all their lives. From the Star on down, they were all children, and they grated on Malachi. "My brother," he said, smile wide and arms open, the Rolex sliding down inside the cuffs of his shirt. "How's it hanging, dog?" Playing the role of the big bad black guy.

The Star flashed white teeth and stepped into the embrace. "Hey, G! Thanks for coming." The room was decked out like a sultan's palace, dangling fabrics and candles everywhere, cushions instead of chairs. "Drink?"

Malachi smiled, shook his head slightly. He unbuttoned his Armani jacket and tucked his hands in his pockets, exposing the shoulder holster. By the way the Star's eyes fell on it, Malachi could tell he loved it, loved the image he had of himself, a tough guy hanging with gangsters. Movie people. Shit. "I'm straight," he said.

"We got Ketel, some Cristal. Oh, I could send down for Hennessy . . ."

"We're good." Malachi smiled. "How's the picture?"

The Star sighed and rubbed at his forehead. "It's a nightmare. Director doesn't have the first clue. I don't know who the guy blew to earn his statue." He shook his head, then said, "You sure I can't get you a drink?"

"I'd as soon get down to business, you got no objection."

The Star smiled. "My man."

Malachi waited. A moment passed, and then the Star caught on, said, "Right, sorry." He adopted the tone of a schoolboy answering an instructor, hamming it up. "I'd like to buy some illegal drugs, please."

Malachi nodded to his man, who set the briefcase on a low table then stepped back. "Here's how we do. Blow, smack, Ecstasy, hydro, painkillers I have anytime. You want something special, I might need a couple hours' warning. I'm available twenty-four hours a day, seven days a week, anywhere in the country. I don't fly internationally, I don't deal for less than twenty-five, and I don't trade in rock." He popped the latches on the case but didn't open it, noting the anticipation in the kid's eyes, playing out the moment. The brunette on the pillows squealed as one of the entourage poured champagne down the front of her dress. She laughed, then moaned when the blonde leaned in to lick it off her tan skin. The boys whooped in appreciation.

"Is it good stuff?" The kid trying to sound hard. "I don't want to pay top dollar for some watered-down shit."

Malachi shook his head. "Pure as a nun's daydream. Guaranteed premium. My prices are high because of the service and quality I provide. Now," he said, and flipped open the briefcase to reveal the rows of neat bundles and colored bottles, "the doctor is in."

JACK LED THE WAY UP. Here, in the bowels of the club, the throbbing music seemed to come from everywhere at once: the walls, the railing, the floor, his heart. He'd been waiting for the rush, and finally it came, the tightness, that familiar hint of joy and panic that never went away. It had made itself at home in 1975, right after he'd shoved Aerosmith's *Toys in the Attic* under his shirt and strutted out of Mel's Records, the shrink-wrap cool against the skin of his teenage chest. He'd gone home and listened till he could sing every note, felt like "Sweet Emotion" was talking straight to him.

The staircase was thin and steep, a pipeline for servers to bring the occupants anything they wanted. There were VIP rooms and VIP rooms, and this was the latter, a private playground for the young, famous, and obscenely wealthy.

He blew a breath outside the door, paused to check the men behind him. They had already pulled on their masks, and in the dim light he could make out only the gleam of eyes and pistols. Bobby and Will seemed anxious, adrenaline jitters, but Marshall had that predatory slowness. Cobra cool, ready to strike.

Jack smiled. Shrugged his shoulders, slipped on his own mask, the fabric trapping breath hot against his lips. Let the rush run through him. Embraced it, that edge when everything was sharp and of consequence.

He put a hand on the knob and turned.

WHAT WAS he *doing* here?

Bobby felt like the veins in his forehead must be about to pop, his heart was banging so hard. He tried to swallow, his throat like sand. He wanted to rub his palms against his suit pants but didn't want to take off the gloves.

This wasn't his first job, nothing like. He'd helped Jack before: late-night warehouse load-outs where the night watchman turned the other way for a C-note. Or jumping the manager of a bar on his way to deposit the night's take. Beating down those two Latinos who had tried to cheat his big brother. Not like he was squeamish. But this, to walk into a room with masks and guns?

It'll be fun. Jack's voice played in his head. *The Brothers Witkowski, rolling hard. Just follow my lead, it'll be over before you know it.*

He took a deep breath.

You're a bad man.

Jack threw the door open, and he and Marshall stormed in.

A group of pretty boys stared wide-eyed from a pile of pillows where two girls were getting it on. Will was right: Both of them were better looking than any naked girl he'd seen outside a magazine. The Star sat at a low table with a well-dressed black guy, a case open between them, the Star holding a playing card an inch from his nose, and his panic exhale sent white powder billowing out like a summer cloud rolling across the plains.

"Go!" Will said, behind him.

Go, Bobby said to himself. *Move your feet.* He felt a trickle roll down his side. His hands trembled.

"Goddamn amateur," Will said, and pushed past, his gun out and up, yelling at the second black guy, a gangster-looking dude who froze with his hand almost to the butt of his pistol.

The scene was surreal, guns waving in this swank space, the beats turning everything into a music video. There were more people than Bobby had pictured, five or six friends of the Star, plus the girls, the bodyguard, and the drug dealers, a lot to manage. Jack was right, they needed four. Hot shame flushed through his bowels. *Go in.*

Then he saw one of the pretty boys starting forward, champagne bottle in hand. He was heading toward Jack, who had his back turned, his attention on the bodyguard. Bobby's legs unlocked. He burst in the door and whipped his gun across the kid's face, putting all his fear and rage into the move, the impact jarring and strangely intimate, something cracking beneath the metal, a sudden warmth against his glove as the boy went down, Bobby half wanting to follow him swinging, break every bone in his face for threatening his big brother.

Instead he stepped back and raised the Smith, swung it in an arc to cover the rest of the entourage. "Don't you fucking move." It felt good, the fear turning to power. *I am a bad man.*

Jack glanced over his shoulder, nodded. "All right." He stepped forward, his gun raised. "All right. Hands on your heads. Do it now."

For what seemed like a long moment, no one moved. Then the black drug dealer lifted his hands slow and laced them behind his head. The motion seemed to jar the rest of them, and they followed suit.

All except the Star.

"THIS IS A JOKE, right? I'm being Punk'd." The little brat smirked, too rich and stupid for his own good.

The tightness in Jack's chest cranked up a notch. Without moving the gun, he wound up and slapped the Star hard with his other hand. The kid staggered, came back up clutching his cheek, eyes wet, lips quivering like he'd never taken a hit in his life. Probably hadn't. "Hands on your head." When the boy did it, Jack said, "The rest of you. Against the wall. *Move.*"

The group shuffled over, fear-dumb. Jack gestured to Marshall and Will, who moved to cover them. Over his shoulder he said, "Get the bags."

His brother kicked pillows aside, grabbed the open sack of cocaine and the playing card and dumped them in the case, then slammed the lid. Jack kept his eyes lasered on the Star. Not blinking. Watching this movie hero fall apart in front of him, turn from a powerful man into a whimpering child.

Bobby whistled. "Holy shit."

Jack let his eyes dart sideways to where his brother knelt over the second case, the one the Star had brought. "What?"

"It's more than we thought. Jesus." Huffing a breath. "Jesus, it's a lot."

Jack raised the pistol to center on the Star's face. "How much?"

"W-what?"

He rocked the hammer back. "How *much*. How much in the case?"

"F-f-four hundred."

He fought to keep his jaw from dropping. They'd gone in expecting about fifty. Split four ways, that would have been a good take for the work. "Four hundred. Four hundred thousand dollars." Jack shook his head. "What the fuck do you need with four hundred grand in cash?"

"It's just, just"—the Star hesitated—"you know, walking-around money."

Jack stared, one lip curling against the mask. "Walking-around money."

The Star looked at him, looked down. "Take it. We won't tell the cops anything, I swear—"

"Cops?" He snorted. "What would you say? That you got robbed buying blow?"

The Star opened his mouth, then shut it, staring down the barrel of the gun.

"Jesus." Bobby whispered again.

"Close it up." Jack kept his voice cool, but the rush pounded through him now, the job, the adrenaline, four hundred thousand dollars. He gestured the Star back to join the others. "All of you. Turn and face the wall." He gave it half a beat, then shouted, "*Now!*"

The civilians went first. One of the boys started to cry softly, just whimpers, but he faced the wall. The drug dealers exchanged a look, then turned around also. Lastly the bodyguard spun.

"Tie them."

Will took plastic zips from his pocket, and he and Marshall started working their way down the line. Jack kept his gun out and up. He looked over at Bobby kneeling on the floor, fiddling with the latches of the case. Their eyes met, and he smiled at his brother, something filling his chest, joy, and he could see it mirrored in Bobby, an unspoken whoop that stretched between them.

MARSHALL STEPPED BEHIND MALACHI, put the .22 to the back of the man's head. "I set the trigger pull on this to nothing," he said. "Tiniest twitch, it's all over."

"I hear you." The man calm.

"All we're doing is tying you."

17

"Go ahead."

Marshall nodded to Will, who took the man's hands from his head, guided them behind his back, and zip-tied them. Then he knelt to do the same to the man's ankles.

"I can tell y'all are pros." Malachi spoke with his face to the wall. "So am I. Just so you know."

"And?"

"Things will go easier all around if you leave my merchandise."

Marshall leaned a little, let him taste the .22. "Why would we do that?"

The drug dealer didn't flinch. "Call it professional courtesy."

"I'll think about it." Marshall gestured to Will. They moved down the line to the bodyguard.

As he worked, Marshall saw double. One part saw backs of heads, knots in muscles, beads of sticky sweat on necks. The other saw the pool at Caesars, a pretty waitress in Roman garb running him whiskey, the sun on his chest and his eyes on the sports boards.

When it happened, it was faster than he'd expected. The bodyguard let Will take one of his hands, started to go along, but then ducked and twisted back, Will yelping as the guard reversed the hold, forcing the smaller man to his knees.

Marshall didn't hesitate. Just blinked back to single vision and pulled the trigger twice. The holes he'd drilled in the barrel muffled the .22, changing a roar to a clapping whoosh and a wet splash. The bodyguard's face crumpled, and he went down.

*   *   *

JACK KNEW THE SILENCE would last only a fraction of a second, so he broke it first, before anybody started screaming. "Don't any the rest of you fucking move." He lashed them with his voice. "Don't move, you don't get shot."

Marshall reached up with his left hand and brushed blood spatter off his face. He shook his head. Panic flared in Jack's belly, but he fought it down. The grip of the .45 was slick. *Goddamnit.* They were supposed to be in and out, ghosts. Easy money. The civilians wouldn't have been able to report a thing, and the dealer wouldn't want to.

Then he saw Bobby. His brother was frozen, one hand to his face. What skin the mask revealed was pale as November. Guilt flooded in to mingle with the panic. He'd promised the kid it would be an easy job, that no one would get hurt. Now there was a corpse on the floor, a murder rap on all of them.

Get control.

Jack looked around the room, hoping for something that could make the difference, some way out of this. Saw only the playthings of a class he had never belonged to. Silk pillows and thousand-dollar champagne. His fingers tightened on the grip.

"You two," he said, gesturing to Bobby and Will. "Get the bags and get out of here. Go ahead the way we planned."

Marshall looked over sharply, but Jack ignored it, his mind working fast. They had the dangerous men under control. The drug dealers were both bound, and the bodyguard, well, he wasn't going to be a problem any longer. The rest were sheep. He and Marshall could handle them. And he had to get Bobby out of here. No way he was letting his little brother stand for a murder charge. "Go. We'll meet up later."

Bobby didn't move, just stared at the ruin on the floor. Jack grimaced, then, keeping his gun on the civilians, walked over and put a hand on his brother's shoulder. "Trust me," he said softly.

Bobby stared at him. Blinked once, then again, then nodded. He ducked down to grab the handle of the case. Will stepped forward and handed him the bundle of zip-ties, eyes unreadable. "You're the boss."

"We'll meet you in an hour."

Will nodded, then grabbed the case with the drugs and headed for the stairs. Bobby followed, stopping at the doorway to look back. Jack gestured him on, then watched him go. He turned back. "The rest of you, foreheads against the wall and don't try anything. We're going to tie you and then we're walking out of here. You stay cool, in two minutes you have the best cocktail story of your life."

WILL WAS BLASTING down the stairs three at a time, and Bobby hurried to catch up. The case was heavier than he would have imagined, banging against his thigh. His heart hit so fast and hard it didn't seem like a pulse so much as a continuous rumbling. The music grew louder as they went.

They'd killed someone. Jesus Christ, they'd killed someone.

At the bottom of the stairs, Will slowed, stripped off his mask. Bobby did the same, tucking it in his pocket. The bouncer was still crumpled beside his stool where they'd left him. Bobby stepped over, and then they were back in the alley, the music cutting off with a slam as the door swung home.

His hands shook like palsy. "Jesus."

"I know it." Will blew a breath beside him. They walked south, away from the stolen Ford they'd arrived in. "That bodyguard."

"What the hell happened?"

"He didn't listen."

"What the *fuck,* man?"

"It's the job. It happens."

"That's it?" Bobby wanted to scream. He couldn't remember the last time he'd ever wanted to scream, to just open his mouth and howl.

"That's it." Will turned left toward a loading dock.

"It can't be that simple."

"It is."

"Wait." Bobby stopped, looked around, seeing the alley for the first time. "This is the wrong way. The Chrysler's over there."

"I know it."

The flash of light registered first, a strobe of white. Then Bobby heard the sound. He gasped, dropping the case, his hands going to his chest, finding it wet. The ground, he could still see the dirty concrete in the afterimage of the gun flare, it was rushing up, concrete and broken glass, his knees hit and the world jerked, and then he fell back, still not understanding, seeing the puzzle pieces but not putting them together until Will stepped over him, holstering his pistol as he reached for the case Bobby had carried.

No. Oh, no, no, no.

For a moment Will just stood looking down, a shape cut out of the sky. He reached up to his ear, drew something from behind it. A cigarette. He snapped his lighter, the flame sucking hungrily through the smoke, the light harsh against Bobby's eyes.

I'm a bad man, he thought, and then his eyes closed.

MAY

2006

2

TOM REED COULDN'T SLEEP for rain and acronyms.

The rain wasn't real. It came from the sound gizmo on Anna's night table. The noise wasn't actually much like rain, more like a hum of static. She said it helped her sleep, and he didn't mind, though it made him smile when she turned it on while real rain fell. Rain from a machine to mask the sound of rain on the windowsill, the same way they had thick curtains to block the daylight and an alarm clock that simulated the sunrise. They'd laughed about it, years ago, how they'd lost the battle against yuppiehood without firing a shot.

But the rain wasn't really the problem. It was the acronyms.

TTC. HPT. IUI. D&C. IVF. ICSI.

At first they'd seemed amusing, if a little precious: TTC for trying to conceive, HPT for home pregnancy test. Anna found a whole community online, thousands of women sharing stories on fertility Web sites, posting their most intimate details on message boards, analyzing basal body temperature and cervical mucus consistency like oracles peering at tea leaves. The Web sites had made

Anna feel better, had provided something it seemed he couldn't. The first acronyms had come from there.

The later ones came from the doctors, and they were neither amusing nor precious. They were cruel and costly. Tom rolled on his side, careful not to disturb her. They used to sleep spooned, the heat of her back nestling his chest, the smell of her hair, the sense that their bodies snapped together like Legos. Sometimes it seemed like a long time ago.

IUI, intrauterine insemination.

He tried to think about work, about the specific, boring mundanity of it. He pictured his office, eight by ten, drop ceiling, metal modular desk, the slim window through which the mirrored side of the neighboring skyscraper bounced a view of his own back at him. But that led to thoughts of the 9:30 status meeting he was going to miss, of sighs and shaking heads. He tried to guess how many e-mails would be waiting when he made it in.

IVF, in vitro fertilization.

The light that slipped past the curtain glowed faint silver. The clock read 4:12. There weren't many reasons to be awake at 4:12. In his twenties, sure: a Saturday night, he and Anna and the old crew, candles burning, beer gone, Leonard Cohen on the stereo, a last joint circling as people fell asleep against each other on garage-sale furniture. In his twenties, 4:12 made sense.

At thirty-five, though, 4:12 was a moment to sleep through. There was only one reason people his age tended to be awake at 4:12.

TWW, two-week wait. Ending today.

*   *   *

ANNA FELT THE bed creak and sag as Tom rolled over. He made faint sounds and nuzzled his pillow. How could he sleep? Her thoughts were loud enough to drown out the recorded rain. She was amazed he didn't hear them, didn't respond like she'd spoken aloud.

This is it. This time is the one.

I'm going to be a mother.

Please, God, let this be it.

But then.

That cramping feels awfully familiar.

Don't be PMS.

I can't do this again.

The hardest part about IVF was that she was indisputably pregnant. Her harvested eggs had been combined with Tom's sperm. This last cycle they had even gone for intracytoplasmic injection, injecting each egg with a single sperm. Of the five eggs they had harvested, three had been successfully fertilized. Three microscopic embryos. Babies.

Because this was their fourth cycle of IVF, the doctors had transferred all of them. Which meant she was not just pregnant, but pregnant three times over. There were babies alive inside of her. But they would stay alive only if they attached to her uterus. If they didn't live, it was her fault.

Stop, she thought, the reaction routine to the point of a mantra. She knew fault didn't enter into it. It wasn't like she hadn't done everything: the diets, the exercise, the post-sex positions, the vitamins, the hormones, the prayer. But none of it mattered to the voice in her head, the one whispering that every other woman could do it, that it was the most basic thing in the world, that to fail at that was like failing at breathing. Women gave birth. That was what made them women.

Stop. This time is the one. You're going to be a mother.

Please, God, let this be it.

SHORTLY AFTER SIX, he gave up, tiptoed across creaky floors to the bathroom. He tuned in WBEZ as the shower warmed: news of the war, the indictment of a telecom CEO, a commercial for *Eight Forty-Eight*, Steve Edwards promising to talk about the governor's latest tax plan and interview a local poet. It felt normal, comfortable, the same sounds from the same tinny radio, the sputter-kick of the water, the faint sourness of morning teeth.

But today could be the last day of your old life. He smiled as he rubbed shampoo into his hair.

Afterward, he quick-dried and wrapped the towel around his waist. In the bedroom, Anna lay on her back, blankets pulled to her chin, hands on her stomach, staring at the unmoving ceiling fan.

"How you feeling?"

"Fat."

He laughed. "Fat's good, right?"

"I think so." She pushed off the covers and started to sit, then leaned back with a groan.

"You okay?" He was beside the bed without realizing he'd moved.

She nodded, took his hand to pull herself upright. "Just cramps."

"Cramps?" She had vicious ones with her period, which was one of those bits of information, like her body temperature to two decimal places, that he'd never anticipated knowing. He could see she was scared, so he put a hand on her shoulder, said, "It's the hormones."

Anna blew air through her nose, then nodded. "You're right." She stood slowly, started for the bathroom. "Tell you one thing, I won't miss sticking myself every day."

He waited till he heard the water, then pulled on slacks and the gray cashmere sweater she'd given him for Christmas a couple of years back. Kettle on, eggs cracked into a pan, bread in the toaster. He left everything going as he unlocked the front door, went downstairs, and stepped out into a crisp spring morning. A haze of clouds sizzled against the beginnings of a bright blue day. He stooped for the *Trib,* then turned, saw Bill Samuelson staring at him, and nearly flipped backward off the porch.

"Jesus." Tom put a hand to his pounding heart. "You scared me."

"Easy to do." Their tenant took a drag from his cigarette, paused to spit a scrap of tobacco. "Don't you ever look around?" His voice was low and rich, a silk-smooth contrast to his generally pissy attitude.

"Just a little jumpy this morning, I guess." Tom shifted from one leg to the other, the cement cold against his bare feet. He itched to bum a smoke, reminded himself that he'd quit. "Kind of a long night."

It was the sort of comment that would prompt most people to say, *Really? Why's that?* But Bill just looked away. Since he'd rented the bottom floor of their two-flat, they'd barely spoken. He kept to himself, never seemed to have guests, disappeared for long stretches of time, and on the rare occasions they did bump into each other, was always right on the verge of rude. But his check hit the mailbox every month, and that was about all Tom cared about.

Back in the kitchen he dumped the *Trib* on the counter, poured tea, flipped eggs, and tried not to think about acronyms.

IT WAS GOING TO BE FINE. The sky was blue, spring was here, and she was pregnant. Sunlight made all the difference. Who wasn't nervous at 4:12 in the morning? A terrible hour to be the only one awake.

She reclined in the passenger seat, the back tilted thirty degrees to take some of the pressure off her belly. Her cramping was a little better, but her breasts were unbelievably sore. She'd had to dodge Tom's hug this morning, and she could tell that had bothered him.

Which was fair. More than. She'd make it up to him. But right now, she could think about only one thing. And all the physical symptoms had to be good signs. She felt different this time than the others.

The morning rush hour was on, and people filled the sidewalks, men and women in business casual. Life casual. Her cell phone rang, and she leaned forward to dig it from her purse, wincing as her breasts swung. She flipped it open, checked the caller ID. Shook her head and tucked the phone away unanswered.

"Who was it?"

"Work."

He cocked his head.

"I'll call them later," she said. "After." She could feel his stare. "It's just a phone call. Don't read into it."

The clinic was in a nondescript office complex. Orange pillars, bland signs, a cramped parking lot. Tom found a spot for the Pontiac and came around to help her out of the car. The air was cool but the sun on the top of her head felt good.

Even at a quarter to nine, the waiting room was packed. She signed in and took a seat. Tom had his BlackBerry out and was punching buttons, mouth curled into a small frown. Anna felt a surge of anger—not like e-mail couldn't wait—but wrote it off to hormones.

She pulled a magazine off the table, a *People* three weeks out of date, the cover given over to the "Shooting Star" robbery. When it had happened, the tabloids had been full of it, and she'd followed the story with that voyeuristic tingle that came from something lurid happening in her backyard. But now, as she flipped the pages and stared at the photos—the Star raising one hand to block photographers, somber police standing outside a dance club, a driver's license photo of the dead bodyguard—it couldn't hold her attention.

When she'd been a kid, Christmas had killed her. The waiting, the anticipation, it was too much. She even had a special Countdown-to-Christmas dance, which basically involved flailing spasmodically in front of the tree, arms and legs flying, dizzy with need. Her parents had found it hysterical. The wait for their name to be called reminded her of that time. *Maybe I should have a Find-Out-If-You're-Pregnant dance.*

Finally a nurse in blue scrubs led them back to an examination room. A poster on the wall detailed her anatomy, uterus and fallo-pian tubes and ovaries and the rest of it, all drawn in pastel colors and labeled.

"How are you feeling?" The nurse busied herself collecting swabs and tape.

"Okay. Some cramping, but I'm feeling better."

The woman nodded. "Roll up your sleeve?"

After two weeks giving herself shots of progesterone, the prick of the needle to draw blood was nothing. Anna stared intently at the dark liquid filling the tube.

"Okay," the nurse said when she was finished. "You can call for your results around noon. Any questions?"

"I know the hormones throw it off, but would it be really stu-pid to hit Walgreens and grab a home pregnancy test?"

The nurse laughed. "Hold out, honey. Just a couple more hours."

Christmas had never been so far.

TOM GLANCED AT HIS WATCH, winced. Shit. He'd told Daniels he'd be late, but this was pushing it. "Can you drop me on your way in?"

"I'm not going."

He paused, then said, "You've missed a lot of work lately, babe."

"I can't sit at my desk and pretend to give a shit about budgets and timelines, okay? Not today."

He sighed, jingled the car keys. Pictured the phone on his desk, the red message light blinking. Then he saw the look in her eyes. "Come on," he said.

They drove downtown and left the Pontiac in an underground garage, rode the elevator up to Millennium Park. The sky was cloudless, and the brilliance of the day had people out in droves: students lounging on the benches, tourists snapping pictures, toddlers playing in the fountain. He got himself a cup of coffee and a juice for her, and they sat on the steps, watching people. Tom used his cup to gesture at a girl with purple hair and a nose ring. "Her."

Anna followed his look. "She's a chef. Her dream is to open a restaurant called Gloom. The servers will wear black eye shadow, and the menu will only have cigarettes, red wine, and fresh suckling pig."

He laughed. "What about him?" An enormously fat man squeezed into a Bulls T-shirt.

"Twelve-inch cock. He makes his girlfriends call him Steel Blue Johnson. Tom, what if it's negative?"

He looked over at her, his wife, this woman he'd known forever. The wind tugged waves of auburn hair around her face, and she used one hand to brush them out of her eyes. "It won't be."

"What if it is?"

"Then we'll try again."

She made a sound that was nothing like a laugh. "We're in debt to our eyeballs."

"Everybody is in debt to their eyeballs," he said.

"Not everybody is dropping fifteen grand a pop on IVF."

He took a slug of cold coffee.

"All this time. The doctor's visits, all the shots. My God, all that *money.*" She shook her head. "If this comes up negative, it was for nothing." Her eyes narrowed, and he followed them to a woman holding hands with a little girl. The girl's hair was so blond it was almost white, and she wore a polka-dot sundress. They looked like they'd been cast by Hallmark. Anna stared, faint crow's-feet etching around her eyes. When had those arrived? "Nothing," she said.

Nothing, he thought, and knew she was right. This thing other people did so easily, for them it came with a long list of costs, not all financial. At first trying for a baby had been fun, had put a charge back into their sex. After a while, when nothing happened, the calendars and thermometers had entered into it. Three days a month became a nonstop fuckathon. He'd had these visions of himself as an oil derrick made of flesh, pumping endlessly and joylessly away. The rest of the month it just seemed like there wasn't any point. And then acronyms had entered their lives.

Somewhere along the path, things had changed between them. He loved her, knew she still loved him. But it seemed like a habit now. The remnants of something.

"It's going to be okay," he said with more conviction than he felt. "It's all going to be okay."

She cocked her head and looked at him. It felt like a long moment before she turned back to the park. They waited. When the clock on her phone read 11:58, she said, "I'm scared."

"Do you want me to?"

Anna took a deep breath, shook her head. "Christmas morning." She started dialing before he could ask what that meant. The steps were cold through his slacks. Tom could feel his pulse as he listened to her tell the nurse her name. She fell silent, put on hold, and their eyes met, both of them thinking the same thing, focusing all their hope.

Then he heard the murmur of the nurse returning, and though he couldn't make out her words, he could read the tone, and more than that, Anna's face, the way she drooped, like everything propping her up had been knocked away, and as he saw his wife begin to cry, Tom Reed added an acronym of his own to the list.

FUBAR. Fucked up beyond all repair.

3

"OH, HONEY," Sara sighed. "I'm so sorry." The younger of the sisters, Sara had always been the cool one, the rebel hitting after-hours clubs and hanging out with actors, but now she had the maternal voice down.

Maybe that's because she is *a mom,* Anna thought, and on the heels of that, *Stop it.*

"What are you going to do?"

Anna shook her head, then sighed into the phone. "I don't know."

"Will you try again?"

"I don't think we can afford to. We're pretty tight."

"What does Tom say?"

"He shuts down, tries to tell me everything will be okay. If you don't acknowledge it, maybe it will go away, right?" She lay on her back on the bed, one hand toying with the fringe of the duvet. Life changed so slowly you hardly noticed. There had been a time they talked about everything. "We really shouldn't have done it this time." Her fingers twiddled on a brass button. "It's just that I thought, one more try, just one more. I was sure it would happen."

There was a silence, and then, "I could probably lend you—"

"No." Anna spoke fast. "Thank you, but no."

"But—"

"No, sweetie." Her sister had a decent job as an editor at a television post house, but it wasn't the kind of paycheck that would earn Donald Trump's attention. And a huge portion of that went to day care for the Monkey. Raising a baby alone wasn't cheap.

Yeah, but at least she— Stop.

"Want me to come over?"

"No. I'm going to take a bottle of wine into the bath and crash. May as well drink, right?" She heard the bitterness in her own voice, hated it, the drama. "Look, it's okay. We'll find a way. And if it's meant to happen, it will, right?"

Sara caught the hint and changed the subject. "You still on for Wednesday?"

"Definitely."

"I could call around, get a sitter instead."

"No, I want to. I love hanging out with Julian."

"You sure?

"Yeah." She made her teeth unclench, got her voice back to normal. "I'm fine, sis. I promise." She took a breath. "Look, I'm going to go. Don't worry about me, okay?"

"Hey, it's what I do. No charge."

Anna forced a laugh, then said good-bye. Hung up the cordless and dropped it on the bed beside her. Stared upward. The blades of the ceiling fan were edged in black dust. It felt like she'd cleaned it not too long ago. Time snuck up on you in the stupidest ways.

She felt the tears somewhere in her throat, put her hands to her eyes. She didn't want to cry. Her breasts were sore and her body bloated, every heave would hurt, and besides, she'd cried so many times.

So it might not happen for them. So what? Lots of people didn't have children. They still lived fulfilling lives. She and Tom could spend more time together. Season tickets to Steppenwolf, pay off their debts, travel. Not like the world lacked kids.

She rolled on her side, pulled a pillow to her chest, and sobbed as quietly as she knew how.

WHEN THE SMOKE ALARM STARTED SHRIEKING, Tom was reading in the den again, and again she was locked in the bedroom. Same house, different worlds. They both had their escapes.

The suddenness of the alarm made him swing his feet off the desk, the chair rocking forward as he did. It was a sound he associated with cooking more than anything else—Anna was a great chef, but their ventilation was for shit, and whenever she pan-seared something, she ended up smoking them out of the kitchen and setting off the alarm.

But tonight's dinner had been cans of Campbell's nuked and eaten separately. The remnants of his beef stew were cold in the bowl, alongside a novel, the spine cracked so the book lay flat.

Once the panic faded, he realized that the sound was different, muted. Like it was coming through walls, he thought, and on the heels of that, he realized that it must be from their tenant's apartment. The ventilation on the first floor wasn't any better than theirs.

Tom sat back down, pinching the bridge of his nose. Muted or not, the screech wasn't helping his headache. One of those lingering mothers that hung behind his eyeballs. When he moved them, it felt like something tugging at his optic nerve, a cold, nauseous ache that made him want to close his eyes. While he was at it, open them to find himself somewhere else. Somewhere warm, with a soft breeze and a hammock. Maybe the smell of the ocean. Sometimes he pictured Anna with him, lying against him: the old Anna, the old him, fresh and in love, before their dreams became a burden. Sometimes he didn't.

He sighed, took a sip of bourbon, and turned back to his book, a novel about twenty-something American expatriates living in Budapest. They were looking for themselves, and for their fortune, and they were beautiful, and so heartbreakingly young it hurt to read, not because Tom couldn't believe he had ever been that age but because he couldn't believe he wasn't still. In that secret center that he thought of as himself, he was in his mid-twenties, astride the intersection of freedom and responsibility. Old enough to know who he was and what he wanted, but young enough he didn't owe anybody or need to get up twice a night to take a leak. A good age.

He planted elbows on either side of the book and rubbed sore eyes. Mid-twenties . . . D.C., the apartment in Adams Morgan, a second-floor unit above a bar-and-grill. He'd still been harboring dreams of becoming a novelist, had typed in the evenings to the smell of hamburgers drifting in the open window. Anna had her own place, but slept at his most of the time. They'd thrown a Halloween party one year, and she'd gone as an abstract painting, naked except for a flesh-colored bikini and swirls of fluorescent body paint. When they'd made love that night, the paint smeared the sheets with flowers, and she'd laughed about it, thrown her head back and laughed that good laugh, then wrapped her painted arms around his back and rubbed color onto him.

He took another sip of bourbon.

There was a tentative knock at the door. He said, "Yeah," and Anna stepped in. She wore cotton pajamas and no makeup. Her eyes were round and puffy.

"Do you hear that?"

The smoke alarm was perfectly clear, but he fought the smart-ass remark, and just nodded. "Bill's, I think."

"It's been going for a while."

"Just a minute or two." Even as he said it, he realized that this wasn't like an alarm clock, something to ignore. Stood up. "I guess you're right." He stepped past her, tracing one hand along her hip as he did.

She fired a tired smile at him. "You want me to come?"

"Nah. Go back to bed." He walked the creaking hardwood hall to the kitchen and grabbed the keys to the bottom unit. He and Anna had fallen in love with the building the moment they'd seen it: a brick two-flat, almost a hundred years old, in Lincoln Square near the river. The neighborhood was great, safe and full of families, and the house backed up to a park they had imagined taking their own children to someday.

Of course, the building ran two hundred grand more than they'd anticipated spending. But renting out the bottom floor let them swing the house payments, more or less. *More or less: the modern way.* Tom opened the front door and started down the steps. *Mortgaging the present to afford the future.*

The smell of smoke pulled him from his reverie. "Shit." He hustled down, yelled over his shoulder. "Anna!" The door to the foyer stuck, and he yanked hard to open it. Behind him he heard her footsteps, but didn't stop, just stepped into the narrow vestibule. A trickle of gray slid beneath the door to Bill Samuelson's apartment. Shit, shit, shit. Tom banged on the door, feeling silly, like the guy was going to hear knocks but not the smoke alarm. He fumbled with the keys, trying one and then another before he got the dead bolt open. Tried to remember everything he'd learned about fire. *Touch the door,* he thought, *see if the flames are on the other side, if you're going to feed them oxygen.* But the wood was cool. Anna stepped behind him.

Tom twisted the knob. The front room was a haze of smoke, the aftermath of a rock concert. The alarm screamed panic. "Hello?" He couldn't see any flames, so he opened the door all the way and stepped in. The room was spartan, just a battered easy chair and a big television propped on a particle-board entertainment center. A halo of swirling yellow clung to the top of the lone lamp.

The décor reminded Tom that he was in another man's apartment, but he pushed the thought aside. This was *his* house, *his* building. He quickstepped down the hallway. The smoke grew thicker and darker. He pulled the hem of his shirt up over his mouth, sucked hot air through it.

The kitchen overheads drilled tunnels of shifting light. Tom could sense heat before he saw flame, primitive instincts feeding dread as he moved toward the stove, where spikes of yellow and green danced. The flames wrapped a blackened teakettle, cloaking it in fire, and for a split second he imagined that the kettle itself was burning, and then he realized that the fire was coming from the gas jets. He lunged forward, spun the knob to kill the gas, feeling the fire like a wave of heat. Nothing happened, and he realized the gas wasn't the source, that the fire came from below and around the metal ring. Months of dribbled grease had caught and pulsed with a sweet black smoke. The wall behind the stove was blackened.

"Shit," Anna said from behind him. "Does he have a fire extinguisher?"

Tom threw open the cupboard beneath the sink. The air was clearer down here, and revealed cleansers, a couple of half-empty liquor bottles, but nothing useful. He stood. There was a mug on the counter beside a jar of Sanka. He could fill it with water . . . Wait. Better. The dishwashing hose. Tom stepped to the sink, spun the water on, then reached for the gun.

"No!" She had to shout over the alarm. "Grease fire."

Grease fire, grease fire, grease fire. Right. Water would just spatter it, send flying blobs of burning oil in all directions. What the hell did you use for a grease fire?

Anna was answering the question for him, pushing past to open the doors of upper cabinets. Canned soup, pasta, a box of Girl Scout cookies. Teas and coffee. Spices with the price tag still on. A ten-pound sack of flour, blue letters on white paper, the top rolled down and rubber banded. She pulled it from the shelf, knocking glass bottles to clatter on the counter. The flames had spread to a second burner. She snapped off the band and opened the sack, then leaned closer to the fire and dumped it, thrusting the bag like she was flinging water from a bucket. An avalanche of powder poured out over the stove, the wall, the counter. The flames sizzled as the flour hit, and then with a *whoomp* were buried beneath mounds of white. Particles rose in the heat, spinning and dancing like dust motes.

Tom felt his breath whistle out, realized he'd been holding it. The world seemed suddenly strange, that post-panic moment when things returned to normal. For a moment they just stared at each other, then Tom said, "Good thinking."

"*What?*" Shouting.

Tom spotted the alarm mounted above the entry to the kitchen. He stretched to spin it off the wall, then yanked the battery. The shriek died without a whimper. He turned back to her. "I said, good thinking." He looked at her and broke into a smile. "Casper."

She stood with the empty bag in her hand, her face and hair coated white. For a moment, she looked puzzled, then saw her arms dusted with flour and began to laugh.

He laughed too, and waving his arms to clear the smoke, stepped over to the stove, preparing himself for the damage. Aligning expectations: the fire had been constrained to the stove, thank God. It would be totaled, the microwave above it as well. The back wall would need fresh drywall, and the whole kitchen would need a coat of paint. He expected all of those things.

What he didn't expect to see, amid mounds of flour piled like snowdrifts, was five neatly banded bundles of hundred-dollar bills.

WHEN TOM SAID HER NAME, Anna had just turned on the faucet to wash the flour off her hands. She had her back to him, and the quiet way he said it scared her.

She turned, saw him at the stove, thought maybe he'd been burned, or that the fire had done more damage than they'd realized. Then she followed his pointing finger.

Packets of money lay in the flour.

The incongruity was startling. Money was something you took care of, folded, kept in a wallet. A dollar bill on the sidewalk leapt to your eye like it was lit by neon. To see bundles of money, *bundles,* the faded green dusty with flour, that chubby portrait of Benjamin Franklin staring up . . . it made something in her tilt.

"Jesus." She stepped beside him. Together they looked down. Her mind was racing, trying to connect dots that didn't seem like they belonged in the same zip code. There was a grease fire. They dumped flour on it. Now thousands of dollars lay on the stove. Alchemy.

She reached out, picked up one of the bundles. Soft and worn and, in the pack of a hundred, heavier than she would have guessed. She rifled the edge with her thumb, and a faint trace of flour leapt up. A hundred hundreds, ten grand. More cash than she had ever held. About two months of paychecks. With the other bundles, nine months' worth of work. Of twelve-hour days, of voice mail and sleepless nights and conference room battles. Nine months in a bag of flour dumped on a fire. The thought seized her, and she grabbed the rest of the money, her fingers suddenly greedy.

"What are you doing?"

She held twenty grand in one hand, thirty in the other. "In case the fire starts again." It was true, that had been her intention, just to get the money and then set it on the counter. But she found she didn't really want to let it go. Looked up at Tom, saw his eyes wide, his mouth open half an inch. After twelve, thirteen years together, she could see the thoughts working across his face, the same equation that was playing in hers. The same questions. "The stove was on when we came in."

"Yeah. I think that's how the fire started." He paused. "Maybe he left, forgot he turned it on?"

She pointed to the mug and the jar of instant. "He started making a cup of coffee and then left?"

"He could have gotten a phone call, something he had to run out for."

She nodded. Moved to the counter, set the money down. "Maybe." Something in her chest was cold. "But maybe we ought to check around."

"Check around for—" He stopped. Looked back down the hall toward the two bedrooms. For a moment, they looked at each other, their eyes locked, the unspoken possibility hanging between them. Then Tom walked to the window and opened it. "We should get rid of this smoke anyway."

It was a flimsy cover, but it was something to cling to. They started with the spare bedroom. The door was open, though the room was black. She hesitated, then reached in and flicked the light switch. Bright overheads revealed a weight bench and a set of cast-iron plates, a portable radio and a tin ashtray overflowing with butts. Inanely, her first thought was that they had told him the building was nonsmoking, that he had to do it outside. That was about the only time they saw him, smoking out on the porch, but apparently it wasn't the only time he did it. Tom opened that window too, and they moved down the hall to the master bedroom.

She knew before Tom flipped on the light. Knew, in truth, back in the kitchen. So when she saw, she didn't jump or shriek or do any of the things useless women did in the movies.

The bedroom was as spare as the rest of the house. A small dresser. A night table: reading lamp, paperback, clock, crammed ashtray, prescription bottle. A queen-size mattress and box spring, no headboard, the blankets faded with age. And Bill Samuelson, his skin pale, lips pursed tight together, curled on his side with his hands against his stomach like he had a bellyache.

The first and last time Anna had seen a dead body was at her grandfather's funeral. She was eleven, and remembered feeling nothing at all as she followed her mother up to look in the coffin. No, that wasn't true—her mother was crying, something Anna rarely saw, and that tore her heart out. But the man in the velvet box, the one with the too-rosy cheeks and the concrete expression, she didn't feel anything for him. He wasn't her grandfather. Her grandfather was a jovial man, a cardplayer, a scotch drinker, a joke teller. The man in the box was just . . . absent.

"Christ." Tom spoke softly.

They stood for a moment in the hallway, as if death were a force field, something that filled space. The body on the bed looked, not peaceful exactly, but sort of calm. Resigned. That was the word. He looked resigned, like a man ready to take his punishment. She stared, the air sticky with grease and smoke, listening to the steady beat of the clock, tick tick tick. Measuring out her time, and Tom's. Their lives subject to the same inane rhythm.

When she stepped in, the floor squeaked like a laugh in church. She froze, then continued. Reached out one hand, slowly. His chest was still, she could see perfectly well that he wasn't breathing, but she needed to know, needed to feel it to believe it. The skin of his arm was cool. Not cold, though. Not too long ago he'd been alive. An hour, maybe? Was that all that separated the two worlds, his and hers? An hour?

Tick tick tick.

"I guess we should call someone." Tom's voice sounding far away.

She pulled her hand from the body, nodded.

The worst of the smoke had cleared from the kitchen, replaced by a chilly spring breeze. The money was on the counter where she'd left it, beside the telephone.

"How do you suppose it happened?"

Tom shook his head. "I don't know. Heart attack? Stroke?"

"He didn't seem that old."

"My uncle had one when he was forty-two. Bill was probably older than that."

She picked up one of the bundles of money, tapped it idly against the counter. "I guess you're right. Maybe he had a condition."

He nodded slowly. "There was a prescription bottle."

"God." She shivered. "He died all alone. No family, no friends. Not even a doctor. Just alone in his bedroom."

"Bad way to go." Tom lined up one bundle of money against another. "But I don't know. Maybe that's the way he would have wanted. Seemed like the way he lived. Kind of a hermit."

They fell silent, both of them staring at the counter, at the money and the telephone. The breeze through the open window was rich with the promise of storm, that sweet electric smell of spring. An idea was forming in her head, hatching slowly, and she was letting it. Not nurturing it, but not quashing it, either. Just giving it space.

She brushed a lock of hair behind her ear. "It's like one of those stories you read about."

"Which ones?"

"You know, 'News of the Weird' kinds of stories. The guy who lives alone in a transient hotel. The neighbors say he was quiet, never had any visitors. One day there's a bad smell. When they break down the door, they find a bankbook with a million-dollar balance."

He laughed. "And a hundred boxes of Kraft mac and cheese."

"And seventeen cats." It was morbid, to be joking, here, in a dead man's kitchen. But it felt good too. Reminded her she was alive, that she stood against the endless ticking.

"The police will take the money," Tom said.

She looked up, startled. Their eyes locked, and she saw that the same idea had been hatching in his head. "He might have family."

"What family? Man never had a visitor, didn't go to work, never had a friend over. Hell, any time we tried to say hi, he'd snap at us."

"True," she said, feeling like she had to argue, though part of her didn't want to. "Still."

Tom shrugged. "Maybe you're right." But he didn't reach for the phone.

She exhaled, ran a finger over the bundle. Almost a year's salary lying on the counter. Enough to pay off most of their debt, the credit cards, the medical bills. Enough to take the pressure off, to relieve that unacknowledged noose that tightened with every envelope marked "Overdue."

Enough to let them try again. Another spin of the pregnancy wheel.

It's not your money. It would be wrong.

Whose money is it? Why not *mine? Why* is it wrong?

Anna looked around the kitchen. It was a mess: the stove blackened and charred, the wall scorched, flour everywhere, cabinet doors open, revealing food and pans and glasses, things Bill Samuelson no longer needed. Then she saw something else. Her mouth was suddenly dry, and she had trouble choking out Tom's name.

"Huh?" He looked at her, recognizing the change in tone, and followed her pointing finger to the cabinet where she'd found the flour—and where another ten-pound bag of flour rested, as well as a big bag of sugar and a clutter of boxes.

EIGHT MORE BUNDLES in the flour.

Six in the sugar.

Seven stacked beneath an inch of sea salt, fitting the box like they were made for it.

One in a box of cornstarch.

The Girl Scout cookies were worth thirty thousand dollars.

They went carefully at first, but as they found more and more, it accelerated, blurring like the scenery out a train window. Ripping open the bags and fumbling inside, pulling out bundles of cash, two months of their life at a time. By the end they were laughing, racing, each of them trying to open things faster, to find more: two bundles taped inside a Frosted Flakes box, another two in the Golden Grahams. One in a box of granola bars. Two upright in an oatmeal container.

Thirty-seven in all. Thirty-seven bundles of ten grand.

Three hundred and seventy thousand dollars.

They piled it on the counter, the money covered in flour and sugar, scraps of oatmeal. A wobbly pyramid of wealth. She stared at it. Around five years of her gross salary. God, more like eight after taxes. More than two-thirds what their whole building had cost sitting in a pile on the kitchen counter amid a sea of paper scraps and spilled food, box tops, and sugar piles. She realized she was smiling, fought an urge to tear open the bundles and throw clouds of cash in the air. "Have you ever—"

"Are you kidding?" He shook his head, the same mad grin on his face. "No. I haven't even held a hundred more than a couple of times."

"If the police find this, they'll take it," she said. "It will end up in an evidence locker."

"Or in the mayor's campaign fund." He straightened, looked down the hall. "We have to call them."

She nodded. "I know. But . . ."

"Yeah."

They stood in silence, staring at the money. It was funny, she thought. In the movies it would have been ten million. Some ridiculous sum. Three hundred and seventy thousand dollars was a lot, no doubt. But it wasn't completely outside the realm of their experience. They had good jobs, each brought in about seventy. Before they'd bought the building, before they'd started the fertility treatments, they'd lived well. Savings accounts and the occasional two-hundred-dollar dinner. An annual trip, Spain, the Bahamas. The fact that it was a graspable sum made it both more and less real. And to see it all in one place like pirate treasure, forgotten and waiting to be found? "I'm not a thief."

"Me either," he said. Then, "But we could always give it back, right? If he did turn out to have a family?"

"Wouldn't we get in trouble?"

"We wouldn't have to tell. Hell, we could leave it on their doorstep."

"Ring the bell. Ding-dong, here's a fortune." She rubbed at her chin. "What if it's stolen?"

"Stolen? From who?"

"I don't know. Maybe he embezzled it or something."

"I guess that's possible." He paused. "But even if it is, it's not like the city is going to be on a campaign to find the rightful owner. It would be like those impounded cars, or houses people lose on back taxes. They'd probably run a two-line ad somewhere, and then when no one claimed it, it would just vanish."

A cool breeze blew through the window, and she hugged her arms across her chest. "It's like finding a twenty on the sidewalk. If someone is looking at the ground, you give it to them, but nobody expects you to walk it to a police station."

"We'd have to be careful," he said. "We couldn't put it in our bank account. They can trace that."

"Sure. We probably shouldn't even keep it in our place." She noticed that they'd moved from *if* to *how*. Wondered if she should feel bad about that, didn't want to.

"Get a safe-deposit box or something."

"Leave it as cash. Keep our jobs, use paychecks for bills."

He nodded, staring at the pile of money. She did the same, her eyes tracing the edges, the geometry of freedom, weathered green, marked with sweat and wrinkled with time. The house was silent, just the breeze through the window and the sound of their breathing. And the faint, imperturbable ticking of the clock from the bedroom.

When she looked up, their eyes met, and she realized they were done talking.

HE LEFT HER IN THE KITCHEN to start cleaning while he ran upstairs for something to put it in. Something to put $370,000 in. Jesus. He felt an urge to giggle, not laugh, giggle, like a little kid or a madman. This was crazy. All of it.

In the hall closet he found his gym bag, unzipped it, and turned it upside down, dumping sour shorts and shoes. He bent to gather the clothes, then decided to hell with it, kicked them into the closet, feeling wildly alive, something nervous and free in his chest. Took the stairs three at a time. He could feel every bump and polished divot of the handrail, could taste the air he sucked in.

In the kitchen, while she used a broom and dustpan to scoop up the spilled food from the counters and floors, he stacked the money in the bag. Each packet was worn as an old blanket. It reeked of humanity, oil from a hundred wallets, a thousand hands. When he was done, Tom zipped the bag. "It's heavy," he said. "I didn't realize money weighed so much."

She leaned on the broom. "Where should we put it? For now, I mean?"

"Maybe in the linen closet, under some blankets?"

"I don't know. If it's in our house . . ."

"What if we hide it in the basement? That way if they find it, it looks like he stashed it himself." He saw her wince. "I'm just saying."

"No, you're right." She didn't sound convinced.

"The crawl space," he said. "I could take the maintenance panel off, stick it way back in there. They'd only find if they searched pretty thoroughly. And if they're searching that thoroughly, they know to look for the money, and it would be better if they found it."

She bit her lip, nodded.

By the time he'd hidden it and climbed back up the stairs, she was nearly done, the boxes and bags gone, cabinet doors closed, oatmeal and sugar and cereal swept from the floor. He looked around. "What about the stove?" Mounds of flour still spilled across it and dusted the surrounding countertop.

"This has to look like we came down, put out the fire, then found his body and called the cops. We wouldn't stop to clean up the flour, right?"

It was a good thought, smart, one of the things he loved about her, one of the reasons he'd fallen for her in the first place. He tended to take problems head-on, bull through them, but she could work it from all angles, find the surprise solution. He stepped forward and pulled her to him. She returned the kiss passionately, arms flung around his back, hips grinding into his, tongue darting and soft, and he felt heat rising in him, alive to every sensation, the pressure and warmth of her body, the cool air against his neck, the bite of her teeth behind her lips. They held it a long time.

"Is this crazy?" She spoke into his shoulder. "Are we crazy?"

"I don't know. Yes." He blew a breath. "It's not too late. We could put it back."

"Do you want to?"

"Do you?"

"Three hundred and seventy thousand dollars." She whispered it, like an incantation. "Three hundred and seventy *thousand* dollars."

"Me either."

ANNA HAD NEVER met a detective before, and hadn't known what to expect. Thus far she was impressed. Detective Halden had kind eyes and a nice suit. You didn't see men in suits anymore. Coupled with an easy calm that suggested he'd witnessed most everything life had to throw at a person, it gave him an air of authority. She found herself trusting him, liking him.

The first cops to arrive had been regular police, two guys in blue uniforms. They'd rung the bell maybe ten minutes after Tom hung up the phone. The sound had kicked her heart into her mouth. As she'd opened the door, she'd imagined that they would see right through her, that they'd pin her and Tom to the floor and snap handcuffs on them. But they turned out to be nice guys. They called her "ma'am," and after she and Tom showed them Bill Samuelson's body, the younger one had chatted with them in the kitchen while his partner radioed for a detective.

Halden swept into the place like a CEO to a boardroom. "Detective Christopher Halden," he'd said as he shook hands with each of them, passed them a business card with a little clip-art drawing of the skyline in blue. He stood in the kitchen and rocked back on his heels, his eyes moving over the counter, the ruined stove, the scorched wall. "I gather you've had quite a night."

Tom nodded. "You could say."

"You both all right?"

"A little singed is all."

"Want to show me where he is?"

They followed him down the hall, the two of them stopping outside the doorway as Halden walked in. He didn't flinch or hesitate, and Anna found herself wondering how long it took before you got there. How many corpses had he seen? What was that like, to have a job where all day you walked in on bodies?

Halden stood beside the bed, his hands in his pockets and elbows out to the side. Sweeping that same careful look around the room. "Check the locks?"

"For what?" Anna asked.

The detective looked over. "I was actually talking to the officers, Ms. Reed."

"Right. Sorry." She could feel sweat in her armpits and on the back of her thighs.

"No sign of forced entry," the older cop said. "The locks are all in working order. Windows are open—"

"We opened them to clear the smoke," Tom said. "Before we found him."

"—but the screens are intact," the cop continued.

Halden nodded. He took a pen from his inner pocket, used it

to poke through the things on the nightstand. "How well did you know him?"

Anna looked at Tom, shrugged. "We didn't, really. He answered our ad about, what, six months ago?"

"What did he do?"

"I'm not sure. He kept to himself."

"You didn't ask?"

She shook her head. "He paid two months up front."

Halden pulled on a latex glove, squatted in front of the night table. He turned on the lamp, picked up the prescription bottle. "He ever mention an illness?"

"No. But we never really talked to him."

"We'd only see him every now and then," Tom said. "Mostly smoking on the porch. Is that medicine something?"

The detective didn't answer, just took a flashlight from his pocket, clicked it on, and leaned down to sweep it beneath the bed. His gun rode high on his belt, and Anna felt her eyes drawn to it. After a moment, he rose, took Samuelson's hands, examined them carefully under the beam. "He have any friends or family? Anybody visiting regular?"

"Not that we ever saw." Tom rubbed his neck.

Halden turned off the flashlight, stood up, and walked out of sight, to the bathroom. Anna's pulse seemed loud, and her hands trembly. *Relax. You and Tom are good people. You have nothing to fear.* She could hear the sound of the medicine cabinet swinging open, imagined Halden rifling through it, aspirin bottles and toothpaste tubes. After a moment, he walked back out, stopped at the foot of the bed. He ran his tongue around the inside of his cheek, the skin bulging out. Stood for a long moment, then snapped the glove off his hand. "Okay." He turned to the officers. "Have the photographer shoot the room, then call for a wagon, get Mr. Samuelson to the medical examiner."

"Want any techs?"

The detective shook his head. "Just the photographer. And bag that scrip." He smiled at Anna. "You look a little shaken up, Ms. Reed. Why don't we talk in the other room?"

They walked down the hall. The air had grown chilly, and she shut the window, the glass rattling in the old frame. "What do you think happened?"

Halden cocked his head to one side. "Well, no indication that anyone broke in, and no sign of a fight, no wounds on his body or hands. That prescription bottle didn't have a label. That usually means that it was painkillers bought on the street. My guess is that he had a health problem, wanted something to take the hurt away, and maybe overdid it. But the medical examiner will say for sure."

"It's so strange."

"What's that?"

"Just . . ." She gestured down the hall. "You know, that he's dead. That someone is dead in a room down there."

The detective nodded. "It doesn't look like he suffered. Believe me, I've seen a lot worse."

"What happens now?" Tom leaned on the counter.

"Well, someone will take him to the morgue. We'll try to get in touch with his family. You have anything that could help with that? Did he give references for the apartment, or have a cosigner?"

Tom shook his head.

"What about his rent? You have canceled checks?"

"No."

"He always paid with cashier's checks," Anna said, and then froze. *Stupid, stupid girl.*

"Cashier's checks?" The detective cocked an eyebrow. "Why didn't he just use a personal check?"

Because he kept his money in ten-thousand-dollar bundles. Bundles that we stuck in an old gym bag and hid in the basement. Her heart slammed against her ribs, but she made herself shake her head as calmly as possible. "Never asked." Realizing as she spoke that she was lying to a cop, a disconnected feeling, like she was watching herself from a distance. It felt somehow like she'd taken a step.

The detective held his gaze for a moment, a question clearly framed in his mind. Then he shrugged, turned away. "I've got some paperwork to fill out, and the photographer will need half an hour or so, then we should have the body out of here." He glanced at the stove. "By the way, you were right not to throw water on the fire, but if it ever happens again, you should use baking soda, not flour."

"Why's that?"

"Believe it or not, it's explosive."

"Really?"

Halden nodded, then opened his binder and started making notes with his pen. "Yup. You got lucky with the flour."

She almost snorted, just barely caught herself. Locked eyes with Tom, saw that he was thinking the same thing, panic laughter tearing them both up inside. Finally, her eyes on her husband's, savoring the words, the connection, the two of them alone in it the way they used to be, she said, "Detective, you sure are right about that."

4

FROM THE STOOL at the end of the bar, Jack Witkowski could look out the narrow window to the apartment building across the street. The blinds were closed, and the blue light flickering behind them had died almost five minutes before.

"You boys want another?" The chick tending bar had the look of a girl who'd dyed her hair too many years in a row. Jack shook his head, but Marshall said, "I'm all right, sweetheart, but set him up again."

"I didn't say I wanted one."

"You didn't have to."

"What the Christ does that mean?"

"You were thinking of Bobby again." Marshall lifted his whiskey, held it under his nose. "A drink'll help."

"Then you fucking have it."

Marshall shook his head, set down the glass, stared out the window.

"Something you want to say?" Jack knew he was being snappy, taking Bobby's death out on Marshall just because he was close, but he didn't care. Three weeks hadn't done a thing to ease the pain. Worst was that when he thought of Bobby, which was all the damn time, he always came back to that last conversation in the car, when he'd told Bobby everything would be fine, that he was a bad man.

Only he wasn't, never had been. He was a lightweight thief taking on a heavyweight job because his big brother asked him to. And now Bobby was dead, killed in a dark alley he shouldn't have been anywhere near, and Jack was left with the memory of talking him into it.

The bartendress returned, set a shot of tequila and a Negra Modelo in front of him. Marshall passed her a ten folded between two fingers. She took it, then went back to her paperback at the other end of the bar.

Jack said nothing, just studied the play of red neon on brown glass. The bar smelled of stale cigarettes and burned coffee. Marshall tapped the edge of his whiskey glass, then pushed it away. "For what it's worth, I'm sorry it went down the way it did. Bobby was a good kid."

Jack said nothing.

"But the cops are tearing the city apart. Will humped us. Once they found Bobby's body, you know they started looking at who he ran with. Your name is top of the list. Mine too. I'm sorry he's gone, but now ain't the time to be running around weeping over it. He was a nice kid, but he wasn't a professional, and that got him killed. That's life."

"Listen to me very carefully," Jack said, then took the tequila properly, no salt, no lime. "If you ever talk this shit again, or disrespect my brother that way, you and I, we're going to mix it up." He turned sideways. "You want to talk professional? Try this on.

The four of us were supposed to leave together. You really think Will would have made a play against all of us?"

"The bodyguard—"

"The bodyguard wasn't supposed to move. That was your job."

Marshall shook his head. "Things don't always work neat, man. That's part of the business. You know that." He paused. "Besides, it wasn't me that sent Bobby out alone with Will."

Jack gripped the neck of the beer bottle hard enough he could feel it creak. "Fuck you."

Marshall said, "The point is—"

"I get your fucking point." He took a swig, the beer tasting foul. Thought about turning and cracking the bottle into Marshall's skull. But a voice told him that the man was right, that the job came with risks. They just weren't supposed to land on Bobby.

He thought of Will Tuttle, that smooth voice and asshole personality, the victory cigarette he tucked behind his ear. The thought filled him with fire. Marshall was right. It wasn't his fault, or Jack's, not really. It was Will that pulled the trigger.

Over the sound system, Mick Jagger sang that ti-ime was on his side, yes it was. Marshall sat silent. Jack sucked on his beer. He stared at the battered bar and tried to pull up his brother's face, found it harder than it should be. It all seemed fragmented: a glimpse of a laugh here, a smile there. Birthdays and moments in cars. The time he'd convinced Maria Salvatore from down the block to give them both handjobs, when fourteen-year-old Bobby had that split look, half fear, half unbearable eagerness. Mostly, though, what Jack came up with was Bobby holding a borrowed gun and saying he was a bad man.

Marshall cracked his knuckles and cleared his throat. When he spoke, it was in a lighter tone, aimed at changing the subject. "Something I always wanted to know."

"Huh?"

"How's two Polacks named Witkowski end up Jack and Bobby?"

"My mother." Jack smiled, remembering her out in the tiny backyard, herbs in pots and paint flaking off the garage, humming while she pinned up laundry. "Big fan of the Kennedy brothers. The whole American dream. Come from a poor Polish family, work hard, do good in school, one day you end up like them." Jack snorted. "Bobby used to say she'd been right—we both grew up to be good-looking criminals."

Marshall laughed, then said, "I am sorry, man. And when we find Will, he's going to be even sorrier."

Jack nodded, took a breath. He leaned back to look out the window. "Light's been off awhile. You ready?"

"Let's work." This time when Marshall set down his whiskey glass, it was dry.

THE APARTMENT WAS FRONTED by a narrow vestibule with two doors, one leading into the ground-floor unit, one to the upstairs apartments. Jack glanced out at Marshall leaning against a lamppost, an unlit cigarette held between two fingers. His partner's head shook, just barely, and Jack went to the mailboxes, took out his keys, busied himself fumbling with them until a middle-aged couple walked by, talking and oblivious. When he looked back after thirty seconds, Marshall nodded.

Jack loved dead bolts. The locks on most doors could be picked in under a minute. But because people had twisted a knob, they felt safe, went to bed believing monsters couldn't get in. As he swung the door open, Marshall fell in behind. They staggered their footsteps, walking on the edge of the stairs to minimize noise as they climbed to the second floor.

The kid had a welcome rug that read, "Hi! I'm Mat." Marshall pointed at it, snorted, then pulled a flattened roll of duct tape from his back pocket and stretched off the first inch. Jack knelt in front of the door, the tension wrench tugging lightly to the side, his pick sliding down the pins. When the cylinder gave that sweet few degrees, he straightened, then twisted the lock the rest of the way open.

The apartment was a Chicago classic, a graystone built on a standard-width lot. Inside the door was a deep living room, furniture barely visible by the light trickling through the curtains. There was a faint depression on the couch where the kid had been watching television without any idea that men sat in the bar across the street watching him. Jack stepped inside, pausing to listen. Dead silence.

The two of them went down the hallway as silent as shadows. The bedroom was dark. Jack took a second to think of Bobby, felt the anger flow into him, the hate.

He wrenched the bedroom door open and the two of them were through it, Marshall snapping the flashlight on, darkness surrounding a brilliant circle, tangled sheets, the edge of the headboard, the guy jerking upright, eyes wide, a good-looking kid in his early twenties, raising one hand out of instinct, trying to block the light, and Jack grabbed the hand and twisted it hard, yanking at the same time, the guy shooting out of bed, mouth opening then closing when Jack palm-chopped his neck, and then they had him, grabbing at his shoulders, his skin soft and warm from the blankets, yanking him up and out of the bed and throwing him face-first on the hardwood, Marshall dropping on him from behind, knees to shoulders as he wrapped the duct tape, loop after loop covering his mouth and flattening his hair in awkward patterns.

Just like that, it was over. Nothing but the whistling of panicked breath through the guy's nose as he turned his head sideways. Pupils dilated in the light. Blinked at them without recognition. Tried to say something, the words muffled syllables behind the tape. He looked like a little boy, all fear and bare skin, and for a second, Jack wavered.

Then he thought of his brother, dead in a dingy alley. He nodded to Marshall, who stretched the arm out and locked it in place at the elbow. Jack took a breath, then raised his right foot and stomped down as hard as he could. The heel of his dress shoe slammed into the guy's fingers. The kid jerked rigid, veins on his neck straining as he screamed against the tape. Jack brought his foot up again. Down again. Howls incoherent and wishbone cracks. With each blow the rigid heel tore skin and muscle, shredded slippery tendons. The boy fought to move, but Marshall held him like a vise. Up again. Down again. Up again. The fingers twitching like worms after a rainstorm, the flesh popping, white bone fragments jutting at odd angles.

When it looked like one of them might be about to come off,

Jack stopped. Panting, he ran his hands through his hair and dropped to a squat. The guy was still awake, still screaming his lungs out against the tape, eyes wide and bloodshot, ropes of snot streaming from his nose.

"Hi, Ray," Jack said. "We're friends of your uncle Will's. And we'd really like to know where to find him."

5

HE FLOATED ON THE EDGE OF DREAM, the world blurry, as
something rubbed against him. Drifting, body here, consciousness there, sensations rolling through him. Skin against his own
in a slow wriggle, neck to ankles. He could smell Anna, the faint
homey hint of musk. The night air was pleasant, and he'd kicked
the blanket off hours before. The sheet was soft as bathwater.

Tom mumbled sleep moans, thought about opening his eyes,
didn't. He felt her back against his chest, a gentle dancing touch,
warm and complete where she moved, cool and wanting where
she pulled away. The press and arc of her bottom. A heat growing
inside, familiar and forgotten. He didn't know what time it was,
hadn't opened his eyes to check, but it seemed late, somewhere
in the lonely hours of the night when the world disappeared. She
moved again, arched against him, and this time his moan wasn't
from sleep. He felt himself taut in his briefs, rigid against the curve
of her.

Tom opened his eyes.

Anna's head was turned to the ceiling, her features faint against
the dark, eyes just a glimmer of reflected light. He saw her smile;

then she pressed backward again, the cleft of her ass grinding against him.

He reacted automatically, wrapping an arm around her, cupping her breast in his hand, warm through the thin T-shirt she slept in, the nipple hard against the roughness of his thumb, and heard her gasp, and it was enough to pull his head all the way back to reality. Habit kicked in, a calendar check. If they managed to conceive tonight, a star would lead wise men to their apartment.

He blinked, groaned as she moved against him, then said, "Baby, it's not time, it won't work." His voice thick and heavy with sleep.

In the dark of the room he saw her flash those teeth again, perfect white teeth, and then she said, "Shhh." Spun against the mattress, his arm still draping her, her lips coming to his neck, his chin, his cheek, her breath sticky in his ear as she said, "I know," and then she was pushing him back, sliding one slim thigh over his hips, ghostly in the dim light, body arching, the T-shirt riding up to reveal pale skin and a dark tangle of pubic hair, her fingers tugging at his briefs, her hand electric, the best thing he could imagine until he felt the wetness of her and slipped inside.

He moaned and thrust upward, resting his hands on the curve of her hips and forgetting about calendars, about rhythms and schedules and optimal ovulation windows.

When at last they were both spent, when she'd collapsed against his sweat-drenched chest and he could feel the pounding of her heart like some trapped and delicate bird, he said, "Wow."

She laughed through her nose and said, "Yeah."

"I mean, wow." He shut his eyes tight, then opened them, blinking. "Jesus." His head felt light, his arms strong. The edges of the curtain were drawn in white light. Dawn must have come while they were making love. "It's been a long time."

"Are you kidding?" Anna nuzzled against him, leaving little kisses on his shoulder. "We've had more sex in the last year than since we were, like, twenty-two."

"Yeah. But. You know what I mean."

She hesitated, and for a second he was afraid that he'd hurt her, that she'd taken it as a rejection. Then she smiled, a wry sort of thing, and said, "Yeah." She put her head on his shoulder, yawned. "Nice."

"Yes," he said. "It is." With his arm wrapped around her shoulders he collapsed into sleep.

HE WOKE WITH ONE forearm flung across his eyes to block the light. Before anything else came the memory of her atop him, and he smiled. Yawned, stretched, shoulders popping. Looked at her side of the bed. The pillow was empty, the sheets in disarray.

Tom rose, snapped off the rain machine on the night table, sat on the edge of the bed with his feet on the floor. Eleven A.M. He didn't sleep that late often. But then, he'd happily trade a couple hours of daylight for her to awaken him like that. Plus, it wasn't every night you found $370,000 and a dead body.

The thought sideswiped him, and his eyes came the rest of the way open. Jesus. Had everything last night been real? He stood, pulled on yesterday's jeans. Opened the bedroom door and started down the hall.

Most weekend mornings he found her in the living room with a cup of coffee and a stack of envelopes, a pen behind her ear. They had an arrangement: He cleaned the bathrooms, she handled the bills. But the couch was bare.

"Babe?"

They'd planned to turn the spare bedroom into a nursery, but all the books said not to do things like that in advance, that it would only add pressure, remind you of the thing you most wanted but did not have. Good advice, except that all they ended up using the room for was scattered storage, a kind of dump for boxes and photo albums that only telegraphed that the room was in transition, served to remind them anyway. She wasn't there. She wasn't at the stove, either, or at their kitchen table. *Maybe she went to get bagels.*

He opened the drawer, rummaged through it. The spare keys were gone. He went out the front and down the stairs. The door to the bottom unit was unlocked, and the air still had an acrid undercurrent of smoke. "Anna?"

Quiet, from the other room. "In here."

She sat on the dresser, wearing a Columbia College T-shirt and a pair of his boxer briefs, one leg tucked beneath. Her hair was loose, and she played with a lock of it, twisting it in her fingers as she flashed an unconvincing smile. "Hi."

"Hi." He crossed his arms, leaned against the door frame. "What's up?"

She hesitated. "I was just thinking about him."

"What about him?"

"I don't know. Not him, really. More that he died. That someone died, right there." She gestured toward the bed. "It's weird, you know?"

He nodded. Waited.

"I mean, we never knew him. And now he's gone. Yesterday he was alive, and now he's just . . . gone." She wrapped her arms around herself. "Maybe he was a really good guy, and we never knew."

"Maybe he was a complete bastard," he said. She glared, but he shrugged. "He certainly didn't go out of his way to be friendly."

"I guess not. I'm just feeling strange about it." Her expression suggested she was referring to more than Bill's death. He looked at the bed, the sheets rumpled. Last night he'd asked the police if they were taking the sheets, and one of them laughed, said no, he didn't figure Bill would need them anymore. "Yeah."

Taking the money, he'd been buoyed by the insanity of it. By the way it could be set against years, against dreams, like time and hope had been transmuted to paper. It wasn't money they were claiming; it was life. Who didn't want more? Now, though, standing in the abandoned bedroom, he found everything seemed less clear.

Then he had a thought. Felt himself smiling.

"What?" She cocked her head. Smiled back, curious. "What?"

"I know how to cheer us up."

"Can I open my eyes?"

"Not yet." Tom leaned forward, passed the cabbie a twenty. "Keep the change." He opened the door, then put a hand under Anna's arm. "Easy. Slide out." He stepped to the curb, guided her beside him, then spun her south, facing down the strip of glittering window fronts. Saturday afternoon, and Michigan Avenue was jammed. On the opposite corner, a good-looking kid danced to a boom box beside a sign reading "Grad Student Discos for Dollars." A crowd of tourists ringed him, snapping pictures and clapping. "Okay. You can look."

Anna took her hands from her eyes, looked down the strip of shops. "The Mile?" She cocked her head. "We're going shopping?"

"Ooooh yeah."

She laughed. "Do you think we should?"

"Why not?"

"What if it turns out he has a family?"

"Then we'll return it. But I think we're entitled to a couple grand. Call it a finder's fee."

She shaded her eyes and looked down the row of stores. He could see her thinking about it, deciding. Then she turned back to him, said, "One question."

"What?"

"Where do we start?"

It was a surreal experience, carrying five grand in his front pocket with the full intention of blowing it. Peeling off the first bill was hard, instinct kicking in to ask what the hell he was doing dropping six hundred on a leather jacket for her, three hundred on sunglasses for him. But by the time he stacked five bills on the counter for two pairs of heels, he was getting the hang of it. And when she leaned out of a Neiman Marcus dressing room wearing a twelve-hundred-dollar Carolina Herrera cocktail dress and a wicked smile, her finger crooked in invitation, he felt right at home. He stepped into the tiny room and pulled the door shut behind him, the two of them fighting first giggles and then moans as they made love against the mirror.

Afterward, laden with bags, they wandered over to State Street. There was a half-hour wait at the Atwood Café, but he slipped the hostess fifty, and suddenly they were sitting at a primo table in the corner of the patio. He started to order a beer, thought better of it. "You have any champagne?"

The air was sweet with spring, sun shimmering off the windows of cabs and the graceful flutes of bubbly. He sighed, closed his eyes and breathed it all in. "Now, this is living."

"I could get used to it."

He laughed. "Don't get *too* used to it. At this rate we could burn four hundred grand pretty fast."

She winked at him over the rim of her glass. They ordered and ate, chatting about nothing. After he'd scooped up the last bite of his salmon and washed it down with the last sip of champagne, he leaned back, crossed his ankle over his knee. "Times like this I wish I hadn't quit smoking."

"Times when you've dropped five grand in two hours?"

"If I had a nickel, right?" He ran his hands through his hair. "You want to talk about it?"

"No, I think it was good you quit smoking."

"Smart-ass."

She twisted pasta around her fork, stabbed a shrimp. Popped it in her mouth and chewed slowly. Shrugged. "What's to talk about?"

"Just want to make sure you're okay with everything."

"I feel pretty good right now. A shopping spree will do that for a girl." She set her fork on her plate, dabbed at her mouth with the napkin. "This was fun. But shopping sprees weren't the reason I wanted to take it."

"I know. Just thought I'd lighten the mood."

"No, I'm glad you did. But . . ." Anna leaned forward, put her hand over his. "Tom, I want to try again."

"For a baby?"

"Not a *baby*, a *child*. People talk about wanting a baby like it's a puppy. I want the whole thing. To raise a child together." She paused. "Don't you?"

"Yeah, of course. It's just . . ." He shrugged, stared out at the sidewalk. "I don't know. It's been rough. I mean, it's not that I don't want a kid. I do. It's just it seems like so much *work* right now. The shots, the waiting, the appointments. Plus . . ."

"What?"

He hesitated. Watched two cops come out of a deli, coffee in their hands. One of them said something that made the other laugh.

"What is it?"

He turned to look at her. She was squinting against the sun, her hair lit gold, and he felt a wave of love for her, one of those moments when he was really seeing what he had, instead of taking it for granted. "This is going to sound silly, but I had fun today. And last night too. It felt more like it used to. Before."

"The sex."

"Sure, but not just that. I mean all of it. The feeling that we're in it together, that it's us against the world. Partners in crime." He laughed. "Literally, now." Her hand was warm against his, and he traced the edge of her index finger. "I guess I feel like the fertility stuff has just stressed us out so much. What if we didn't go for IVF again? What if we thought about adoption?"

She opened her mouth, then closed it. "We talked about that before. After everything we've been through . . ."

"There are a lot of kids out there."

"There really aren't," she said. "You know that. There are a lot of older kids, but not a lot of baby-babies. The process can take a long time, if it happens at all, and meanwhile, the odds of me ever being able to get pregnant keep declining. And I don't want to go all Madonna and adopt from another country. It seems like it could put too much on them when they grow up."

He played with his spoon. "I just don't want to lose you in all of this."

"I know what you mean. I do." She squeezed his hand. "But things are different now. So much of the problem between us had to do with money."

"You think?"

"Are you kidding? We've got three credit cards maxed, a fourth on the way. The mortgage. We work sixty hours a week. Add all the fertility stuff on top of that? Yeah, it had a lot to do with the money."

He rocked his head back and forth. She had a point. Every time things hadn't worked out, every procedure, every visit to the clinic, some part of him was punching buttons on a mental calculator. Now that wouldn't be a worry. They could pay their bills, get themselves even, and still have maybe three hundred grand, enough for as many tries as it took. It would help. "It's not just the debt, though. I've missed . . ." Tom held an empty hand up. "Us."

"I know." She shrugged. "I know. But now it can be different. We can make a point of it. Only now we won't have to worry about anything. No bills, no panic that it's a waste. Besides." She leaned forward. "Imagine holding a child in your arms. Our child, yours and mine. Can you imagine how *beautiful* she'll be?"

"She?" He smiled. "I thought we'd worked this out. You're having a boy."

"No chance. You'll be a complete sucker for a little girl, and I like seeing you squirm. Now," she said, and leaned back. "Pay the nice lady. I want to go home and try on my new dress."

"I'm just going to end up taking it off you again."

Anna cocked an eyebrow. "Why do you think I'm putting it on?"

6

THE CAR WAS A HONDA CIVIC, ten years old, black and in need of a wash. It was exactly like five or six others on the block, which was why they'd chosen it. Jack had stood watch while Marshall jacked it from a parking deck down on Lake. The deck was an art deco trip, the façade designed to look like the grille of a car. The Honda had been parked smack in the middle of what would have been the radiator.

Jack reached for his coffee, took the last cold slug, then tossed the empty cup in the back and squirmed in his seat, trying to find a more comfortable position. Three hours parked and staring at everyday people hurrying off to their little jobs was enough to put a crick in anybody's back.

"Still no sign of Will." Marshall tapped an unlit cigarette against his thigh. Man didn't smoke, but always carried a pack. Claimed they were useful, an easy way to get close to somebody or to start a conversation with a chick. "You don't think the little prick lied to us?"

"No."

"I guess you're right. Number you did on him, he'd have ratted on Jesus Christ." Marshall scrunched his face up like he was in pain, cast his voice high. " 'Ohgodohgod, please, not my other hand, I'll tell you where he is, just not my other hand, *please*!' " He blew a breath. "That was heavy shit, you doing it anyway, after he told us."

"Had to be sure." Something queasy happened in Jack's stomach, and he had an image of the boy the way they'd left him, cruciform, facedown, a pool of blood spreading fast, pouring out of his neck to darken the hardwood like a hose left on the concrete. He pushed it away, a mental twitch that was becoming easier. The boy hadn't been his first.

"Poor Ray. Just bad luck, him being Will's nephew."

"Yeah." Jack closed his eyes, rubbed them with his fingertips. "Poor Ray."

"Funny, the way luck works. Going about your business, thinking about what car to buy, whether you want to stay with your girl or look for a new one, and *wham*! Head-on collision with fate."

"Fate?" Jack shrugged. "It wasn't fate. It was us. We did it."

"Sure. Fate's messengers." Marshall spun the cigarette between his fingers. "Let me ask, how many times you pull the trigger on somebody?"

"A few."

"You remember the second?"

"Huh?"

"I got this theory. The first you're always going to remember. Like losing your cherry. I remember the first time perfectly. Julia Buckley. I was fifteen, she was fourteen, in her parents' basement. They had this orange shag rug, and we did it right on top." He paused. "Thing is, I can't remember the second time we fucked. Already started to lose the novelty."

Jack ran his tongue between his teeth and his lips, shifted in the seat. "I remember the second time."

"Second time you killed or the second time you fucked?"

"Both."

"Huh." Marshall stared out the window, spoke slow. "You notice how none of them believes it's happening? Take your toughest tough guy, he won't believe it. But it's like getting hit by a bus. Anybody can get hit by a bus, anytime. Bus don't care what you're thinking, that you aren't ready. It's just getting from A to B." He jerked his chin toward the windshield. "There's the other neighbor."

Jack followed his stare to the brick two-flat forty yards down. A woman was stepping out of the door that led to the second-floor apartment. When they'd first arrived, he'd gone into the vestibule that fronted the place and checked the mailboxes. The first floor read Bill Samuelson, close enough to "Will" that it'd be automatic to respond when people said it. The second floor listed a Tom and Anna Reed. A guy Jack could only assume was Tom had left earlier, wearing rock star shades.

They watched her lock the door and head down the block, her low-rise jeans tight enough to show off the sweetheart of her ass. She climbed into a late-model Pontiac and pulled away.

Jack reached in back and pulled the shotgun, handed it to Marshall.

ANNA COULDN'T GET used to how easily she'd gotten used to it. The money. Only a couple of days since they'd found it, and everything felt different already.

Like her job. Normally, given all the time she'd missed for doctor's appointments, today she would have gone in early. Tried to make some headway against the mountain of e-mails. Butter up her boss. Spend some time schmoozing the client, letting them feel they were involved without letting them muck anything up.

There'd been a time when she'd loved it. Loved the hours and the excitement of a downtown ad firm, loved wearing heeled boots and working on the forty-first floor, loved the free lunches and Friday-afternoon beer. But lately it had come to seem so . . . pointless. Working sixty-hour weeks to create advertising—the one product people actively tried to avoid.

And this morning she just couldn't face it. So after Tom had left, she'd called in to say that she was wiped out from the treatments. Then she'd put on her favorite jeans, gone to the basement, and taken eight bundles of their money.

Their money. That was another funny thing. She no longer thought of it as Bill's. From the moment she lied to the detective, it had started to become theirs. Little images popped up against her eyelids when she closed them: the house paid off, a baby girl in her arms and another on the way, an annual vacation to South Carolina to play in the surf. Nothing elaborate, no jet-set life or movie-star parties. Just a family and the security to enjoy it. That was all she had ever really wanted.

She flipped her signal, turned onto Lincoln. A lovely spring morning, the trees suddenly green along the neighborhood blocks, sunlight playful off storefront windows. A perfect day to play hooky. She decided to treat herself to lunch. Maybe even call her sister, see if Sara wanted to join.

But first, errands. She dropped off the dry cleaning, filled the tank with gas. Swung through a hardware store for some cleanser and rags. Then spun east toward Uptown.

The neighborhood was an in-betweener, an economically depressed zone—trash bags in piles, men lounging against the wall, shops that sold incense and hair extensions—nestled between affluent neighbors. It was an area she didn't often hit. It wasn't dangerous exactly, but it didn't offer much reason to visit, either. But today she found exactly what she was looking for on a Clark Street corner.

She parked at a meter, glancing around to make sure no one was watching. An empty taxi was two spaces up. A pedestrian waiting on the light to change glanced in her direction, then up at a billboard for a cell phone company. Anna narrowed her eyes, but the man didn't look over again. Down the block the El rattled overhead, throwing flickering shadows across gray stone.

She hadn't been inside a Currency Exchange in a decade. The last time was before Sara lived in town, when she and a boyfriend had come to visit. Neither of them had remembered to deposit their paychecks before running to the airport. Considering that was half their drinking fund for the weekend, it had seemed problematic until Tom had suggested visiting an Exchange.

This was a different location, but they all seemed pretty much the same. Garish neon, the inside faded linoleum and too-bright fluorescents, a counter fronted with inch-thick Plexiglas. A shuffling line of people looking as though they'd like to be elsewhere. A closed-circuit camera was mounted on the back wall, and it made her nervous. She took sunglasses from her purse and put them on.

It took about five minutes to make it to the counter, where a bored woman popped her gum, then asked what Anna wanted.

"I'd like a cashier's check, please." She pulled the envelope from her purse. "Made out to Citibank."

"How much." The clerk's voice so level it hardly seemed a question.

Anna glanced over her shoulder, then said, "Fifteen thousand, four hundred and twelve dollars, and fifty-seven cents."

"Sure thing, lady." The clerk rolled her eyes, then gestured to the customer behind Anna. "Next."

"Wait." Anna didn't budge. "Is there a problem?"

"Only with you being crazy."

"Why do you say that?"

"You serious?" The clerk stared. "You want a cashier's check for fifteen thousand, four hundred and twelve dollars?"

"And fifty-seven cents."

"How do you plan to pay for that?"

Anna reached into her purse, took out a bundle and a half of hundreds. Set them down on the counter, then smiled to see the clerk's jaw drop.

THE SHOTGUN WAS a Remington Tactical 870 configured with a pistol grip and loaded with three-inch magnum slugs. Marshall liked it. At this range, it would tear a fist-sized hole in the door and eviscerate anyone standing on the other side. Of course, fired inside, it'd leave them both half-deaf for hours too.

Jack knocked, and they both watched the peephole set in "Bill

Samuelson's" door. Seconds clicked by. There was a faint odor of smoke. Jack knocked again, then rocked from foot to foot. "He's not here."

There was a hint of disappointment in his voice, and that irked Marshall. Professionally speaking, Will not being here was a good thing. It would give them time to search the place, find the money if it was inside. He was more than happy to help take care of Will—man had stolen from him too—but you had to have priorities. He put up the shotty. "How's the dead bolt?"

Thirty seconds later, the door swung wide. The living room was spartan, just a lamp, a La-Z-Boy, and a television on a pressed-wood entertainment center. Marshall went first, sweeping the room and then the hall. Behind him, he heard Jack lock the door.

The apartment radiated that unmistakable feeling of emptiness, but Marshall moved carefully anyway. The bedroom had a cheap box–spring–and–mattress combo, the blankets ruffled like someone had been sleeping on them. The second bedroom had been converted to a weight room, with a crammed ashtray and a bench sporting iron. A hall bathroom had the lights off, toilet in need of cleaning. In the kitchen, the stovetop was scorched and the wall blackened. The source of the smoke, apparently. A back door led to a narrow stairwell. "Looks like he took a powder."

Jack didn't answer, just wandered back down the hall. Stepped into the weight room, looked around. He picked up one of the cigarettes, inspected it, the butt smudging his white surgical gloves. "What kind of an asshole smokes while he's working out?"

"Will's kind." The hunter in him could *feel* Will here, could see him lifting, pausing between sets to fire a cigarette. The man would have been nervous, jumpy. Feeling a constant pressure behind his eyes, that sense he was being watched, that someone was getting closer. Marshall let the shotgun dangle, checked the load on the bench. 120. Pussy. "Why didn't he blow town?"

"I don't know," Jack said. "Maybe he figured we'd leave first."

Marshall nodded. If Will thought they didn't have a way to find him, then holing up wasn't a bad idea. Without the cash, and with CPD working doubles to find them, leaving was a good call. The job had been all over the newspapers and the tabloids both.

"Damn it," Jack said, slinging his .45.

"It'll take a while to search." Marshall shrugged. "Maybe we'll get lucky, he'll drop by, you two can have yourselves a chat."

SHE HIT FIVE MORE Currency Exchanges in the next few hours. It seemed safer to spread it out. Then she stopped by the clinic and stunned the receptionist.

They'd figured it the night before, sitting at the kitchen table, a half-empty bottle of three-buck-Chuck between them. "It should work," Tom had said. "If we never deposit the money, never declare it, the government doesn't know to look for it. Cashier's checks."

As it happened, Anna had found an even better twist. The cashier's checks were good for the clinic and their medical expenses. But Currency Exchanges would let them pay their credit card bills directly, immediately depositing the money.

That morning, they'd been almost seventy grand in debt. By noon, they were even.

The feeling was strange and wonderful. In their wildest hopes, they hadn't imagined being able to pay that down for years. They'd become resigned to it, this ethereal burden that trailed behind them, and suddenly they were free. It was like dropping ten pounds. She felt a radiance, a glow that made her smile, made her nod her head and tap her fingers as the Mountain Goats sang from the CD player, John Darnielle telling her how he was gonna make it through this year if it killed him.

Anna parked the Pontiac on their block, slung her purse over her shoulder, and took the hardware bag in her other hand. Leaves rustled in a hundred shades of green above her head, and the air was sweet with the smell of dirt and sunlight. She walked down the street, taking it all in, breathing beauty. She skipped up the steps to their front porch, hummed as she opened the door to the vestibule. She had a feeling she hadn't had in years, one that used to come naturally, back in the days when a job was just a job, when the future was nothing but options. A simple, wonderful feeling that everything, *everything*, was going to be okay.

She pulled the keys from her purse and started for the stairwell door. Then paused. No point hauling the cleaning supplies up to their apartment. May as well just leave them in the bottom unit. Anna stepped to Bill Samuelson's door and slid the key in the lock.

Still humming, she stepped into the living room and shut the door behind her. The place smelled like smoke, though not as badly as before. She set down her purse and the bag from the hardware store, then went to the bay window, unlatched it and hoisted it rattling upward. That was better. She started down the hall, intending to do the same in the kitchen, get a little cross-draft going.

The door to the bedroom was closed. That was odd. She didn't remember closing it after they left the other day. Maybe they'd left a window open, and the breeze had slammed the door. Anna turned the handle, pushed the door open.

The drawers were all pulled out of the dresser, and the closet doors were open. The mattress lay askew on the box spring. Ghostly feathers traced her back. "Tom?" Had he come home early to start clearing out the apartment? She stepped into the bedroom like the floor might crack beneath her weight. "Honey?" Anna took another hesitant step, conscious now of her breathing, of the weight of the purse strap on her shoulder and the pinch of boots against her toes. She could smell something foul, a rotten stink that made her nostrils twitch. It was coming from the bathroom.

Slowly, she peered around the corner. The vanity lights were on, hot white spilling across the room. Below, the cabinets gaped, revealing the lonely leftovers of a life: air freshener, plunger, half-burned candle. The medicine chest doors hung wide, their mirrored faces throwing fragments of the room. Bottles had been knocked over, and the toothpaste and toothbrush lay on the floor. The room looked like someone had gone through it in a hurry.

The smell was worse here. It took her a moment to realize why, and then she noticed the toilet. Ughh. Why would Tom walk away like that, forget to flush—

Suddenly it hit her all at once. The disarray, the closed bedroom door, the toilet, Jesus, the disgusting toilet, left filthy by someone. Someone not Tom. The muscles in her neck tightened, and she threw one hand up to cover her mouth. Whirled around, realizing her back was exposed, sure someone was behind her.

The bedroom was empty.

She had to get out. Fast. But what if whoever had done this was still inside? Her temples throbbed, and her armpits went moist. Did she dare risk running for the front door? She'd come in humming, called Tom's name, done everything but telegraph exactly where she was. He could be creeping down the hallway now, a skinny man with long dirty fingers, a knife in one hand, the other on the zipper of ragged pants, stroking slowly—

Get a grip, get a grip, goddamnit, get a grip!

The best thing to do was get out, get out fast. Front door or back? The front, the way she'd come. Chances were if the burglar was still here, he was heading away from her, for the back door. Okay. Simple, then. Pull out your keys. Good. Grip them so you can punch with them, stupid as that seems. Good. Now just turn and walk out the way you came. Don't panic, don't run and risk falling, just walk out of here right now.

I said, just turn and walk out of here—

Anna Reed lunged for the door, threw herself into the hallway, and sprinted for the front, her heart slamming till she thought her ribs might crack.

JACK STARED THROUGH THE WINDSHIELD at the woman they'd seen earlier. She'd just thrown open the door to Will Tuttle's place, then the front door to the vestibule, and was tear-assing down the block like the bogeyman was behind her.

"I guess she realized we'd been there," Marshall said dryly. "What do you think she was doing in his apartment?"

"I don't know," Jack said.

"You think she's in on it?"

He spread his hands, said nothing.

"Lucky thing you saw her coming." Marshall pulled the briefcase onto his lap. "If she'd just walked in on us . . ."

Jack started the car, glanced over his shoulder, and then pulled the Civic onto the street. The Reed woman would be dialing the police. Best to be moving. Marshall popped the latches on the briefcase and lifted the lid. Rows of neatly ordered bundles and prescription bottles fit together like a puzzle. "What do you want to do with this shit?"

"You know anybody who can move it?"

Marshall sucked air through his teeth. "Maybe Mikey Cook?"

"Trust him?"

"I wouldn't let him fuck my sister or anything, but he's good people."

Jack nodded. "Fine. We can unload it when we're finished."

They rode in silence for a momen; then Marshall said, "Will's going to be spooked now."

"Yeah." Jack signaled, then turned south. "We'll have to keep a close watch, make sure he doesn't bolt." He kept his face and voice calm, but behind them his mind surged and raged. *You better be spooked, Will. I'm coming. I'm coming for you and for my money, and nothing is going to stand in my way.*

Nothing.

7

THERE WAS A POLICE CAR in front of his house.

Tom had been away from his office when Anna called. It was one of *those* mornings, the kind where by nine-thirty he knew he'd be lunching at his desk, and by eleven o'clock he realized he wouldn't be eating lunch at all. The kind where he wished he'd stuck to his dream of writing books, instead of getting a corporate job doing technical writing. The Vice President in Charge of Fucking Up People's Day had had a change of heart on a program Tom's team had been set to roll out next week. Typical bullshit, just ego cloaked in platitudes about "forward-thinking design" and "going another way," but it tanked ten weeks' worth of work. After a meeting like that, seeing the red voice-mail light burning didn't brighten things up.

Then he heard the message, and it got worse. Anna was panicky, breathless. All he could make out was something about someone in their house, and to come home right away. He'd stood with the phone in one hand, his lips clenched, staring out at the city street far below, boxy yellow cabs and ant people. Part of him was thinking about how this was going to complicate things here, and wondering what the hell she was doing at home in the middle of the day anyway. The other part was already racing for the street, hailing a cab, offering the driver forty on a twenty-dollar ride if only he'd go fast.

He went with the latter, spent the ride praying that nothing was wrong. But there was a police car in front of his house. Tom threw two bills at the driver and leapt out of the car. He ran straight through the rows of tulips his neighbor had planted, and took the steps to their porch two at a time. "Anna?" He started to unlock the door to their apartment, then noticed that the one to the bottom unit was a few inches open. He pushed it wide, looked in. "Hello? Anna?"

"Tom?" The voice came from down the hall, followed by loud footsteps, and then she was there, throwing her arms around him, her grip tight, her hair in his face, and something in his chest loosened, a fist he hadn't realized was clutching his heart.

"You okay?"

"Yes. Yes, I'm fine, just . . . " She sniffed. "Someone was here. In this apartment. I was so scared—"

"It's okay, baby. It's okay." He held her, stroked her hair. "You're okay. Just tell me what happened."

She stepped back, took a deep breath. "I decided to call in. Ran some errands, took care of our bills"—giving him a meaningful look—"you know, like we'd talked about."

They had talked about it, though he hadn't intended for her to miss yet another day of work to do it. Not like Currency Exchanges weren't open twenty-four hours. But that wasn't important. He nodded.

"When I came home, I was dropping stuff off in here. I went in the bedroom, and the drawers were open, the closets, there were things on the floor." She locked eyes with him. "Tom, they went through everything."

The fist moved from his chest to his gut, his stomach going wobbly. "Are you saying—"

"They were looking for something. Whoever they were."

He realized his mouth was open, and closed it. "It was probably just someone robbing the place." He saw her uncertainty, kept talking. "Looking for jewelry, money, that kind of thing."

"They didn't take the TV, the—"

"They didn't take it *yet*. You probably startled them."

She started to protest, then stopped as footsteps came down the hall. A cop, tall and barrel-chested in his bulletproof vest. "Are you the husband?"

"Yes. Tom Reed." He put his hand out.

"Al Abramson." The cop shook hands, then rested his right on the butt of his gun and turned to Anna. "Ma'am, we've checked the whole place, including your apartment and the basement. There's nobody here."

She sighed. "Thank God."

"Any idea who would have done this?"

"No," she said. "Tom?"

He shook his head.

"Well," Abramson said, "the way they went through everything, I'd guess it was junkies. They hit the medicine cabinet too. Pretty common. Get strung out, need a fix, they'll try anything. I wouldn't worry about them coming back."

"What about the . . ." Anna hesitated, then pointed toward the bathroom.

Abramson shook his head. "These guys are animals. At least they used the toilet. I've seen places they did it right on the living room carpet." His radio chirped, and he said, "Excuse me a moment," then stepped down the hall and answered it.

"Did what?" Tom cocked his head at Anna.

"Uh," she said. "You don't want to know."

"Are you sure you're okay?"

"Yeah. Just shaken up."

He hugged her again, wrapped his arms around her, the smell of her filling his nostrils. "Anna, maybe we should tell them—"

"No."

"I'm just saying."

"No." She pulled away. "That's our child. I'm not giving it up, not without a reason."

He was saved from replying by Abramson's return. "Sorry about that, folks. I didn't realize, I guess you had an incident here the other night?"

"Yes," Tom said. "Our tenant died. This was his apartment."

The cop nodded, not overly interested. "Well, that was my dispatcher, wanting to let me know a detective was on the way. Guy named Halden?"

"We met him that night. But he's a homicide detective, right? Why is he coming?"

Abramson shrugged. "Have to ask him. Meanwhile, you want to take a look around, see if anything in particular is missing? I need to know for the report."

"We didn't know our tenant very well," Anna said. "I wouldn't know what to look for."

"Well, just take a glance, see if you spot anything."

They shrugged, started walking around. Tom figured unless the refrigerator was gone, he wasn't going to notice much difference, but it gave him time to think.

What he'd said to Anna, about it being thieves, that had been automatic, just him trying to calm her down, to make things better. Male problem solving. But in his own head, he had to wonder. They'd never been robbed before. Lincoln Square was pretty quiet. And as he took in the gaping cabinets, the cans of soup and containers of pasta spilled across the counter, the open drawers, it was hard not to get the feeling that this was a pretty thorough search for a couple of junkies.

Maybe they hit this unit instead of ours because it was on the ground floor. Maybe the place is torn apart because they were looking for cash, or for pills. Maybe they were thorough precisely because they were desperate. There's no reason to think it's more than that.

Except, of course, that there were reasons. Several hundred thousand of them.

DETECTIVE HALDEN made Anna feel good about paying taxes. Justice in gray pinstripes, he was in charge the moment he stepped into the room. The other cops clearly deferred to him, their posture improving. Halden spoke to the officers, nodding and asking questions. He squatted by the front door and focused a flashlight into the lock, then repeated the process in the back.

"Hello again," as he shook their hands. "Officer Abramson

gave me a rundown, but would you take me through it again, Mrs. Reed?"

"Anna, please."

"Anna. I'd like to hear it from you."

She nodded, sitting at the kitchen table now, the three of them having coffee, the uniformed cops gone. Told him about running errands—leaving out the part where she leveled seventy grand in debt—then coming home, finding the place ransacked. The foul smell in the bathroom, the insult of it, the violation, someone they didn't know leaving that floating in their toilet. Her fear as she realized they might still be around, then her flight, right past her purse with her cell phone, and finally dialing 911 from the corner market. Halden nodded, scribbled the occasional note. His posture straight, a good-looking guy, clean-cut as a recruiting poster. Her gaze kept pulling to the gun on his hip, a matte black thing that made her shiver. When she finished talking, he nodded, said, "When you arrived, the door was locked?"

"Yes."

"You're sure?"

She thought back, remembered setting down the plastic bags to dig out her keys. "Yes."

"And the windows were closed and locked as well."

She nodded. Then caught where he was going, said, "Yes. So how did they—"

"Neither door shows signs of force. My guess would be that they either had keys or jimmied the lock."

"Who would have keys?"

"A friend?" Halden stared at her. "Tell me, have you remembered anything else about your tenant?"

She made herself bite her lip before shaking her head, wanting it to look like she was thinking hard. "I'm sorry. We really didn't know him."

"You said the other night that you didn't know what he did for a living."

"No."

"Did you ever notice him going to work? Bump into him in the hallway?"

She thought about it. "You know, I guess I didn't, really."

"Why do you ask?" Tom lifted his mug by the rim. "Could whoever broke in have something to do with him?"

Damn it, don't go there. Why even plant the seed?

Halden rocked his head in a noncommittal gesture. "Hard to say." He set his pen down on top of his notebook, the edges perfectly parallel, then leaned forward with his hands laced. "Usually we don't disclose information about active cases, but given the circumstances, there's something I should tell you. Your tenant, the man you knew as Bill Samuelson, that wasn't his name. His real name was William Tuttle. When we ran his fingerprints, the record came up." He paused. "I'm not going to lie to you. Tuttle was a bad guy."

"What do you mean, bad?" Tom asked.

"He'd been arrested for assault. Did a little time, couple of years, on an armed robbery. He was questioned in several more, and was picked up on a distribution charge out in California, though that eventually fell apart." Halden leaned back, spread his hands. "I should say that he wasn't wanted for anything when he died. Just because he had a sheet doesn't mean he was still a criminal. That's why I was asking about a job."

Anna could hear the ticking of the wall clock, could feel her pulse outpacing it. The money. It wasn't what they'd thought, a quirky story, a recluse who didn't trust banks. That money was stolen. And not in the victimless embezzlement scenario they'd spun, either. Will Tuttle was no pension scammer or white-collar embezzler. He was a dangerous man who worked with others like him. She met Tom's eyes, saw the same calculation in them.

They had to get Halden out. The longer he was here, the greater the chance they'd slip in some way. She could tell that Tom half-wanted to just give in, to announce the truth to the detective. But it was more complicated than that.

She realized that Tom and Halden had continued talking. Shook herself, tuned back in.

" . . . an overdose," Halden said. "That prescription? It was a drug called fentanyl, a very serious painkiller. It's not normally available in pills like that, but this was re-cooked for the street."

"So it was suicide?"

The cop shook his head. "No. He probably figured it was something he could handle, OxyContin. But the dosage was powerful enough to trigger a heart condition. Chances are he didn't even know he had heart problems. People usually don't, until it's too late. But here's the thing." Halden sipped his coffee. "To get his hands on stuff like that, he would have known people. Dealers, other junkies. It's very possible one of them knew where he lived."

"And decided to see if Samuelson—I mean, Tuttle—if he had any drugs to steal," Tom said.

"Exactly." The detective nodded. "That's my thinking."

She crossed her arms, leaned back. Looked away. Hitting the body language hard, trying to get the detective to see it was time he left. But Tom kept talking, asking, "Is there anything you can do?"

"Do?"

"To catch whoever was here. Fingerprints or something?"

Halden smiled, shook his head. "If you want, I'll get a team out. They'll make a big mess, stain up your nice white walls, but if it'll make you feel better, I'm happy to do it."

"There's really no point?"

"Guy who knows how to pick a lock but not to wear gloves? Or even if he had keys." Halden shrugged. "I mean, you think they don't watch TV too?"

"So should we be worried?"

"That they'll come back? No," the detective said. "They'd have gotten a pretty good scare. Besides, they probably found what there was to find."

Tom looked at Anna, then reached out to cover her hand with his own. "Good."

A silence fell, and then the detective picked up his mug, took a last sip, set it down. "Well. I best be on my way. There will be some follow-up paperwork for your insurance, but you should be in good shape."

They stood up, followed him to the door.

"Thanks again, Detective," Anna said, thinking, *Almost, he's almost gone.*

"My job," he said. He tucked his gold pen inside his suit jacket. "One more thing."

Tom cocked his head. "What's that?"

"Will Tuttle was a thief. Who knows what he might have stolen, what might have been lying around his place. Jewelry, drugs. Hell, maybe even cash."

"So?"

Halden shrugged. "Life's funny. Sometimes situations land in front of you that you don't know how you'll react until you're in them."

"What does that mean?"

"Well, just hypothetically, say that someone found whatever it was Will had. It would be the easiest thing in the world to decide to keep it. I mean, he's dead, so it's not stealing." The detective's eyes were searchlights. Anna felt something squeezing her lungs. Her mouth was dry and her palms were soaked. She stared, trying to think of something to say.

"I'm not sure where you're going with this." Tom sounded steady, even the tiniest bit offended. It gave her strength, her partner in crime covering when she slipped. "Are you suggesting we took something?"

Halden just hit them with the gaze again, steady, knowing; he was seeing inside her, knew what they'd done. He was smarter than she'd guessed, smarter and more in tune, and he'd known while they sat at the table and chatted, had maybe known from the very beginning. Anna felt a mad urge to open her mouth and let truth pour free. Forced her teeth to grind.

After a long moment, the detective shrugged, said, "Tell you what. If you remember anything else useful, give me a call, would you? Sooner would be better." He reached for the door handle. "Thanks for the coffee." Then he stepped out, letting the door fall behind.

8

"ARE YOU FUCKING *SERIOUS*?"

"Yes." Anna sat on the kitchen counter Indian-style and watched her husband gulp a bourbon and water that was pretty much sans water.

"You still want to keep it."

"Yes."

Tom stared with that expression he got when he couldn't decide whether to be baffled or angry. It wasn't his most attractive look to begin with, and over the years she'd come to associate it with their fights. He blew a breath, shook his head, took another hit off the bourbon. "We should never have taken it in the first place." Something in his tone accusatory. A hint that maybe she was to blame, that he'd been talked into it. She thought about setting him straight, didn't see the point. Instead she shrugged, said, "We're past that now."

"If I had known the truth—"

"If either of us had, we would have left it alone and called the cops. But how could we know? I mean, really? Bill was a bit of an asshole, okay, but who looks at their neighbor and thinks, *Gee, I bet he's a violent criminal*?" She shook her head. "Like you said, he was a hermit. It made more sense to imagine him saving his pennies than waving a gun at some clerk."

"Clerk?" Tom shook his head. "Don't be naïve. This didn't come from a register. I don't think you can get four hundred grand from a *bank*. This was stolen from a person. Maybe the one who took a shit in our bathroom this afternoon. You think of that?"

"Of course."

"And you still want to keep it."

"Tell you what, honey. I won't be naïve if you won't be dense." She leaned against the cabinets. "It's not as simple as giving it back and saying we're sorry."

He shook his head, threw back the rest of his drink in a swallow, then opened the Maker's and splashed in two inches, forgoing the water completely this time. He capped the bottle but left the drink on the counter, put a palm up to rub his forehead. When he spoke, it was from behind his hand. "Maybe we can get that money back."

"How?"

"Maybe the transactions can be canceled. Or, wait," he said, "it went to credit cards. We can just pull it out against them."

"Twenty-five thousand went to the clinic. We can't pull that back. And the rest, do you really want to take a fifty-thousand-dollar cash advance? We were close to broke, to having to sell the house. We'd be worse off than before."

"Okay, so we keep what we've spent and return the rest. The cops don't know how much was there to begin with."

She stared at him, her brow wrinkled. "And all it takes is one smart detective to pull our bills. Detective Halden seems pretty smart."

"Yeah, but he was warning us. Trying to help."

"Trying to *help*? He wasn't trying to help, he was fishing. Hoping we'd screw up, tell him something. He's a cop. You think if we hand over the money, he's going to tell us all is forgiven?"

"I can't see us going to jail over something like that."

"Maybe not. But how much do you think the lawyer will cost?" Anna shook her head. "If we give up now, we'll end up in twice as much debt, have to sell the house, maybe even declare bankruptcy. All for nothing but a dress too nice to wear and a pair of sunglasses you'll lose in a month."

He glared at her. "Someone broke into our house today. I couldn't give a shit about our debt. Get your head straight." Accusation in his eyes.

She met the glare, bounced it back. "How's this for having my head straight? Someone broke in, searched the place, *and they didn't find it*. Now they know it's not here. There's nothing connecting us to the money."

"You think they're just going to back off?"

"You think giving it to the cops will back them off? Not like we can post a sign, 'We gave the money back, please leave us alone.' Anyway"—she shrugged—"think. Why would they assume his *landlords* have his stolen money? Whoever they are, they probably think he stashed it. They checked his apartment to be sure, and now they'll start looking elsewhere."

That shut him up. He leaned over the counter from the other side, his elbows on it, the drink between them. She knew the posture—God, after years, what posture, what gesture, what expression couldn't she read like a billboard—knew that it meant he was thinking about it, that the hotter emotions were draining away.

"Look." She uncurled her legs, pins and needles, then slid off her perch and stood across the counter from him. "I know it's scary, but we have to ride it out."

He sighed. Looking at his drink, he said, "I just don't want anything bad to happen to . . ." He trailed off, leaving the *you* unspoken. Trying to protect her. It was sweet in a way, but irritating too. She didn't need a knight in business casual right now; she needed a partner, someone on the ball and working the problem.

"I know, babe. I know." She took his hand. "But nothing is going to. We'll be careful. We won't spend any more. Forget we have it, live like normal. We won't give any hints that we took the money, give anyone a reason to suspect us. And if things get worse, we can always give it back then."

He played with the whiskey glass, spinning it on its edge, his eyes focused on the swirl of gold.

"Are you okay?"

He shrugged. "I hate this. I don't even care about the money. Not really."

She snorted.

"You don't believe me?"

Anna shook her head. "I don't believe you felt like you had to say it." She put a hand up to his cheek, the skin rough with blue-black stubble. "I know you, baby. Better than anybody." She smiled at him, saw the crinkle around his eyes, the lines in his forehead. "Don't think of it as money. It's never been about that."

"What has it been about, then?"

His question shook her. She'd thought they were in it together, that there had been one simple reason to take it, the simplest reason in the world, the one that was only complicated for them. For a moment, she stared at him, then she stepped around the counter so that they faced each other. She reached for his hand, the fingers larger than hers and rougher, and with her other hand she pulled up her shirt and pressed his palm against her belly, let him feel the heat of it. She stared at him and didn't say a word.

Finally he nodded, a slow, reluctant gesture. "Okay."

She was still awake.

Tom was on his back, one arm thrown off the bed, the sheet bunched around his hips. Anna leaned on an elbow and looked at him, the faint trace of his features by the light of the clock. How many nights had they gone to bed together? Thousands. Too many to count. Thousands of nights of brushing teeth and washing faces, of conversations about bills, funny anecdotes, trembling embraces. She could smell his skin, his hair. His faint snore rose and fell against the steady drone of the rain machine. She'd told him she liked the machine for the rhythm, never had the heart to tell the truth, that it drowned out his snoring.

The hardwood floor was cool underfoot. She stepped lightly, dodging the squeaky spot. Closed the bathroom door and peed in the dark, then flushed the toilet and turned the light on. Stared at herself in the mirror, naked except for a pair of cotton panties and a white T-shirt, her hair tangled, skin red from the pillow. Stared and stared, and then when she was tired of thinking about it, she pulled her robe from the bathroom door, killed the light, and crept out.

The house was inhabited by night. The familiar surroundings seemed different, the counter looming, the kitchen table and chairs a beetle with a tangle of legs. She eased the back door open.

The stairwell was old, lit only by a high Plexiglas window, and she moved carefully, wishing she had thought to put on slippers, her bare feet tracing the edge of the wood steps. The light faded the lower she went, until she closed her eyes and just let her feet guide her, one gentle motion at a time: slide, ease down, touch the next stair. When she felt concrete, she opened her eyes and fumbled around left-handed for the light switch.

Dusty yellow pushed against the darkness, but not very hard. The mass of the water heater sat to her left, their barbecue grill, draped in spiderwebs, to the right. The air smelled old, with a faint tang of bleach from the washing machine. She moved forward, the concrete cold, careful to watch for pebbles and nails, the detritus of a hundred years. The furnace was a dark tentacled shape. She stepped past it, then moved to the wall and lifted off the plywood panel that sealed the crawl space. The scrape was loud and accusatory.

It's not stealing. It's not. I'm not taking from him, I'm not even lying to him. I'm just looking out for our best interests. He wants it as badly as I do, and for the same reason, but he's scared, thinks he has to protect me.

I have to protect us from him protecting me.

She squatted down and reached into shadow, fumbled against the pipes and dust until she found the strap of the duffel bag. She pulled it out, surprised again at the weight, at how she had to drag it until it was clear enough for her to get a good angle and haul it to her shoulder. She replaced the panel and stood up. Walked back the way she came. When she flipped the light off, blackness fell like a blanket.

If he thinks he's protecting me, he might do something stupid. He might panic and just give it up without thinking. We can't afford that. We have to think. To plan. We have to move carefully. That's all I'm doing. Being careful.

Her mouth tasted sour as she unlocked the outside door. The air was cool, heavy with the smell of growing things. A truck went down their street too fast, the engine revving. She hesitated at the edge of the building, conscious suddenly of wearing nothing but a robe and panties, her hair a mess. But it was after three, dead hours, and no one was on the sidewalk. She went to the car and did what she had to do, covering the bag with a pile of clothes she'd been meaning to donate.

Walking back to the house, she felt an absence in her chest, like she was hollow, a vacuum in there that was tugging at the rest of her. Her heart beat quick, and the night air found its way past her robe to tighten her nipples and send a shiver down her spine.

This is the right thing. I love you, Tom. I do.

She hurried up the steps and snuck back into her own home.

9

No. No, no, no, fucking *no*!

Jack's hands shook, and he set the newspaper down on the diner counter so that he could read it properly. Like the problem had been the tremor of his fingers, and not the plain black and white of the *Tribune*.

Will Tuttle stared up at him. The shot was a couple years old, Will back in his Hollywood days, hair frosted and mussed above the standard Screw-You-Pig expression everybody wore in a mug shot. And beside it, a headline that changed everything.

MURDER SUSPECT FOUND DEAD IN LINCOLN SQUARE APARTMENT

The story went on to say how Tuttle was a prime suspect in the recent "Shooting Star" robbery that had left two dead. How he was a felon with a history of assault and armed robbery who had been living under a false name. How his landlords Anna and Tom Reed, hearing a smoke alarm, had let themselves into his apartment to find him dead, victim of an apparent overdose. How police had no comment at this time, other than to say that they were diligently pursuing all leads in the Shooting Star case.

For days they'd been watching the house, and all the time Will had been dead already. Jack clenched his hands into fists, let the nails bite into his palms. Bobby dead, and now there was no one he could repay for it, no way to balance the score. By dying, the prick had forced a stalemate.

"It's time we thought about leaving," Marshall said.

Jack snatched the paper from the counter, crumpled it up into a ball, watching Will's face wrinkle and distort. He mashed it tight, then hucked it at the trash can on the other side of the counter. A trucker sitting two down from them looked over, his expression hard. Jack stared back. "Something on your mind?" The man shook his head quickly, turned back to his eggs. Jack kept his gaze locked until the trucker's fork started to shake.

Marshall cleared his throat. "Are you hearing me? With him gone, it's highway time."

"An overdose, for Christ's sake. Drifted off like he was taking a nap."

"Look, you've got blood for blood. His nephew went hard."

"It's not enough."

"You want to piss on his grave?" Marshall shrugged. "Fine. We give the fucker a twelve-pack salute to float him into the afterlife. But then we split."

Jack rubbed at his eyes, pushing hard. Blood-purple stars whirled and spun against his lids. "There's nothing in the paper about the money."

"They wouldn't announce that."

"Maybe. But if it was there, we'd have found it."

"So he stashed it somewhere. It's a big city."

Jack picked up his coffee, took a cold and bitter swallow. Tried to think what he knew about Will. Not much, not when you came down to it. They'd worked a few jobs together, but the guy generally kept himself to himself. If he'd passed the money on to a friend, Jack couldn't think how to go about finding out. And it could always be somewhere untraceable. A safe-deposit box, the rent paid years in advance, four hundred grand just sitting there. He had a memory of Bobby, that night, staring down at the case, his face lit up with wonder. His brother had died for that money.

"He's not going to beat me," Jack said.

"Who?"

"I'm not leaving. Not without the money."

"What money?" Marshall shrugged. "It's gone, man."

"We could check his place again."

"For what? You said it yourself: If it was there, we'd have found it."

"There'll be something. Something that will tell us where to look."

"You think he drew a treasure map?"

Jack shook his head. "An address book, maybe. We can start working through his friends. Or a receipt for a storage locker." He had a vision of his father, rough hands moving easy as he bent over one of the wooden airplanes he spent hours on. Using a scrap of balsa to trace the glue onto a wing strut. Looking up to see his son watching him, and smiling, saying in accented English, *One foot, then another,* synu. *Do this, you do anything.*

Marshall sucked air through his teeth, drummed his fingers on the counter. "I don't know, Jack."

"Wait a second. Maybe they were friends. Maybe they know who his other friends are." Another thought hit, and he rubbed his hand against his chin. "Holy shit. More than that. They were *in* his place. Before us. Before the cops."

"Who was?"

"His landlords." Jack looked over. "Tom and Anna Reed."

"BELIEVE ME, I'm not any happier about it than you are." Christopher Halden leaned back, his feet up on the desk he shared with Karpinski, the detective working the opposite shift. Halden's side was tidy, ordered: an inbox of folders, a pen set, a list of the ME's phone numbers pinned to the half-cube wall beside a photo of the cabin he rented in northern Wisconsin. Karpinski was a slob. The remnants of a tuna sandwich rested precariously atop a teetering mound of papers.

"How could this happen? Why didn't you tell us first?" Anna Reed's voice sounded thin over the phone.

"We didn't tell you because it's only a theory at this point. Your tenant, Will Tuttle, is what's called a known associate of a man who was found killed at the Shooting Star scene. That means—"

"I've seen *Law & Order*."

"Okay. So you know that just because they'd been known to work together in the past, it doesn't mean that Tuttle was involved in that case. But someone, probably someone in the medical examiner's office, got excited and called a reporter."

"But they used our *names*. How could they do that?"

"Your names are a matter of public record. It would only take a phone call to find out you own the property. And the details of how you found the body were part of the accident report."

"So you're saying that someone just—"

"I'm saying someone who likes attention leaked it to the press. If I find out who it was, I'll have their head. But that's about all I can do at this point." He fought a sigh. It got tiring, the pose of calm assurance, the coddling. Sometimes he just wanted to scream at people to stop *whining*. To try a week in his job, investigating bodies three weeks dead in the heat of August, or eight-year-olds that caught stray bullets in a drive-by, and then see how heavy their little problems weighed.

There was a long pause, and then she spoke again, her voice nervous. "Do you think he was involved in that case?"

"The Shooting Star?" Halden picked up his pen, spun it between his fingers, the gold bouncing highlights. "Why do you ask?"

"Well, I was thinking the people who broke in might have been looking for the money."

"What money is that?"

"The money they stole," she said. "Right?"

"Let's not get ahead of ourselves, okay?" Halden put on the voice he used to talk to bereaved family members. "The men who committed that robbery were hard guys. They had a *lot* of known associates. No matter what the paper says, there's no reason to believe that Tuttle was in on that."

She started to say something, then stopped herself. Like she'd been about to argue but changed her mind. "Okay. You're right."

"Look, Mrs. Reed, if you don't feel safe, my advice is to go somewhere for a while. Stay with family. Or buy a dog."

"We're having an alarm system installed now."

"Good. That's good." He looked at his watch. Twenty after twelve. If he was going to get anything done today, he needed less time on the phone with high-maintenance citizens and more time on the street. "Now, unless there's anything else I can do for you . . ."

"No." Anna Reed caught the hint. "Thanks for your time. You'll let us know if you find out anything more?"

He promised he would, and then hung up, shaking his head. For the tenth time that morning, he looked at the photo, the cabin up west of Minocqua. It'd been built for hunting, but he'd done more than enough hunting without leaving Chicago. No, when he hit his twenty-nine-and-a-day he was going to buy that sucker instead of rent it, move up with a dog, a box of books, a twenty-pound sack of coffee beans, and maybe Marie, if he could convince her that 75 percent of a detective's salary was enough for them both.

There was a time he'd hoped he might go out at a higher grade, but that had faded as years rolled by. Lesser cops who kissed ass, worked the political angles, they moved up. Not him. It didn't matter. One glorious day he'd pull the Chequamegon National Forest around him like a blanket on a February night and not crawl out again. Just read and hike and make love. Head into Iron River on Saturday night for a couple of Budweisers.

He closed the folder he had spread in front of him, rapped it against the desk to even the edges, and set it in the inbox, wondering idly if Will Tuttle had been part of the Shooting Star. Not caring much; the case was a mess, and he was delighted to have no part of it. Sure, if someone did close it, it'd be a golden ticket—promotion, newspaper ink, commendations, the works. But the hitters had been pros, and nobody had a lead. Dollars to dough-nuts the bad guys were right now in Key West, kicking back on four hundred grand.

Wait. The money.

No information about it had been released. All the public knew was that the Star had been robbed, and that a bodyguard and a criminal had been shot. They didn't know about the missing cash. The Star's five-hundred-dollar-an-hour lawyer had made certain of that. But Anna Reed had said, *maybe they were looking for the money.*

Could be nothing. The offhand comment of a citizen with an active imagination.

Or it could be a lead.

He rubbed at his chin. The phone rang, but he ignored it. He couldn't just start digging around. The detectives in charge would welcome the help, but if he turned out to be wrong, he'd have committed himself, tied his name to a case that showed every sign of being a loser. Not a good thing for somedays.

Besides, all he had was a gut feeling. To do it properly, he'd need a lot more than that. Halden stared up at the fluorescents. Tapped a forefinger against his lips.

There was a way to check, of course. It wasn't precisely legal, but no one needed to know about it. Once he had what he needed, he could work backward to do it properly. He picked up the phone and dialed.

"Christopher Halden? *Detective* Christopher Halden? To what do I owe? You ready to lay a hundred against the Cubs?"

"Never happen, Tully. This is our year."

"God loves an optimist."

"That's what they keep telling me. Listen, you still snooping through people's private business?"

"You still playing with dead bodies?"

"Man's gotta make a living. I need you to run a check for me."

"Let me grab a pad." There was the sound of a chair creaking, and then Lawrence Tully said, "Okay, go."

"Reed, R-E-E-D, Thomas and Anna. Address is . . ." Halden opened his notebook, flipped pages, then read it off. "I'm curious to see if Mr. and Mrs. Reed came into any money recently."

"Got it. You just want the easy stuff, or should I lube up?"

"Somewhere in between."

"No problem. When should I expect the paperwork?"

"No paperwork on this one, Tully."

There was a pause. "I know it's been a long time since we were partners. I know I'm just a lowly information broker with a few friends here and there. But I could swear I read somewhere that unless you had a subpoena or written consent from a judge—"

"This isn't for court."

Another pause. "A personal matter?"

"Not exactly. Just checking a hunch. It'll be off the books."

There was a sigh. "You mean you won't be paying."

"I'll buy you a steak and offer my eternal gratitude."

"Lucky me." Tully cleared his throat. "All right, fine, you're good people. Gimme a couple of days. Freebies get slotted where I get time."

"Owe you one."

"Yeah, yeah. Remember me when you hit the Mega Ball."

*　　*　　*

THEIR MAILBOX WAS EMPTY. Considering the flood of junk mail they regularly got, it was odd, but Anna didn't worry about it. Probably just a new carrier. She climbed the stairs and pushed open the door to their unit.

The new alarm panel beeped, and she keyed the code quickly. The system freaked her out a little bit. She'd never lived anywhere with one, and while it seemed straightforward enough, she also figured it was only a matter of time before she forgot to disable it, or entered the wrong code, and ended up pinned to her own floor by a burly security guard.

Tom had called and set up the appointment the day of the break-in. Protecting her again. Of course, they could come only during business hours, and of course, he had a big meeting, so once again, she'd called in sick. Luckily, she got her boss's voice mail, left a message there. Lauren wouldn't be happy, but it couldn't make much difference. After all, Anna had already scheduled the afternoon off to babysit her nephew.

So all morning she'd watched a team of polite technicians cut into their drywall and run sensors to their windows. One of them had walked her through the system, showing her how to enter the code, how to change it. Tom had asked for the top of the line. It even had a feature that let her enter her code one digit higher. The alarm would shut off, but it would shoot a panic signal to the police. Slick. And once she took care of the money, they'd be safer still.

The thought sent guilt coursing through her, but she pushed it aside again. She was just being careful. If Tom found out, he'd be pissed and hurt, and she didn't want either. But then, they had agreed that it would be safer if neither of them touched the money. It kept them above suspicion. So the only way Tom would find out what she had done would be if he cheated, tried to act without her.

No victim, no crime.

Her cell phone rang. The office. She looked at it, thought about answering, didn't.

"WHY NOT JUST GRAB HER?" Marshall spoke around a mouthful of chips. "She knows anything, it's not going to take long to get it."

"We don't know if they're connected. Not for sure yet." He waited for her Pontiac to turn from Racine to Wolfram before he merged to follow, a couple of cars between them. "She gets hurt, the cops will assume it had something to do with Will. They'll come down hard, and we'll lose our shot." He always called them cops, never pigs, had known too many good Polacks who went that route. "We need to be sure."

"She's stopping."

"I can see." Jack slowed beside an empty spot. God bless the city. In the suburbs, even a civilian might notice they were being followed. Here, especially in this stolen black Honda, they were anonymous. Just neighbors. Jack flipped his signal and reversed. Anna Reed didn't even look in their direction as she closed the trunk of the Pontiac, slung a duffel bag over her shoulder, and strolled up the walk to one of the graystones. He watched her go, the good sway of her hips. A nice-looking woman, with that serene glow that came with a sense of safety.

"Now what?"

Jack spread his hands. "We watch."

"RAGGEDY ANNA." Sara threw the door open, then stepped forward with her arms extended. She wore a men's flannel shirt, something from an ex-boyfriend no doubt, and her hair was pulled into a ponytail.

"Hey, honey." Anna dropped the duffel bag and let Sara gather her into her arms. Tom had once said Sara was the best hugger in the world, and though at the time it had slammed a spike of jealousy into Anna, now she thought of it whenever Sara embraced her. The girl just had a way of squeezing without reservation.

"How are you?" The question whispered, concerned.

"Good." With everything that had happened in the last few days, it took Anna a minute to realize that Sara was talking about the failed IVF. Normally the thought would have had jagged edges, but things were different now. "Better than last week."

Her sister leaned back from the hug, smiled. "I'm glad." She squeezed Anna's arm, then stepped away. "Come on in."

Anna followed, knowing what was coming. Bracing herself, trying to grit her teeth without actually moving them. The apartment smelled of milk and diapers and talcum powder, of late nights spent soothing and cooing, of afternoon naps for two. Of hope and promise and dependence and love. Of spit-up and sweat and late golden sunlight.

It smelled of baby.

And as always, something in Anna just broke, fluttered away

like a kite cut free. Same as all the times she'd been invited to showers, or had to buy onesies for near-forgotten college friends, or sometimes even when she just saw pregnant women, that happy flush as they neared the end. To cover it, she did what she always did, which was say meaningless things. "Place looks nice."

Sara, on her way to the kitchen, threw the words over her shoulder. "I know, right? One minute I'm dropping E with the shower boys at Spin, next I'm Betty Crocker." She shook her head. "Sometimes I'm not sure how I got here."

Her voice was weary, but there was nothing like regret in it. Anna forced a smile. "Yeah, well, I don't know about Betty Crocker. She can cook." A baby seat hung from bungee cords in the hall entrance. She tugged at it, and the thing bounced up and down. "Where's the Monkey?"

"Julian's sleeping, thank *God*. Coffee?"

"Sure." She moved a bright plastic rattle and sat at the table. Sara returned with two mugs and a box of Girl Scout cookies pinned beneath one arm. "What's in the bag?"

"Sweats," Anna said. The lie came easily, just falling off her tongue. "I thought I might stop by the gym afterward."

Sara nodded, tore open a sleeve of cookies. "So how are you really?"

"I'm okay." She sipped at the too-hot coffee. "It gets easier every time. That's a terrible thing to say, isn't it?"

"Oh, honey."

"I don't know. Maybe next time."

"You guys are going to try again?"

"Yeah. Sooner or later the odds have to work in our favor, right?"

"But I thought . . ." Sara cocked her head.

Shit. She'd forgotten talking about how broke they were, how they couldn't afford to pay their bills. "Well, you know. We can live on credit cards for a while."

It sounded lame, but Sara didn't pursue it. They sat in awkward silence for a moment, and then Sara said, "Come on. I need help picking an outfit for my interview." She grabbed the coffee and led the way. Anna dropped on the bed while her sister went into her walk-in closet.

"So how are things with Tom?" Sara's voice disembodied.

"Okay. It's tough." She fiddled with the edge of the duvet. "We've been together forever, and we love each other, but sometimes marriage seems like so much work."

"That, sweetheart, is why I've got a strict six-month dating policy."

Anna laughed. "It's weird. The longer you've loved a person, the harder it is to articulate why." She looked up as Sara stepped out, holding a bright red dress cut for cleavage. "No," she said.

"No?"

"Not unless you're applying to be a secretary-with-privileges."

"If I could only find a boss that looked like George Clooney." She vanished again. "So what does that mean, hard to articulate?"

"It's just, you get so used to loving each other as an idea, you sometimes forget to *do* it." She leaned over to look at a picture on the night table, Sara and three girlfriends in a bar booth, her sister's head flung back in laughter.

"Can I ask you something?"

"Sure."

"Are you sure Tom wants a baby as much as you?"

She was glad Sara couldn't see her wince. "I don't know. How much is him wanting one and how much is him doing it for me gets kind of murky."

"How about this?" Sara's arm extended out the door, holding a pin-striped suit.

"Mehh."

She pulled her arm back. "Does that scare you?"

"Are you kidding?" Anna opened her sister's night table drawer, peered in, part fidgeting, part nosiness. Lip balm, tissues, a silver vibrator, okay, didn't need to see *that,* some postcards. "Of course it does."

"Don't get me wrong, I think he'd be a great dad, but—"

"I know," Anna said, cycling through the postcards: a black-and-white shot of a flamenco dancer, a pattern in avocado and orange, a flock of birds in flight. "I get scared by it, like I said. But to be honest, I don't think that's the problem. Have you ever seen him with kids? He goes totally—" She turned to put the cards back in the drawer, and her mouth fell open.

"Totally what?"

"Why do you have a gun?"

"Huh?"

It lay beneath where the postcards had been. A revolver, short, like the kind cops in old movies carried. Anna stared at it, wanting to touch it, wanting not to.

Her sister stepped out with a white blouse and a guilty expression she covered by going aggressive. "Snoop much?"

"Why do you have a gun, Sara?"

She shrugged. "A cop friend gave it to me when I moved into the city. He said, you know, a woman alone."

"A cop friend?"

"Okay, a cop *boy*friend."

"And you kept it?"

"It seemed kind of romantic at the time. After we broke up, I didn't know what to do with it."

"What about Julian?"

"He's too little to be going through drawers."

"Are you fucking kidding?" She stared at her sister, feeling her face scrunch up. "I wonder how many parents say *that* just before their kid has an accident."

"That's a little dramatic."

Anna held the gaze, raised her eyebrows. After a moment, Sara rolled her eyes. "Fine. I'll get rid of it."

"Thank you."

"I mean, that is way out of his reach—"

"Sara."

"Okay, okay." She held up the blouse. "What do you think?"

Anna shook her head, dropped the postcards to cover the pistol, then shut the drawer. She sighed, then said, "With the gray skirt."

"The short one?"

"The long one."

Sara tossed the blouse on the bed. "You're no fun."

They finished the coffee, then went to peek at Julian. He lay flat in his crib, doughy arms splayed out, hair mussed. His eyes were open and staring at a mobile of black-and-white shapes. When he saw Anna, he giggled and smiled and farted, and thin needles tore into her heart.

"Look who's awake," Sara said, in that exaggerated baby voice.

"Look who it is!" She leaned in and picked him up, one hand behind his head, and straightened with a groan. "You're getting so *big*."

"Hi there," Anna whispered. She held out a finger, and Julian's tiny fingers closed around it, and she knew. They would make it happen. The money would make it possible. It was like something out of a fairy tale. A magic lamp that could grant wishes. And she had only one.

THE LINEN CLOSET? Too frequently opened.

On top of the armoire? The quarter inch of dust was good. But there wasn't enough space.

Her cell phone rang, but she ignored it. Under the bed? Too risky.

After Sara left, running out the door in a whirl of curses and instructions, Anna had burped Julian and changed his diaper, wiping his little bottom and dusting him with talcum powder. He'd cried for a while until she'd put a CD on, Cake's *Prolonging the Magic,* and danced around her sister's house bouncing him to the beat and singing that sheep go to heaven while goats go to hell. She had him giggling and grinning, waving his little fists like he was cheering.

"Ten months old and already a rock star," she'd said. "You're going to break a lot of hearts, kiddo."

When he'd grown tired of their duet, she'd put him in his "office," a plastic ring of bright toys with a canvas seat suspending him in the middle. He banged things happily. She dragged it into the hallway so she could keep an eye on him as she paced.

The living room didn't offer many options. A coat closet, a couple of cabinets filled with DVDs, a bookshelf. Besides, it seemed too exposed. The bedroom felt better psychologically, deeper in the house, separated by another door. But she couldn't find a good spot there, not somewhere she was sure Sara wouldn't come upon.

It felt a little dirty, looking at her sister's home as a place to hide stolen money. She'd considered renting a safe-deposit box. But something in her rejected it. For one thing, it felt too risky. Cameras and security, police on call. And the banks must have master keys to open their own boxes. It was irrational to think that they would, of course, but it just seemed better to have the money stored somewhere no one else knew about. A place she could get to anytime.

The kitchen had potential. Her sister considered mac and cheese challenging, had often joked that her culinary skill began and ended with ordering. The cabinet beside the stove was filled with shoes. The oven held two loaves of Wonder Bread. Anna squatted down, peering into a cabinet that held one skillet, a saucepan, and one pot large enough to boil pasta. Maybe if she put it all the way in the back? She leaned in, feeling around. There was plenty of space, and the angle as the counter met the wall made for a blind spot. It might do. With a grunt, she hoisted the bag in, then pushed, the weight of it cumbersome, all those stacks of bills moving and shifting. It took a little arranging, but she got it out of sight, then put the pots back in the same positions.

Not bad. Anna stood, checked it from other angles. Decided to leave it there for the moment, see how she felt as the afternoon wore on. She opened the fridge, grabbed a Diet Coke, popped the can as she walked to the living room. It was a gorgeous day, one of those right on the blurry edge between spring and summer, and she watched the sunlight trip over trees and bushes to fall in the angles of afternoon shadows. The street was quiet, just a woman in shorts walking a dog, the faint banging of a construction project. Two men sat in a black Honda down the block. As she watched, the car started and they pulled away.

The money would be safe here. If Sara happened to stumble on it, she'd recognize the bag and call Anna. It would make for an awkward scene, but she was sure her sister would understand. And now their house was clean.

She sat down cross-legged in front of Julian, who was repeatedly pushing a button that made a cow go moo. Every time it did, he would gurgle as if surprised. She wondered if it was the sound that startled him or the fact that he made it happen. Probably the latter, she decided. That was the beautiful thing about babies. As they discovered the world, you got to watch them, and to rediscover it yourself. They were so helpless, and yet they had a greater capacity for—

What the *hell* was she doing?

She'd been so focused on finding a hiding place that she hadn't thought about anything else. But now, sitting with Julian, watching him press a button over and over, reality sideswiped her. Was she really hiding stolen money in her sister's house? Money men had already died over?

She stood in a dizzy rush of blood. Sprinted down the hall to the kitchen, tore open the cabinet, knocked the pans out clanging, then grabbed the strap and hauled the duffel bag out. No. No way.

She believed everything she'd said to Tom, that there was no reason that the thieves would draw a connection to them. The odds against it seemed astronomical, and considering the benefit, it was a risk she was willing to take. But for herself.

Her cell phone rang again. Still thinking of what she'd almost done, she answered it without checking the number.

10

AS HE BIT INTO THE DRIPPING SANDWICH, Tom supposed he ought to be angry, but he wasn't. Actually, he felt good. Better than good. Great. Buoyant.

Which was unexpected. The morning had been a disaster, seen him called out on the carpet by his boss's boss. Internal politics, a turf war two levels above him, but today he'd had to serve as the whipping boy, getting questioned in humiliating detail about the project he'd headed for months. A project Daniels had signed off on at every step, by the way, though of course today his boss sat silent and stern, like he was disappointed in Tom.

All of which should have pissed him off, and did, but didn't dampen his mood. The reason was pretty simple—halfway through the meeting, he realized that it didn't matter. That if he wanted, he could tell everyone in the room to sit and spin, punch up a Dropkick Murphys album on his iPod, and stalk out with middle fingers in the air. It was a silly vision he hadn't indulged in years, not since he was first starting professional life. A kid's dream, the kind of fantasy that could only belong to someone without responsibilities.

Or to someone who had three hundred thousand dollars in a duffel bag.

He took another bite of Italian beef, chewed with relish, loving the crunch of hot peppers amid the soggy mess of meat and bun. Grease glistened on his fingers as he turned the page of his novel. Mr. Beef was a Chicago institution, and though the walk from the office cut an hour's lunch break thin, today he didn't give a rat's ass about getting back in time.

At first he'd thought Anna was crazy for wanting to keep the money, especially after the break-in. Oddly enough, what had settled his stomach was the story in yesterday's paper linking Will Tuttle to the Shooting Star case. Yes, the money was stolen, and he supposed that, in some black-and-white way, that made him a bad person for wanting to keep it. But it had been taken from a movie star who commanded fifteen million a picture, even for that last piece of dreck about the asteroid. Not only that, but from the beginning, the tabloids had been full of rumors that the Star was buying drugs.

"You mind?" A sharp-dressed black man gestured at the empty bench seat opposite Tom's. The lunch crowd was thinning out, and there were other seats available, but Tom shrugged, said, "Be my guest."

Considering where the money came from, why shouldn't it end up theirs? Better them than either a Hollywood brat or the thieves who targeted him.

Across the table, the man carefully tucked a silver tie between the fourth and fifth buttons of an orange shirt. "I love a sausage now and again, but they are messy."

Tom didn't say anything, just dipped a fry in ketchup, popped it in his mouth. He ate pretty healthy overall, but sometimes you needed grease.

"Yes, sir," the man continued. "And nobody likes a mess. Am I right?"

Without looking up, Tom nodded.

"A mess"—holding the bun in slender fingers—"is a sign of a disordered mind. And a disordered mind is a sign of weakness."

Tom put a finger in the margin of his book. The man didn't look crazy. The suit was expensive and clearly tailored, and the thin mustache against his dark skin gave him an air of gravity. He looked like an entrepreneur, or a particularly stylish politician. "Do you agree, Mr. Reed?"

"What?" How did . . .

"Do you agree that a disordered mind is a sign of weakness?"

"I'm sorry. Have we—do we know each other?"

"And here's the problem with weakness. You show weakness, you open yourself up to your enemies. The world is defined by strength. When you're strong, actual violence isn't much necessary. The threat is plenty. But for that to work, you can't be seen as weak." The man took a bite of sausage, chewed slowly. He picked up his napkin and wiped his fingers carefully, then said, "Do you love your wife, Mr. Reed?"

Something icy slid down the back of Tom's thighs. Caught between fear and anger, he decided on the latter. He started to rise, saying, "Excuse me? Who the hell—"

"Anna. She's lovely."

Three words. Just three words, but the world warped under the weight of them, like the restaurant was tilting. He sat back down, his hands shaking. The money. This had to be about the money. Jesus. "Who are you?"

"Generally, I'm too busy to read as much as I'd like," the man said, ignoring the question. "But I do a fair bit of business in Los Angeles, and I like a book when I fly. Mostly history. Coming in from LAX my last trip, I went through something on Genghis Khan. Interesting stuff. His empire was bigger than Rome, you believe it? Genghis, he marched *all* over the world. Fought his whole life. Got so that countries were so scared of him, they'd lay down arms just because they heard he was coming. And if they did, you know what happened?"

Tom felt a vein jump in his forehead. He looked around the room. The exit was only a dozen feet away. But between him and escape sat a muscular man in a maroon track suit. An untouched basket of fries lay in front of him. His hands were large and scarred, and his eyes, lazily half-open, were locked on Tom.

"I see you've noticed Andre. But are you listening, Mr. Reed?"

He found his voice. "What happened?"

"Nothing." The man raised his eyebrows. "Nothing. The Khan would welcome them into the empire. I mean, there'd be slaves taken, some tribute due. Basically, though, everybody could go on about their business. But if they resisted him, well. He tore cities down to nothing. Killed everybody, women and children, even livestock. Had the earth salted so crops couldn't grow. Know why?" He leaned forward. "Because by resisting, they had tried to make him appear weak. So he had to look especially strong in victory. Had to look like anybody who cost him reputation, what they call face, would suffer. And not just his enemies, but everyone who loved them, helped them, even sheltered them."

Some part of Tom wanted to just say, *Take the money. I'm sorry, we're sorry, take the money and go.* But remembering what the man had said about weakness, he tried to keep his voice even, to give nothing away. "What does this have to do with me and my wife?"

The man in the suit steepled his fingers. His eyes were steady and his voice was calm. "Not long ago, a group of men cost me face. And as I've explained, world I operate in, that can't happen. So I'm burning cities, and I'm salting earth. Understand?"

Tom swallowed hard, nodded.

"Good. Now. I'm going to ask you a question, and I suggest you think hard."

Here it comes. He felt a hollowness inside, a mix of fear and adrenaline and loss. Perhaps it shouldn't hurt to give up what had never been theirs to begin with. But it would. It would rip away the safety net they had begun to enjoy. It would cripple their dreams of a child. Plus, he realized with a rush of fear, they had spent so much of it. Would he be able to convince them that this was all they had found? He remembered the way this stranger had said his wife's name, pronouncing the syllables as if he owned them, as if he could do with them what he liked.

Then the man spoke, and Tom wondered if he'd understood correctly.

"Whose side are you on?"

"What?"

"I suggested you think, Mr. Reed, and you'd better start. Because you have sheltered my enemies." The intonations like a preacher reading scripture. "Now, it may be that you're just what you look like. A perfectly normal man. But even so, you have sheltered my enemies, and for that alone, I could regain face by punishing you. So I ask again, whose side are you on?"

Tom took a breath. Tried to think of an answer that would satisfy. All he could come up with was the truth. "I'm not—we're not on anybody's side. We're just . . ." He spread his hands, palms up. "We rented our apartment, that's all."

"You rented it to Will Tuttle."

"We only just found out that was his name. After he was dead, I mean. He told us his name was Bill Samuelson. We barely knew him. He paid his rent every month, lived quietly."

"Who else do you know?"

"What?"

"Jack Witkowski. Do you know him?"

"No."

"Marshall Richards."

"No. We don't know anyone."

"You don't know anyone? In the whole world?"

"I mean—"

"You're not convincing me, Mr. Reed."

The skin on the back of his hands itched, and his neck burned. "I swear to you, we didn't know anything about this. We're just . . . we're trying to have a baby. I'm on my lunch hour, for God's sake." Tom stared, not sure how he got here or how to get out. If it were just him, he'd make a run for it, maybe start yelling. But they had mentioned Anna. "Listen, it's been a bad couple of weeks. First there's a fire, then our tenant dies, then we find out he's a criminal. Now you show up and threaten my wife? I don't *know* those people. I don't know anything about anything. I'm just, just a guy." He glanced at his watch. "Hell, I have a meeting in half an hour."

For a long moment, the man opposite just stared. Finally he gave the ghost of a smile. "A meeting, huh?"

"Yeah," Tom said. "Work is killing me."

The man chuckled, shook his head. He folded his napkin, set it on top of his half-eaten sausage. Looked over his shoulder. "Work is killing him."

Andre smiled, wet lips parting to white teeth. Something in Tom went very cold.

"Here's the thing." The man pushed his food aside, set his hands on the table. "Even if I believe you, that only gets you so far. Because if you're not on a side, then you're not on my side."

Tom swallowed hard. Stared across the table. Tried to force his mind to order. Finally he said, "What can I do for you?"

"Now see, that's a good question. I knew you were smart." Fingers slow-tapping the wood like piano keys. "Without getting specific, I sell a product the police would prefer I didn't. Will Tuttle had a sizable quantity of my merchandise. I'd like it back."

Merchandise. The tabloids had whispered the Star was buying drugs. It all came clear. This guy wasn't one of the thieves. He wasn't chasing the *money*—he was chasing the *men*. The men and the drugs they stole from him.

"Now, if you were to find what I've lost, well . . ."

"You'd know which side I was on."

"Exactly."

Tom nodded. The guy must believe the drugs were in Will's apartment. Which meant that all he had to do was find them. For half a second he had hope. Then he remembered the break-in earlier that week. The place had been searched. The drugs were probably gone.

On the other hand, he'd been given a possible out. The guy had made it clear he was willing to kill them even if they were innocent. If he rejected the one lifeline thrown his way . . .

Besides, maybe whoever broke in had missed the drugs. There was no way to know how long they'd had to search. And Tom knew the building better. "I understand."

The man in the suit nodded. "Good. Andre?"

Standing, Andre wasn't as tall as Tom would have guessed, maybe just under six, but moved like a boxer, his sleeves tight with muscle, hands held ready. He reached into an inner pocket with two fingers and pulled out a slim business card, which he set on the table.

Tom hardly noticed. Hardly saw the man opposite him stand, the two of them walk out. Because as Andre had opened his jacket, Tom had seen something inside. A shoulder holster and a big black gun.

HE DIDN'T MAKE his meeting.

With traffic, it took almost thirty minutes for the cab to deliver him home. Thirty minutes of staring out the window, fingering the business card. It was elegant in its simplicity: heavy stock, textured cream, with a phone number embossed. No name. Thirty minutes thinking of that gun. When he arrived, he didn't bother going up to their place to drop his bag. Just opened the door to the bottom unit and went to work.

He wanted to tear the place apart, yank boxes from cabinets and overturn them, throw books off the shelf, bang at the bottoms of drawers and the hollows of walls. But if the place looked like a tornado had hit, Anna would assume they'd been burglarized again. He'd have to explain about the bodyguard who looked like he was hoping Tom said the wrong thing, and the drug dealer who knew Anna's name. The memory brought bile to the back of his throat. He wasn't a violent guy, but if he'd had a gun, a weapon, even a baseball bat, he'd have—

You'd have gotten yourself killed, is what you would have done. You work in Corporate America. They sell drugs. What do you think the odds on that one are?

He turned and kicked the La-Z-Boy, the impact jarring up his leg, rocking the chair up a couple of inches to pause, hesitate, and then fall back down. He kicked it again, then again, then stepped forward and grabbed the back of it and threw it sideways, the heavy chair tipping, then crashing down.

For a second, he imagined it breaking open to spill bales of cocaine across the floor. But all that happened was that it landed with a muscular *whoomp,* kicking up a cloud of dust and revealing cigarette butts and a patch of grimy hardwood. He sighed, sat down on the edge of the overturned chair. Rubbed his forehead, closed his eyes.

Then he stood up and went to work.

MARSHALL LEANED AGAINST THE TREE, hands in his pockets. A woman passed pushing a stroller, and they exchanged smiles. He checked her figure as she went by, then returned his attention to the brick two-flat. The angle of the sun off the windows made it hard to see any detail, but he could make out the man's silhouette.

Marshall took out his cigarettes, pulled one free. When he'd decided to quit, nine years ago now, he'd gone out of his way not to be around smokes or smokers. Shopped at the Whole Foods because they didn't sell cigarettes, stopped going to bars. Then one night, it had hit him—he wasn't beating the addiction. He was just avoiding it. The smokes were winning.

After that, he started carrying a pack, always. Fuck them.

He drew the cigarette under his nose, smelled the tobacco. Originally, he hadn't planned to get out of the car. But after he saw Tom Reed not only come home in the middle of the day, but go into Will's apartment instead of his own, it'd seemed worth a look. He was considering the risks of getting closer when he heard a heavy thudding sound from the house, like something dropped from a height.

What the hell. He tucked the cigarette behind his ear and started forward. A path ran between the building and the one next door, and he started down, head facing forward but eyes on the window. The reflection kept him from making out detail, but he could see that the man had his back to the world.

Careful to be quiet, Marshall leaned against the window, one hand shielding his face so he could see inside. The La-Z-Boy was on its side. Beyond it, Tom Reed squatted in front of a cabinet. He was going through it, hands moving fast. As Marshall watched, Tom closed one cabinet and moved to the next, and then the one after that. When he finished, he stood and started rifling the shelves. The guy was clearly oblivious to everything else, and Marshall felt safe watching for several minutes.

Finally, he turned and stepped away, retraced his steps to the car. He sucked air through his teeth. Glanced around the interior:

the coffee cup in the holder, the stack of mail in the passenger seat, the cherry air freshener dangling from the mirror.

Tom Reed hadn't just been going through a former tenant's belongings. He hadn't been cleaning, or considering what was worth selling and what was trash. What he'd been doing was searching for something.

Marshall fired up the car and pulled away.

TOM CHECKED EVERY CABINET, every cupboard. Fingered the contents of every drawer, then pulled them out and looked behind. Flipped the mattress up, stripped it, checked for slits. Felt the pockets of every item of clothing. Opened and closed the freezer, then opened it again and checked each container.

He took the lid off the toilet tank to see if anything was suspended within. Aimed a flashlight up the narrow chimney. Braced the extension ladder against the top of the rear stairs and climbed through the trapdoor to the roof. Fetched his toolkit and opened the back of the oven. Peered into the hollow behind the medicine cabinet.

Think.

If the drugs had been here, then whoever came earlier had found them.

Think, man. Try and see the big picture.

Okay, the corollary, then: If the drugs hadn't been here, that meant Tuttle had hidden them somewhere else.

That thought gave him a fresh burst of energy, and he returned to the unit, looking for clues, starting with the mailboxes. Their own was completely empty, kind of odd, but the other was crammed with catalogs and junk mail, all in the name Bill Samuelson. In the kitchen he found a grocery list (eggs, olive oil, smokes) and a week-old *Tribune*. Dog-eared delivery menus. A copy of *Perfect 10* in the bathroom, the cover proudly proclaiming "The world's most beautiful natural women!" Ten or twelve matchbooks from ten or twelve bars.

What he didn't find was the key to a safe-deposit box. A day planner, or a little black book full of phone numbers, one of them circled in red. A map with a spot marked X.

No drugs, and no clue as to where Tuttle might have stashed them. After three and a half hours, the only thing he was certain of was that whatever the man in the suit wanted, it wasn't in this house.

THERE WAS ONLY ONE THING to do.

Tom noticed dirt under his thumbnail, and picked at it with the nail of his middle finger. He smelled sour, his dress shirt marked with sweat stains. The clock on the bedside table read just after five. Anna would be home soon. Home from babysitting the Monkey. That was always a delicate time for her; she loved the kid with all her heart, but seeing what her sister had that she did not, it was tough. Tended to leave her jaggy, on the edge of tears.

The man in the suit hadn't given a deadline, hadn't told him to have the "merchandise" in forty-eight hours. But why would he? He would have known Tom would rush right home and tear the place apart. Would have counted on it. He'd probably give him the night, maybe the next day. But there wouldn't be any point in waiting longer. Either Tom could deliver or he couldn't. Which meant that very soon, two dangerous men were going to come looking for something he did not have.

He took a breath, held it, blew it out. Tried to steady his thoughts. He was scared, absolutely, but it was more than that. Or beyond that, maybe. This whole situation felt surreal, and he was struggling for context. Trying not to just give in and go with it, hope that things worked out for the best.

He saw Andre's smile again, wet lips and white teeth, and he stood up, walked into the hallway, rubbing at his neck.

All right. Go through it again. One more spin round.

The drugs weren't here. And there was nothing that gave him an idea where to look. Worse, because he hadn't mentioned the robbery, he'd painted himself into a corner. Been too clever. It had seemed like a good idea at the time, but now if he tried to tell the truth . . . Jesus: *Our house was actually ransacked a couple of days ago. Sorry—didn't I mention that?*

He didn't even have anything to offer; matchbooks and last month's cable bill wouldn't save their lives. He had nothing to give the man in the suit.

Wait. That wasn't true. He had three hundred thousand dollars in a duffel bag. Tom stood in front of the bay window, looked out on the street. The money was a possibility.

Except, what happened when you gave a sack of cash to a killer? Maybe he'd shoot them just to clear the last ties. Or maybe he'd smile, say thanks, and leave. How the hell should Tom know? This wasn't his world.

There was only one choice.

Tom walked out, leaving behind the faint smell of fire.

Climbed the steps, limbs heavy with the effort of the last hours. Unlocked his door, and was surprised to hear a short double beep. The new alarm system. Anna had left the code on his voice mail, and he keyed it in to the pad, thinking how it was funny that just yesterday this seemed like it would protect them. In the kitchen he poured a glass of ice water and drank it slow. Knew he was stalling, hoping that some other idea would occur to him.

But nothing would. Over an Italian beef sandwich, his whole life had changed. He was an amateur in a game whose rules he didn't understand. All he knew for certain was that if he waited too long, the man in the suit would come back, telling tales of Genghis Khan and threatening everything Tom loved.

He set down the glass of water, took the business card from the drawer where he'd stowed it, picked up the phone, and dialed. After one ring, it went straight to voice mail. As he listened to the message, the tone deep and calm, he told himself that he was doing the right thing. Or at least the best thing he could see.

When he heard the beep, he said, "Detective Halden? This is Tom Reed. I've been thinking about what you said the other day, as you were leaving. We need to talk. Please call me as soon as possible." He left his cell number, then hung up and leaned his elbows on the counter, head in hands, trying to imagine how to tell his wife that in order to save her life he had to destroy her dreams.

11

THE INTERIOR OF KAZE was designed in a style Tom thought of as space-age Zen: white walls, white tables, white light, minimalist plates and glasses. They'd ordered a bottle of sake, which the waitress had poured into a funky decanter that was a cross between a vase and a bong. Personally, he could take or leave sushi, but Anna could be buried in the stuff and chew her way out smiling. Tonight he needed all the help he could get in the smile department.

Or he would, anyway, once he manned up enough to say what needed saying. After he'd called the detective, Tom had stripped off his business clothes and hopped in the shower, made a plan as he sluiced grime off his body. After hanging out with Julian, Anna would come in tired and sad. So the first order of business was dinner, a good meal at a quiet corner table. A bottle of wine. Strike that. Two bottles. Then, when Anna was mellow with fresh yellowtail and bacon-wrapped scallops, soft with good booze, he would take her hand, and ask her to listen and not speak until he was done. Tell her that they'd been wrong about everything, that they were out of their depth. That they had made a very big mistake, and that now it was time to stop hoping to keep something that wasn't theirs, and focus on surviving.

But Anna had thrown him. She didn't so much walk in as float. Her eyes were bright and clear, no sign that she'd stopped halfway to cry. Instead of the usual quick hug and peck, she'd wrapped her arms around his back and pulled him tight as her lips parted, her tongue dancing against his, the swell of her breasts against his chest. The kiss lasted thirty seconds, and he was hard by the end of it. She'd given him a knowing smile, said, "Hi," with Marilyn Monroe breathiness, then pressed her pelvis against him. "Did you miss me?"

"Always," he'd said.

She laughed, said, "Yeah, yeah," and stepped away with a smile. "Prove it. Buy me dinner."

Her good mood had continued through the evening. She'd hummed while she changed from a T-shirt and jeans into a summer dress and flip-flops with silver bangles. She'd pulled her hair back into double ponytails, a style they joked was her Inga-the-Exchange-Student look. It had been a long time since he'd seen her so happy, so unequivocally in the moment. Knowing he had to smash that was like knowing he had to strangle a puppy.

The evening was warm, and they'd decided to walk the two miles to the restaurant. She was irrepressible, pointing at flowers and smiling at the smell of barbecue, talking about their nephew, describing how big he had gotten, how he giggled when she made funny faces. At one point, strolling down a row of well-tended bungalows, she'd looked at him sideways. "You okay?"

"Huh?"

"You're kind of quiet."

"I'm just . . . mellow," he said. She accepted his explanation without comment, went on talking about Julian, and then about the summer night and their plans to get away for the Fourth of July, while he walked beside her, hating himself for the lie. He decided he would tell her right after they ordered.

But they'd started with martinis. Then appetizers. A short bottle of sake, and a first round of sushi. Another bottle, another round. Tom splurging as if an extra half-dozen pieces of nigiri could somehow make up for the loss of the money and their plans.

Now there was nothing but scraps of pink ginger on the bamboo plank, and he was trying to convince himself that they needed dessert. Some sorbet, or a cheese plate. She looked so lovely by the candle glow, features soft and eyes sparkling.

Do it. You have to do it.

He couldn't believe she hadn't noticed how quiet he'd been, hadn't dug deeper than the one question. In fact, she'd talked all night, not in a domineering way, but energetically. Like they'd been apart for a month instead of an afternoon.

The waitress came by, picked up the decanter, and refilled their cups, first Anna's, then his. "Interest you guys in dessert?"

"No," Anna said, at the same time he said, "Yes."

Both women laughed, and the waitress said, "How about I bring you the menu and you can take a glance?"

"Fine." He fiddled with his chopsticks, picking at single grains of rice strewn on the serving board.

His wife looked at him across the table, cocked her head. "You still hungry after all that?"

"I thought you might want something."

"God, no. I couldn't eat another bite. You're going to have to roll me home." She turned sideways, pushed her belly out. "See? I look like I'm four months pregnant."

He glanced up fast, expecting to see her face falling. It happened all the time, people firing little jokes they didn't realize had barbs. Sometimes, like now, it was even one of them who slipped. But the smile on her face didn't curdle. She caught his look, said, "What?"

"I . . ." He spread his hands.

She shrugged, her eyes still bright. "I'm tired of everything being a minefield." Held up her sake cup in a toast. "To us."

He raised his. Started to clink, then stopped. "Anna . . ."

"Wait." She leaned forward, tapped her glass to his, then drank it in a swallow. Set it down but didn't release it, her fingertips rolling around the rim. She hesitated, then said, "There's something I have to tell you."

His first thought was that she was pregnant. He'd often imagined how she would tell him, how she would probably tease her way into it, surprise him. But the way they'd been drinking, it couldn't be that. He sipped his sake and waited.

"I want you to hear me out first, okay?" Her words echoing the ones he had planned to say himself.

"Sounds serious."

"It is. It is and it isn't. I guess that's why I've been talking like an idiot all night. I've been afraid to tell you. It's going to sound like a bad thing at first. But it's not."

Feeling nervous, he said, "Okay."

She took a deep breath. Looked up from the table. "I lost my job."

"*What?*"

Anna held up a finger. "Let me finish, okay?" She waited for him to nod, then continued. "You know I've been missing a lot of work. All the appointments and everything? Well, I guess today was the last straw. Lauren called this afternoon. She said she was sorry, but that she had been getting complaints from the client. The agency promised we'd deliver this quarter, but we're way behind schedule. The truth is, that's mostly because of client delays, but you can't tell *them* that. Lauren needed to hang it on somebody, and I'd missed a lot of work, so . . ." Anna shrugged. "She picked me."

"Wait. They can't just fire you. Not without a warning."

"She did warn me. A month ago."

"You never told me."

"I know. I'm sorry. We were in the midst of everything with the doctors, and I just didn't want to talk about it."

He didn't like that she was keeping secrets, but let it go. "Still. You could go to HR—"

"Let me finish." She twisted her napkin in her lap, then caught herself, folded it, put it on the table. "Tom, I wasn't happy there. I haven't been happy for a long time. I'm sick of advertising. I work so many hours, and for what? To dream about Excel spreadsheets? To convince people in Wichita to buy cheap jeans they don't need?" She shook her head. "You made me realize that the other day."

"Me?"

"When you said you missed us. Missed the way we used to be." She looked at him, her eyes a bridge she invited him to cross. "You were right. I've been working too hard. *We've* been working too hard. But before, we couldn't do anything about it. With the house, the medical bills, the credit cards—there was no way either of us could take a breath, much less try and figure out what we really wanted to do. Now . . ."

She didn't finish the sentence. Didn't have to. The words rang in his head. *Now that we have the money . . .*

The same thought he'd had this morning, he realized. As he sat through his stupid meeting, taking a beating that wasn't his, he'd found comfort in realizing that the money gave him an out. He hadn't taken it, but then, he hadn't been forced to.

"I'll get another job," she said. "I'm not saying I want to stay home and eat bonbons. But now I can take time, a little, to figure out what I want to do. Maybe teach, or go back to school for nursing. Something where the work *matters,* you know? Now that we're okay financially, think how much better this could make everything. We'll be able to spend more time together, to get back to being the people we want to be. You and me against the world. Like tonight." She smiled, then reached across the table and laid her hand on his, slim fingers cool, the diamond on her ring alive in the candlelight. "It will even help us conceive. Stress is one of the big factors. If I'm happier, more relaxed, it's going to make the odds better. This could turn everything around for us, baby."

His head was a whirl. He understood everything she was saying. It all made perfect sense. He knew that she had stopped enjoying her job a long time ago, that she was doing it for the mortgage, and the health insurance, and the bills that came every week. They had both been sacrificing the present to the future.

And, man, how she glowed tonight. Smiled and laughed in a way that he had feared lost forever . . .

He thought of the man in the suit and his bodyguard. Of wet lips and white teeth and a big black gun. Of the call already placed to the detective, the message he couldn't take back. He had to tell the truth. He had to. Even though it would kill her.

"What do you think?" Her face traced in candlelight, a hint of cheekbone, the delicate hollow of her throat. He remembered one time kissing that hollow, telling her he wanted to pitch a tent and spend the rest of his life there, and her laughing, laughing against him.

"Tom?" Her lips slightly parted, as if she were preparing to smile, or to cry.

"I think it's great," he said, and squeezed her hand.

12

THE LADDER WAS THIN and wobbly and impossibly tall, and he was at the top. The whole thing swayed with every breath, then swayed further when he tried to compensate. He smelled dust. Put his hands up to brace against the ceiling, but the motion only made the ladder lean further. A long, creaking shudder. The wood groaned. Everything started to topple. He scrabbled for purchase, fingers tracing slickness, straining to hold, but the weight was too much, and the ladder tipped, falling toward the surrounding dark.

And as it went, as he lost all hope, as his calves and the inside of his pelvis shivered with the electric anticipation of falling, and even as his body tumbled free, deep inside and delineated by fear, Tom Reed felt something like relief.

His eyes snapped open. The pillowcase was wet, and Anna was beside him, her breath faintly sour with sleep. He took a breath, flipped the pillow, and turned on his side.

Doesn't take a genius to figure that one out.

After dinner, they'd grabbed a cab. Anna had taken his hand and held it the whole ride, smiling to herself. He'd opened the window, and the rush of air and blur of lights and pressure of her hand had combined to allow him to forget everything but sensation. A moment outside of time, and for the brief ride home, he let himself soak in it.

But after they trudged up the steps and opened the door, the alarm had given its quick succession of beeps, and every fear had tumbled back into his head. They brushed their teeth and fell into bed, too tired and buzzed to talk or make love, and she had drifted off almost immediately.

For him, sleep didn't come so easy. He lay staring at the ceiling, trying to think of a way out. A way to keep the money and lose the bad guys and have the life they wanted, simple and happy and complete. He replayed the conversation with the man in the suit a hundred times. Each time, he almost woke Anna to tell her everything; each time, he decided against it. It wasn't about deception. Tom just wanted to make everything right first. Between the pregnancy attempts, and the break-in, and now her job, she had enough on her mind. He'd tell her when he'd figured out what to do.

He stared and thought and wished he still smoked. His mind seemed to be working in circles, slow orbits around wet lips and white teeth and a big black gun. Around a threat, and a promise, and a hope. Around a voice-mail message. Around a tomorrow approaching too quickly.

Sometime after three, it had come to him. A possible way out. So simple he'd overlooked it; the truth, of all things. More or less. He'd slipped into a shallow sleep broken by dreams of falling.

It took most of the day to get hold of Detective Halden. They traded voice mails until nearly three o'clock. When they did finally connect, Halden suggested that Tom come by the station. They could have a cup of the world's worst coffee, he said, and talk in one of the interview rooms.

"I'm in for the coffee," Tom said, "but could we meet halfway? There's a Starbucks on the corner of North and Wells. I need to talk as soon as possible." A partial truth; he did want to talk soon, but he also didn't want to do it in a police station, on the cop's home court.

The coffee shop had that standardized coziness, the same anywhere in the country. Tom supposed that was one of the comforts of chains, but it was one of the horrors too. Soon there'd be no point going anywhere. He ordered a coffee, no whipped cream, no flavored syrup, no caramel, just coffee, in a large cup—did anybody actually feel more international by saying "venti" instead of "large"?—and took a seat at a corner table by the window.

Halden arrived a few minutes later. He nodded at Tom, then got a coffee of his own, sweeping back his jacket to reveal his silver star. The girl at the register smiled, and Tom noticed she didn't charge him.

"Mr. Reed."

"Detective. Thanks for coming."

The cop sat down, crossed his legs ankle-on-knee, and sipped at his cup. He didn't start firing questions, just leaned back and let Tom take his time.

Remember, you're scared and confused and have nothing to hide. It wasn't a hard role to play. Two of the three were dead accurate. "I'll get right to it. Someone is threatening my wife and me."

"Who?"

"I don't know. I was having lunch yesterday, and this guy I've never seen before sat down, started talking. He knew my name, and my wife's. And he asked me if I loved her."

Halden ran his tongue around the inside of his cheek. "Your names were in the paper."

"It gets worse." Tom paused. "He was part of the Shooting Star robbery."

The cop leaned forward. "How do you know that?"

"He bragged about it." Tom gave it a minute, let the lie—not lie, exaggeration—sink in. "He said that some men had cost him face. He said that Will Tuttle was one of them. He said that because I had sheltered his enemy, I was now an enemy myself."

" 'Sheltered his enemy'? He say it that way?"

"Yeah. He had a story that led up to it, about Genghis Khan. I think he was trying to scare me." Tom took a sip of coffee, went back to that moment, the man saying Anna's name, that she was lovely. "It worked. I'm scared shitless. He had a guy with him that looked like a gangster, big guy with a gun."

"He drew a gun?"

"No. Just let me see it in his holster."

The detective nodded slowly, his face giving nothing away. "What then?"

"He said that I had to pick a side. That the men who had done the robbery had taken some of his merchandise. He didn't say what, I assume drugs. That's what the papers have been saying. Anyway, he said it was in my house, and that if I didn't give it to him, he would kill us both." Another helpful exaggeration, the more-or-less version of the truth.

"This was yesterday?"

"Yes."

"At lunch, you said."

"Right."

"So why did you wait to call me?"

Tom sighed, shrugged. Looked at his fingers tracing shapes on the table. "I thought maybe if I found what he was looking for, he'd just leave us alone. I went home and tore the place apart."

"And?"

"If it was there in the first place, then whoever broke in earlier this week took it. The other bad guys." He shook his head, put on his best victim expression. This was the moment he had to sell through. "Detective, I don't know what to do. We're normal people. All of a sudden we have drug dealers and murderers coming after us. My wife is terrified. So am I. We need help."

Yesterday, when Tom had left the first message for Halden, his plan had been to come clean. Give up the money and beg for help. It had seemed the only way. But as he'd lain in bed last night, he'd remembered that the drug dealer didn't know about the money, or didn't know that Tom and Anna had it, at least. All he wanted from Tom was his drugs back—and that was an opportunity.

It was risky, bringing in the police. It would certainly count as choosing sides in the drug dealer's mind. And if Halden decided to take a close look at them, he might come across the bills they'd paid. All of Anna's predictions about bankruptcy and even jail time might come true.

But the man in the suit had already made it clear he was willing to kill them. Going to the cops couldn't make it worse. Besides, Tom had just handed the detective a lead on Chicago's highest-profile robbery in years. It was misdirection, sure, but it was essentially accurate. It would put them on the right trail. And so long as the cops were following the bad guys, they couldn't be looking too hard at the good ones.

Halden gestured with the coffee cup. "This man, he tell you his name?"

"No."

"How were you supposed to contact him?"

"He gave me a business card." Tom took it from his back pocket, set it on the table. He'd stared at the number so long he had it memorized, suspected he'd know it in twenty years. "He said to call. To do it soon, or he would . . . hurt . . . Anna." The worse he made the guy seem, the more time pressure he applied, the better it was for them. "Can you get his name from the phone number?"

Halden shook his head. "I doubt it. It'll probably be a disposable." The cop leaned forward to pick up the business card, holding it by the edge. Looked at it for a long moment. Then he said, "You know, when I got your message, I thought maybe you had something else to tell me."

Tom held himself steady. He'd gone round and round trying to remember exactly what he had said. "What do you mean?"

"You mentioned you'd been thinking about what I said."

"That these were bad men? That's why I called."

"No, what I said as I left."

"What was that?"

Halden's eyes narrowed. "Don't jerk me around."

"I'm not."

The detective sipped his coffee, set the cup down. "Mr. Reed, by now you're starting to understand the type of people involved in this. These aren't forgiving guys. You don't want to mess with them. If you've got anything to tell me, anything at all, now would be a good time. Maybe your last chance." Halden stared, letting the moment hang. Tom's palms were wet. The little kid inside of him, ever afraid of punishment, wanted to give in, to just tell the truth. To fall off the ladder and bask in the relief of falling.

But what he said was "Detective, I didn't know what you were talking about then, and I don't now. All I know is that someone is after me and my wife. And we need your help. Please."

The cop stared at him, gaze level. Didn't blink, didn't look away. Finally he said, "What else can you tell me about this guy?"

They talked for another half hour, Halden having him run through it again and again. Tom had expected that, and kept his story to almost exactly what happened. Where the drug dealer had been smooth and professional, his violence implied, Tom made him rougher, meaner, more explicit. Other than that, he recounted every detail: the cut and color of the man's suit, the Rolex he wore loose on his left wrist, the manner of his speech, his "associate" Andre, even the story about Genghis Khan. He remembered the names the guy had asked about, Jack Witkowski and Marshall Richards, and thought he saw something quicken behind the cop's eyes.

Halden took it all down in the same binder he'd used in their kitchen, precise handwriting flowing from a gold pen. Finally he said, "Okay."

"What will happen?"

"I'll run this up the flagpole and get back to you as soon as possible."

"But what—"

"I'm not sure yet, Mr. Reed. If this guy was involved in the Shooting Star, he's going to be a top priority. My guess is that we'll set a trap for him, maybe ask you to call him and say that you found his product. You'd be willing to do that?"

Tom had anticipated that, but made sure to hesitate visibly before saying, "Yes. If that would mean you catch him."

"It may. I'll be back in touch with you soon, probably later today. Keep your cell phone on."

"What about us?"

"Why don't you and your wife check into a hotel? It won't be more than a night or two."

"What if he finds us?" No need to fake the concern in his voice.

"He won't." Halden set down the cup, adjusted his tie. "He knew your names because he read a paper. He probably staked out your house, followed you to work, then waited for you to go to lunch. Supervillains are comic book stuff. This guy just has a *Tribune* subscription."

Tom nodded slowly. "I guess we could use the rest."

"There you go. Pamper yourself. Pamper that wife of yours."

They stood up, Detective Halden passing him another business card, telling him to call immediately if anything more occurred, his tone stern. Tom nodded, shook hands, and they walked out together. Halden was dialing his cell phone even before he opened the door to his pale blue Crown Vic. Tom smiled.

The risk had paid off. The promise of closing the Shooting Star case was too tasty an opportunity for Halden to miss. It was a sexy case, the kind of thing that would no doubt earn him a lot of credit. Like anybody else, Halden wanted to move up. He'd be focusing on the drug dealer, working his bosses, trying to set a trap as quickly as possible. It would keep his attention where it belonged.

Feeling ten pounds lighter, Tom dug out his own cell phone.

"Hey, baby," she answered.

"Hey," he said. "Where are you?"

"Running errands."

"Meet me back home. Let's grab a few things and go check into a hotel."

"A hotel? What's up?"

"I'll tell you when I see you."

"Everything okay?"

"Yeah," he said, smiling. "It is now."

He walked three blocks to the Sedgwick station and waited for the Brown Line. Had the platform almost to himself, just a bag lady and a beefy guy who climbed the stairs after him. From the raised platform, he could see the Sears Tower marking the skyline. Maybe they'd go downtown tonight, a four-star, the Peninsula or the Ritz, someplace with fluffy bathrobes and a fancy pool. Splurge a little.

The train clattered up. It was almost five, and the car was packed with rush-hour commuters. He fought his way to the back and leaned against the door separating two cars. As the El rocked and swayed, he thought again of the detective, how intent he had become once Tom mentioned the Shooting Star. This was going to work. Better still, he could tell Anna now. She'd be scared at first, mad at him for concealing it, but she'd be happy with the resolution. With the cops after the drug dealer, and no one after the money, they were clear.

By the time they made Rockwell, the crowd had thinned. A dozen people got off, everyone in their own world, folding newspapers or glancing at watches, hurrying in different directions. The air was cool after the stuffy embrace of the train. He walked the few blocks to their home, listening to the wind toy with the leaves, smelling food and flowers on the night air.

"Excuse me, buddy." It was the man from the Sedgwick platform, a biggish guy, not fat but hefty, with eight o'clock shadow and dark hair. "I got a question for you."

"What?" Tom asked.

As he did, his stomach exploded. His knees went wobbly and he doubled over, retching. Struggled desperately to suck air into his lungs, his mind running a mile behind, trying to process that this total stranger had gut-punched him with a fist like a chunk of concrete.

The man said, "Are you right- or left-handed, asshole?"

13

JACK TOOK A HANDFUL of the douchebag's hair and dragged him up the steps of his building. At the moment the street was clear, but it was just after five, an hour when people walked their dogs and fired up their grills. No point hanging around.

He opened the door to the entryway, then yanked the guy in and flung him at the wall. He didn't have time to get his arms up, and hit hard. Staggered back, dazed, that sheep look, like if he blinked enough the badness would go away.

"Open the door," Jack said.

The man coughed, straightened slowly. "Who are—"

Jack slapped him openhanded, *whack,* right across the cheek. Same thing he'd done to the Star, and with the same reaction. Fear and helplessness crept into Tom Reed's eyes. Fear and helplessness were good. They were loud emotions, static that interfered with thinking. The stupidest thing this guy could do was to open the door and let himself be taken into a private space, away from prying eyes. What he ought to do was run for the street, yelling his lungs out. But fear and helplessness kept him from thinking properly. "Open the door."

The guy nodded, reached into his bag, and came out with a ring of keys. He turned and inserted one into the door to the stairs.

"Not that one. The other door."

"What?"

Jack pulled his chrome .45, let it dangle at the end of his arm. Tom Reed's eyes widened, and he said, "Look, take my wallet."

"Open the other door, Tom."

For a moment, the guy just stood there, finally catching on. Then he stepped sideways and unlocked the door to Will Tuttle's apartment.

"Inside."

Jack followed, waited until they were in the living room and the door was closed behind them. Then he drove the butt of the pistol into the guy's right kidney.

Tom Reed collapsed like every muscle had failed at once. He hit the floor fetal, clutching at his side and his belly and wheezing a thin animal sound. His legs spasmed like a frog's. Jack turned to snap the dead bolt shut. He stood for a moment, watching the man writhe, and then he said, "Let's have a little chat, shall we?"

HE COULDN'T MOVE, couldn't think. A dark sun burned in his back, spitting lances of flame, gobs of lava that burned and sizzled. Tom fought to breathe, just to breathe, the world wobbly and wet before his eyes. He could see the pattern of the hardwood floor, smell the earthy dirt of a thousand footprints. From somewhere came a crisp metallic snap. The lock being twisted. It was the scariest sound he had ever heard.

"Let's have a little chat, shall we?"

Tom grunted, gasped. The voice was above him. The man from the Sedgwick platform. Big, not fat. With a gun. A guy who knew his name. He tried to force his thoughts into order.

The man said, "We haven't met, but I feel like I know you, Tom. Amazing, the things you can learn about somebody by going through their mail." Paper fluttered down. White paper, with something printed on it. "You know what that is? It's a Visa receipt. The kind they send when you make a remote deposit. It says you paid down fifteen grand in debt last week. Fifteen thousand, four hundred twelve dollars and fifty-seven cents, to be exact."

Their mail. He'd noticed it was empty the day prior, and Anna had mentioned something about it as well. They'd assumed it was a new carrier, just a typical post office glitch. Now he understood. This man had been stalking them for days.

"What kind of a person can pay fifteen thousand, four hundred twelve dollars and fifty-seven cents at once?" A boot nudged him. Tom pulled away from it. The motion made the world spin, but at least the level of pain seemed to have stabilized. He found he could draw air. He gulped it, trying to clear his head.

"I'll tell you, it would take a real asshole. We're talking grade-A stupid here, the kind of person who had everything handed to them their whole life and thought they deserved it. The kind who could find four hundred grand and think he gets to *keep* it."

Tom put a hand on floor, tested it. The shift spilled boiling oil down his spine. Slowly, he pushed himself to his knees, half-expecting to get beat back down. But he couldn't just lie there.

"You think that's the way the world works?" The voice nearer, coffee breath in Tom's face. He blinked until he could focus, see the man bending down, the gun still in his hand. It was a big chrome thing, heavy. "You think four hundred grand lands in your lap and you get to keep it? Do you?"

Tom coughed, straightened his back. Tried to imagine lunging into the man, throwing him against the door, wrestling the gun from his hand. Tried, but couldn't make himself believe it.

"Didn't your mother ever tell you bedtime stories, for Christ's sake? You find a chest of gold, you better know there's a monster guarding it. *That's* the way the world works. You want something, you have to take it from someone like me." He swung the gun up fast, leveled the barrel so that Tom could stare down into the darkness. It looked enormous. His body throbbed and his head ached. The man said, "Do you think you can do that?"

Tom forced his gaze upward, away from the gun. The guy looked Polish, had that wide pork chop face and dark hair. The thought led to another, and he scrambled for it. A name. Jack Witkowski. The man in the suit had asked if Tom knew a Jack Witkowski.

"Well?"

Tom forced himself to look Jack in the eye. Slowly he shook his head.

The man smiled. "Good." He holstered the pistol, then held out his right hand. Tom took it, clambered to his feet. Nausea swept through him, making his whole body tremble, but he forced himself to stand straight.

"Now," Jack said, "where's my money?"

An hour ago, he'd have answered differently. He'd have hedged or tried to lie. Pretended ignorance. Now, though, he was suddenly and profoundly aware of two simple facts. First, he was in shit deeper than he'd ever imagined. Second, Anna would be home soon. "It's in the basement."

"Show me."

Tom pictured it, concrete ceilings and walls, a solitary window at the far end, the dingy light of a single overhead bulb carving a slow attenuation to shadow. He imagined a body facedown on that dirty floor, a camera panning out on a slow tide of blood flowing from what was left of his head. An image borrowed from a Scorsese film, only it would be his body, his blood. Then he thought, again, of Anna. "This way."

"You go first. Carefully."

It took enormous effort, but Tom forced himself to turn his back on the man and the gun. His wounded kidney sang with pain. He took one step and then another, eyes darting. The pattern of the wood grain, the smell of his own sweat, the dings and cuts in the molding, every little thing seemed to hold enormous portent, and yet there were so many of them, the world so very present that he couldn't possibly sort through it.

The back stairs smelled faintly of trash. He started down, the wood squeaking and groaning with every step. There were cobwebs in the corners, and scraps from where a garbage bag had split a year ago. His mind like it was watching from a distance. He watched himself fumble to turn on the light, dusty yellow like faded lace. Saw himself walk to the back, past the washer and dryer, past the furnace, to the plywood hatch that covered the crawl space. He turned to look back at the man following him.

Looking at Jack snatched away that comfortable distance. Put him back in his body. Tom stared at the broad shoulders and ready posture, the pistol out and steady. Jack looked like a man at ease, a man who did this for a living. Tom said, "My wife and I, we're trying to have a—"

"Don't." Jack's eyes narrowed. "Where's my money?"

Tom swallowed, acid ringing in his nostrils and the back of his throat. "In there." Pointing to the crawl space. "In a duffel bag."

"Get it."

He took a breath. Maybe once he gave up the money, this would all be over. Jack Witkowski would take what was his and leave them alone. They could go back to their old life, to bills and work hassles and making dinner and watching reruns, all the silly moments that took up a day, took up a life. Every precious thing they had thought they wanted to get clear of.

Tom stepped forward, gripped the edges of the plywood panel, lifted it up and off, then set it against the wall. A musty smell rose from the darkness. He squatted and reached in. His hand fumbled for the strap of the bag. Nothing. He started patting around in the crawl space, hand clanging against the metal of pipes, triggering spills of dust. He leaned in to the shoulder, felt in both directions, thinking maybe they had just tucked it farther than he remembered. Nothing.

Tom ducked down to peer into the dim space. As his eyes adjusted, he saw chalky piles of dust, abandoned spiderwebs, the faint, slick darkness of the pipes. But no duffel bag. It simply wasn't there. He stared, trying to understand.

The burglary, he thought. But then, no—after the cops had left, the first thing he and Anna had done was come down to the basement to check on the money.

Everything stood still. Tom crouched on the ground with his

head in the crawl space like a child hiding. Some part of him praying that by not seeing the threat behind him, he would make it somehow go away.

Then Jack said, "Lay down and stretch your arm out."

JACK WATCHED the man stiffen. Idiot civilian. Most guys, a solid kidney blow taught every needed lesson. But not this stupid son of a bitch. He still felt entitled.

The click of the hammer cocking back was loud in the confined space.

"No, wait, please!" Tom Reed spun on his knees, hands in front of his face. He looked desperate, had that animal panic, all darting eyes. "It was here. I *swear,* it was here."

"Lay down," Jack said, "and stretch out your arm."

"We got robbed," Tom blurted. "Earlier this week. They didn't find the money then, but they must have come back. They must have realized they'd forgotten the basement. We didn't notice because they didn't go into either of the units, but they must have come here and—"

"Tom." Jack spoke slowly. "Who do you think broke into your house?" He shook his head. "You want to do it the hard way, we'll do it the hard way. Now lay the fuck down."

For a long moment, the man just stared at him, the blood draining out of his face, a thousand horrors flowing in to replace it. Nothing was scarier than the monster you conjured in your own head. He started to argue, but Jack moved the pistol from his face to his stomach. "Now."

Slowly Tom Reed lay down on the dirty floor. He unfolded his knees from beneath him, then eased himself back onto his elbows. Held the position for a second, then rocked onto his back. He extended his arm. His eyes were on the ceiling, but seemed like they saw through it.

Jack eased the hammer down on the 1911, but kept it on Tom Reed's stomach. He put the ball of his size-twelves on the guy's arm, just past the elbow. Leaned in hard. The guy's lips were moving without sound, something rhythmic and steady, a prayer, maybe, or a promise. The old tightness came back, exhilaration and fear and a surge of power, of living on the thin edge of life, where the world was made minute by minute. He let the moment stretch, let the man's fear thicken and curdle.

Finally he said, "Tom, where's my money?"

The guy twisted his head sideways. His skin looked clammy. His eyes were all pupil. He said, "I swear to God. It was in there."

Jack shook his head. Leveled the pistol just in case. Then he lifted his right foot, the heel of the dress shoe angled down.

DON'T BE AFRAID, *don't be afraid, don't be afraid, oh God, what's he doing, why is he, his leg, why is he, oh God, is he, he can't, oh God, don't be afraid, don'tbeafraid, dontbeafraid,dontbea—*

The man slammed his foot down, and Tom's world exploded. "We put it in the crawl space, we put it in the crawl space, I swear to Christ, we put it right there!" Screaming the words to fight the agony.

Jack lifted his foot again, and Tom sucked in a deep breath.

He yanked against the shoe holding him in place, saw the finger tighten on the trigger of the gun, forced himself to stop.

The second time he noticed the sound, just as bad as the pain, a meaty horror with a slick-sick backslide as his knuckles ground concrete. A crack, like breaking a twig, and his little finger was twisted all the way over. He looked at it and felt something heave in him, fought not to vomit, *the pain, the pain, the burning shrieking jagged-glass ragged-edged pain.*

"Where is it?"

"We put it in the crawl space!"

The third stomp caught the edge of his wedding ring, the stainless steel band they'd picked out at a jeweler's off Michigan Avenue, caught it and deflected most of the force, but it was enough, enough, more than enough. Tom stared and fought against the black spots in his vision, thinking of his ring, his ring, his wife, his sweet ring and wife, Jesus, Anna, she would be home soon.

"I swear to fucking Christ," screaming, bellowing, eyes bugging, "we found the money in his kitchen, in the flour and the sugar and we put it in a duffel bag and took it down here, just my wife and me, and we haven't fucking moved it, I swear, I fucking *swear.* I don't know where it is, no matter how much you hurt me, I fucking do not know, because *we put it in the crawl space.*"

The man raised his foot again. Narrowed his eyes and paused. He was looking down, and Tom put it all in his eyes how he'd never been more sincere in his life, never. To make Jack believe. To keep that foot from coming down again. Heartbeats lasted decades; just the cool of the concrete, and the smell of blood and dust and bleach, and the inferno that was his hand.

Then Jack lowered his foot. Slowly. He took his other off Tom's arm, and dropped to a squat. Held the gun loose and casual, and Tom considered going for it, but the mere thought of moving his fingers made him almost vomit. Jack stared, hard features hollowed by the overhead light, eyes more suggestions than anatomy. Finally he said, "Huh," and stood up, stepped back. He ran a hand through his hair.

Free to move, Tom rolled over on his side, cradled his left hand in his right, holding it gently, like a limb that had fallen asleep, only instead of pins and needles, it was spikes and sawblades. His fingers were bloody and torn, savaged by the concrete. The little one was clearly broken. There was a wicked gash in the index finger. They were red and swollen as sausages.

They'll be okay. You'll be okay. Fingers heal. You put them on ice, you bind them, you go to the hospital. But first you have to get out of this.

Slowly, trying to use only his stomach muscles, Tom sat up. He was dizzy, and his head ached hollowly. "I swear," he said. "I swear, we put the money down here. I don't have any idea where it is."

Jack nodded slowly. "You know what? I believe you. You don't know where it is." He squatted down beside Tom. "But you know what else? I bet Anna does."

Before Tom could process what that meant, Jack's gun hand lashed out, and everything went away.

THROBBING.

His hand hurt furiously, in steady pulses tied to his heart. His head too. As he grasped at the straws of consciousness, his first thought was that he hadn't had a hangover this bad in a long time. Had he fallen asleep on the—

It all came back. Tom's eyes snapped open. He sat up sharply, but a slap of pain thrust him back. Slow. Take it slow. He was in a chair. A La-Z-Boy. Will's apartment, their downstairs unit. He was sitting with his hand propped up on the arm. Alone. Where was Jack?

And on the heels of that, where, oh God, where was Anna?

The fantasy played itself out in a fraction of a breath, a flickering horror show: Anna's arm extended, her mouth wide, head thrown back, Jack raising that foot. Another: Jack throwing her to the ground, unbuckling his pants, his wife screaming for help, while Tom lay unconscious in the chair . . .

He sat up again. The pain came in a white wave, and he made himself ride it, eyes closed, teeth clenched. The pain didn't matter. If she was here, he had to help her, had to get to her. Even if she wasn't, she would be soon.

A sound came from down the hall. The refrigerator door opening. Jack was in the kitchen. He must have felt safe with Tom unconscious, left him here. Just lucky timing. Tom stood, holding his left arm in his right. The world wobbled, then slowly steadied. Now what?

He might be able to make it out the front door, but what if Anna came home before he could get the cops here? He could try her cell phone, but what if she was on the El, or the battery was dead?

No. He couldn't leave until he knew they were both safe. So what then? The phone was no good; the extension was in the kitchen. His cell was in his bag, but he didn't see it. The room was spare, just the chair, an entertainment center, a TV, a lamp. His eyes roamed the fireplace, the shelves, the hallway. His toolbox. He'd left it in the hallway after looking for the drugs.

He didn't let himself think. Just ordered his feet to move. One step. Two. Heart racing, Tom bent down by the orange plastic toolbox. The latches were unfastened. Thank God he'd been in a hurry the other day. He reached for it, automatically using his closer hand, his left. The broken pinkie grazed the lid. Stars burst behind his eyes. He wanted to gasp, to howl, to scream curses and kick the wall. He held his breath and didn't make a sound.

Don't stop, you don't have time, go, go, be strong. Teeth grinding, he forced his right hand into motion. Opened the lid gently. Inside the top tray lay a collection of small tools: needle-nose pliers and a current detector and a miniature flashlight and a handful of misfit screws. And a four-inch Buck knife. Tom picked it up with two fingers. He'd originally had the hammer in mind, but this was better, faster and concealable. Carefully, he lowered the lid of the toolbox.

He heard a noise from down the hall and jerked upright. It took a minute to process the familiar pop and hiss. Jack had gone to grab a beer, like this was no big deal. The rush of anger that brought was amazing, hundred-proof hate at the sheer arrogance. The guy had clearly written Tom off as nothing.

Lips twisted, Tom took the few steps back to the chair. He opened the knife and slid it gingerly into his front right pocket. Then he sat, closed his eyes, and waited. He might be down, but he wasn't nothing.

*   *   *

JACK TOOK A LONG SWALLOW of Old Style. The cold beer slid easy down his throat. He glanced at his watch, saw it was nearly six. The woman would be home soon. Almost done.

He walked down the hall. Tom Reed was still in the chair. His position was a little different, though, and his breathing didn't have the regularity that came with unconsciousness. His left hand burned red, angry flesh and drying blood. "You awake?"

The guy didn't answer, but his eyelids twitched. "Yeah, you're awake." Jack stepped past him, to the front window. Glanced out at the quiet block. A pretty little street. Vintage graystones and two-flats, a couple of bungalows stuck in between. Plenty of trees, but still in the middle of things, restaurants and bars an easy stroll. The people walking dogs smiled at each other, stopped to chat. "Lemme ask you, what does a place like this run?"

There was a long pause, and then Tom said, "You've got to be kidding me."

"What? You think I don't live somewhere?" He turned back from the window, walked over to the door. Unlocked it. "How much?"

"I don't know."

"You don't know? You bought it, right?"

"Yeah."

"So how much?"

Tom rubbed at his head with his right hand. "There's a place for sale down the block for five and a quarter."

"Half a million dollars." He whistled, traced the woodwork of the molding with the palm of his hand. "You know the house I grew up in, my dad bought for something like thirty grand? A little place off Archer, with a postage-stamp yard and a crooked roof. My brother and I shared a bedroom until . . . shit, until I moved out." He sipped his beer. "It was a big deal, though, him being able to buy at all. Most of the Polacks we knew were renting."

"What did you mean when you said you thought Anna knew where the money was?"

Jack walked over to the wall, leaned against it. "Two people put something somewhere, one is surprised to find it gone?" He shrugged.

"She wouldn't do that."

"Better hope you're wrong." Jack rolled his shoulders to loosen them. Long jobs were the hardest. Too much time for foul-ups. A neighbor looking through the window, a civilian growing a spine, you never knew. Forty-three years old now, and more work than he could remember. Time to quit. Once he and Marshall split the money, he was heading for Arizona. See if Eli was still interested in a partner for his bar. Jack unclipped his mobile phone from his belt, flipped it open. The reception was fine. "I know, I know, it's a bitch. Hard to believe something like that. But it's funny how money changes people. Even people you trust."

"If Anna does know where the money is . . ." The man hesitated, and Jack could see that it hurt him to think like that. "Will you just take it and go?"

"You have a gambling problem or something?"

"Huh?"

Jack finished the beer in a long swallow. "You've got a building in a neighborhood that runs half a mill." He set the can on the ground, then stomped it flat. Saw Tom Reed wince at that. He chuckled, then bent to pick up the can and slip it in his pocket. "You've got a job that pays solid bank, and a good-looking wife."

"So?"

"I'm just wondering, why would you take the money?" He paused, locked eyes with the guy. "I really want to know. I mean, what is it you want"—he gestured in a circle—"you don't already got?"

"It's not that simple."

"Why not?"

Tom shook his head, said nothing.

"Okay, sure, it's tempting. Money is always tempting. But you had to know life didn't work that way, right? In your heart? I mean, it was a bag full of money."

"We . . ." Tom hesitated. "We didn't know where it came from. We thought it was his. Like he'd saved it, didn't trust banks."

"That make it better?"

"He was dead. We weren't hurting anybody."

"That's the problem with you people." Jack cracked his thumbs. "I'm not saying I wouldn't have taken it. I would. Did, as a matter of fact. But I didn't tell myself it wasn't hurting anybody. I wanted it, so I took it. You get my meaning?"

"No."

"Let me put it another way." He cocked his head. "You really believe you didn't bring this on yourself?"

Tom opened his mouth, then closed it. The moment stretched. Then Jack felt the phone vibrate on his hip. He drew the .45. "Don't fuck around. Get me?"

Tom gave the barest of nods.

Jack opened his phone and read the text message.

ANNA FLIPPED ON HER BLINKER, waited for a white construction van to pass, then put the Pontiac in reverse, turned the wheel hard, and backed into the narrow space. Before she moved to the city, parallel parking had seemed like an arcane art. Now she could do it in her sleep.

The sidewalk was dappled with spring sunlight, little patches of flowers beginning to bloom beside the road. A red BMW was offset by an explosion of white tulips, and a flowering bush half obscured a black Honda, the engine running, a man inside fiddling with a cell phone. She strolled easy, thinking about Tom's voice as he'd suggested they go to a hotel. He hadn't seemed worried—just the opposite, in fact. Like he'd solved a problem that had been bugging him, and wanted to celebrate. Odd.

Still, a hotel sounded nice. They used to do that every now and then, check into a place downtown just for the change. A vacation in their hometown, complete with big fluffy robes and a swimming pool. It had been years. Should be fun.

She climbed the steps and dug for her keys. Checked the mailbox out of habit—nothing, again, which was getting ridiculous—and figured she'd pack her green bikini with the blue flowers, order room service and a movie.

The door to the bottom apartment yanked open, and a burly blur came through it, a man, she could see that much as she threw her hands up in panic, and then he grabbed her, fingers steel on her arm, and yanked her inside, her feet tangling, struggling just to stay vertical as he half pulled, half tossed her through the open door. She took three or four steps to catch her balance, and was opening her mouth to shriek when she saw Tom starting to force himself up from the overstuffed chair, his hand held at an awkward angle. What was he doing here? What was going on?

The door closed behind them. "Don't scream, Anna."

There was blood on Tom's left hand, and the way he held it was odd, a swollen mess, the pinkie off-kilter. Her nerves felt like she'd bitten metal. She gasped, one hand covering her mouth, and started forward. Then she saw the look on his face, and stopped.

Sometimes it felt like they had known each other for a hundred years. She knew his every gesture, every expression. She could render them in her mind: the easy smile, tilted a little to one side, that drew crinkles around his eyes. The half-lidded head loll, lips barely parted, as they made love in the night. His precise squint when reading, meant not to bring the words into focus but to put the rest of the world out.

She had never seen the look that was on his face now. She recognized fear around the wide eyes. Pain marked in the press of his lips. And concern, concern for her, in the cock of his head and the readiness of his body. But there was something else too. A guardedness like a metal gate drawn across a store window. And through the slats of that, a sharp and sparkling accusation.

And so she wasn't surprised when the man behind her said, "Funny thing, Anna. Tom really believed it was in the basement."

She turned, her lips curling in a snarl at this creature, this monster who had hurt her husband, who had smashed his hand and drawn a screen across his eyes. She found herself staring directly into the barrel of a big gun. The hole shallowed the depth of field until everything behind that black circle was just blurry shapes, and one of those blurry shapes said, "Anna, where did you take my money?"

IT WAS TRUE. Jack had told the truth, and his wife had lied.

At first, when Jack had yanked open the door and snatched Anna, snapped her into the room like he was cracking a whip, Tom had reacted on instinct, struggling to get out of the chair. Ready, as always, to catch her should she fall. But then their eyes had met, and he saw what was in hers. She had taken the money.

She had taken the money and she hadn't told him. As a result, he'd been held at gunpoint on the dirty basement floor. He'd had his fingers smashed and broken. Had a gun held to his belly by a man clearly willing to pull the trigger. And worse than the consequences was the action. His wife had betrayed him.

Stop. Now isn't the time. He didn't try to forget his feelings. He just pushed them down. If they were going to get out of this, he needed to focus.

Anna stood a few feet away, one hand still holding her keys, the other at her side and behind, as if preparing to catch herself. "What money?"

"You know what money, Anna."

She hesitated, then said, "It's not here."

"Where is it?"

"Somewhere safe."

No, Tom thought, *no, don't get cute with him, he'll—*

Jack's left hand lashed out in a wicked slap. From his chair, Tom saw her head jerk sideways, saw the force ripple through her body, and he leapt to his feet without thinking, instinct mingling with pure hate. But Jack was a move ahead of him, the gun swinging over to point at his chest. Tom thought about going for it. Wanted to. But there was no way he could cover the distance.

Icy. He had to be icy. Cold and hard and able to bear what Jack dealt, so that when the moment came, he could act. He lowered his arms.

Jack nodded, kept the gun where it was, but looked at Anna. "Let's try this again, honey. This time, if I don't like your answer, I'm going to shoot your husband. Now, where—"

"Upstairs. It's upstairs." The words tumbled from Anna's lips.

"Show me." He gestured with the pistol. "You too."

Tom's mind was racing. Once they gave him the money, there was no reason Jack wouldn't kill them. They'd seen his face, heard him talk. And for a man who was used to pulling the trigger, what were two more bodies? He would have to move first. Soon. The weight of the knife in his pocket was a comfort. His fingers screamed to reach for it, but he made himself stand still.

"Let's go." Jack gestured. Tom moved to the entryway of their building. Through the glass doors of the vestibule he could see their porch, and beyond it, the street. A woman walked by with a dog, a blue plastic bag dangling heavy from one hand. Normal life, ten feet away. It made him want to scream.

"Move."

Anna opened the door and started up, Tom following, and behind them Jack. Like they were landlords again, just showing the place to a prospective tenant. *Two baths, plenty of street parking, a washer and dryer in the basement. Want to see the back porch, or would you rather just shoot us?* Panic thoughts he didn't have time for. The steps fell away one at a time. His legs tingled, and his palms itched. Soon. He'd never used a knife in anger before, wondered how best to hold it.

But when Anna opened the door, hope quickened in Tom's chest. Besides the usual squeak of the hinges, there came a series of three quick beeps. The alarm system.

Jack heard it too. He hustled them inside, closed the door behind, his mouth set hard. "Turn it off."

Beep.

Anna started for it. Tom said, "Don't." She hesitated. Jack whirled on him, stepped forward, raising the gun.

Beep.

Tom said, "He's going to kill us. After we give him the money, he's going to kill us."

Jack said, "Turn off the alarm, Anna. Do it now."

Beep.

The three of them stood frozen. Tom had his hand against the hem of his pocket, but couldn't move, didn't dare, not while Jack stared at him.

Beep.

"Goddamnit," Jack said, his voice irritated more than angry. He stepped forward and put the barrel of the gun under Tom's chin, then turned to Anna. "Turn it off."

It was the best chance he was likely to get. Tom dug into his pocket, fingers grazing the ridged plastic of the handle, twisting his body at the same time, his first thought to get out of the line of fire, his second to bring the knife up. Time went liquid, and he could see everything at once without any of it really registering, a twitch around Jack's eyes as he sensed Tom's motion, the counter-slosh throbbing of his head as he jerked back fast, another beep from the alarm panel, Anna's mouth opening to scream, the faint hitch as the knife snagged the edge of his pocket, slowing him down. His chin passed over the gun even as Jack pulled the trigger, a roar like the world breaking, but no pain.

Then he had the knife clear of his pocket, and lunged forward, not planning anything fancy, just stabbing underhanded as hard as he could. He saw Jack twisting too, left arm coming down, and Tom tried to adjust, to make it to the stomach, but Jack was too quick, his forearm slammed into Tom's hand, weird with resistance and suddenly wet as the blade cut flesh. Jack roared and spun, bringing his gun hand up in a gut punch. The breath blew from Tom's lungs, and he struggled to swing the knife again, but Jack stepped into him, a hard shoulder-check that knocked him back. His feet caught, and then he was down, the knife bouncing away. Jack dropped to crouch on his chest, the gun unwavering on Tom's forehead. He was panting, and his eyes blazed, and something wet dripped onto Tom's face.

Everything was still, just the three of them locked in the ear-ringing aftermath of violence.

Beep.

Jack said, "Turn off the goddamn alarm."

"Okay," she said, stepping to the panel. "I'm doing it. Don't

hurt him." Her fingers danced quickly over the keys, and the beeping died.

MARSHALL JERKED UPRIGHT IN HIS SEAT, one hand on the shotgun, one on the door handle, lips open, leaning forward, poised,
waiting. To a civilian, that might have sounded like anything, a
firecracker, a truck backfiring, but he knew it for what it was. He
waited to hear the second shot.

Nothing. He sucked air through his teeth and stared down
the block. One shot. That was strange. The plan had been that
after Jack got the money, he'd tell Tom and Anna to lie down,
then put a bullet in each of their brains. Nothing personal, just
business.

Maybe Jack had needed to kill one of them to coerce the other.
Marshall leaned back in the seat. One shot wouldn't bring the cops.
Neither would a second or a third, most likely. It was the kind of
neighborhood where people never assumed the worst.

Still. If he was wrong. If one of them had managed to get the
gun away from Jack or get to a phone. Sitting on Will Tuttle's
block with an illegal shotgun and half the police looking for him?
Bad place to be. The smart thing would be to take off. But the
money was inside that house. He knew it, knew it in his gut. If he
left now, he cut himself out of the take.

Marshall took out a cigarette, spun it between his fingers.
"Come on, Jack," he said. "Come on."

*　　*　　*

JACK'S LEFT ARM THROBBED, a heat timed to his heartbeat. Without taking the gun off Tom, he twisted his arm to get a look. Shit. It was a pretty good slash, five diagonal inches across the top of his forearm, the skin puckered and pulled away to reveal pink tissue. Blood came free, and wiggling his fingers sent shocks down his spine.

Where had the fucker gotten a knife? If it hadn't snagged as he was pulling it out . . . Jesus. Something nagged at him, but he couldn't place it. No time. Things were getting out of hand. "Now."

Anna said, "It's in the heating vent."

"Which one?"

"The kitchen."

He nodded, stood slowly, his eyes on Tom. "Let's go." Forcing the pain away. Let them think he couldn't be wounded, that he was stronger than they could imagine. Fear was good. He tried to think things through, see every angle. The gunshot would have been heard for a block. Marshall would have heard it. Would he split?

If he did, he did. One thing at a time. The vent was high on the wall, just shy of the ten-foot ceiling. "You have a screwdriver?"

Tom said nothing, but his wife was smarter, said, "There's a cordless in the toolkit."

The toolkit. He'd noticed it downstairs, in the hallway. Of course. That was where the knife came from. Tom had seemed so cowed, Jack had figured him for a wimp. Turned out the guy had a backbone after all.

Focus. "Do you have one up here?"

She hesitated, then said, "There's a regular one in the kitchen drawer."

"Get it. Quickly."

She nodded, her eyes on his as she backed toward the counter. A good-looking woman, seemed smart. A shame. Jack looked back and forth between her and Tom, his adrenaline running, tuning him up. He could feel the faint ache in his toes, the heat in his armpits. City sounds came through the windows, the bark of a dog, a faraway siren.

"You," he said. "Drag the table over to the wall."

Tom grimaced, then took the edge of the table in his right hand and scraped it across the floor. A faint line dug in the hardwood marked the passage.

"Get up on the table. Anna?"

She was still rummaging through the drawer. "I know it's here." She threw a handful of delivery menus up on the counter, dug back in with both hands.

Jack stepped away, widening the margin and putting his back to the wall to keep them both covered. "Hurry up."

Anna nodded, then said, "Here it is." Came out with it, started to walk toward Jack.

"Give it to him."

She hesitated, then stretched to pass the screwdriver. When his fingers touched it, it knocked from her hand and clattered to the ground. She froze, then bent, picked it up, shaking. She passed it to Tom.

"You know what to do," Jack said. Tom turned to face the wall. With his good hand, he stretched the screwdriver above his head and went to work on the return vent. The table rocked slightly as he moved.

Jack watched, gun level, mind steady. Probably two minutes,

maybe three, since the woman arrived. Figure another few to get the cover off and dig out the money. His ears buzzed in the aftermath of the gun blast, a rhythmic whine that rose and fell. Tell the couple he was going to tie them up, to lie down. With a .45, one shot each would be plenty. Collect the brass. The guy had the vent cover off, finally.

Anna said, "It's really far back there. You might need a ladder."

The guy went up on tiptoes, his arm all the way in. A hollow rumble sounded as he hit the walls of the vent.

What else? His gloves should cover him on fingerprints. He'd been bleeding up and down the hallway, but there wasn't much he could do about that. The cops could match his 1911 to the one at the club, but it would be going over the Skyway Bridge on their way out of town. The whine grew louder, and he realized it wasn't in his ears, but outside, sirens. As always, there was that moment of automatic panic, but he put it aside. Chicago was a big city.

Still, there was something missing. Something right in front of him. Jack stared at Tom, saw the guy digging as far as he could. Looked at the wife. She stared back at him. Why did that seem wrong? Wasn't it human nature to be looking up at her husband? Especially if he was pulling money out of the wall? It was almost as if she were—

The sirens stopped, and Jack realized what he'd missed. "Oh, you cunt." How had he not seen this? Had he been that distracted by pain and surprise? It was only the sirens stopping that triggered him. The cops did that when they wanted to roll up quietly. Screaming sirens to get close, then silence for the final approach. The alarm had a panic code.

Tom Reed was frozen, his right arm lost to the shoulder, his neck twisted to look down at his wife. Anna stood straight-backed, defiant. Jack sighted down the barrel of the 1911. "I still have time to kill you."

Her eyes widened, but she said, "You'll never get the money if you do."

Fuck, fuck, *fuck*. His eyes darted over the kitchen, taking in the windows, the rear door. The cops might be a mile away. They might be a block. No way to know. His cell phone rang. Marshall. He grit his teeth.

"You don't want to do this," he said. "Just give me the money."

Anna Reed said, "They'll be here any second."

Jack ran.

14

THE RETREAT OF IMMEDIATE DANGER was like a break between waves at the beach. Tom had been leaning into horror, bracing himself against it, and the sudden absence left him weightless. He pulled his arm out of the vent, shoulder creaking. Stood on the table he and Anna had bought together at a flea market, staring around his kitchen. Everything the same, only viewed from an angle that made it all strange and threatening.

"Are you okay?" Anna stared up, eyes wide. She didn't seem to know what to do with her arms, first reaching for him, stopping herself, almost crossing them over her chest, and finally letting them dangle awkwardly.

He didn't answer. Just sank to a squat. His left hand throbbed a warning, and he caught himself in time. Put the handle of the screwdriver in his teeth, then picked up the vent cover with his right hand. Slowly he rose, fighting dizziness. The cover was hard to manipulate with one hand. It had been easy to take it off, but putting it back together was tricky. The way of things.

"Tom?"

He managed to fit it into the open hole. The edge of the drywall held it in place just enough for him to let go, take a screw from his pocket and gently insert it. The handle of the screwdriver was slippery. He slotted it and began to turn, rightie-tightie.

"Tom, don't bother with that now. We have to think. The police are coming."

A dozen twists, and the screw was sunk. He pulled the other and went to work on it.

"Honey—"

"Why did you take the money?" He kept his eyes on the vent. The table rocked lightly as he moved.

"I didn't."

He laughed.

"I mean, I didn't *take* it. I just moved it."

"Why?"

"I was afraid you would give it to them. The police. Trying to protect me."

He nodded, habit more than anything else. Now that the adrenaline was fading, everything was starting to hurt. Warming up like an orchestra, all discordant and garbled. His hand led the way, hot swelling throbs of brass-thick pain. Right behind it, his head, a metronomic ache from the blow of Jack's gun. His back and stomach hummed and warbled, and across his body came a hundred faint stabs and ripples like the twinkling of flutes. He grit his teeth and worked on the screw.

"Tom, we have to get ready for them."

A final twist, and the cover was in place. For a moment he badly wanted to unscrew it, take it off, and then put it back on again. To repeat the process all day long.

"Honey." Her voice pleading, strained. "We have to think."

"You lied to me." He tucked the screwdriver in his pocket, dropped to the edge of the table, and stepped to the floor.

"I know. And I'm sorry. I wish I hadn't. I didn't think anything like this would ever happen. How could I know?" Her eyes pleading. "I'll tell you everything, answer any question you like, but right now we have to talk about the police."

Tom looked away. "What about? We tell them the truth."

"We can't."

He snorted. Gripped the edge of the table with one hand, began to pull it back where it belonged.

"Tom, listen to me. Would you just—" She grabbed the other side, pulling away from him. "Just *stop*."

He yanked harder, and she braced herself to resist. The table came off the ground, wavered back and forth. He glared, and she glared back. All of it spilled out between them, the lies, the pressure, the slow tectonic shifts of their relationship exploding in a tug-of-war over a table.

Then a buzzer sounded, loud and insistent. The doorbell from downstairs. The police.

He dropped his side, started for the hallway, where the intercom would open the downstairs door. She was closer, hurried to block the hallway. "Just listen for a second, okay?"

"Get out of the way, Anna."

"*Listen.*" She spat the word, then took a breath. "There is no way to tell the cops why that guy was here without telling them about the money. No way at all."

"I don't care." He started to push past her.

She put an arm against either side of the hall to block him. "Damn it, think!" Her eyes pleading. "Later, we can talk all we want. We can figure out what to do, you can be pissed at me—I don't blame you—but right this second *there are cops coming to our door,* and we need to be together."

"Why?"

The buzzer sounded angrily and long.

"Because if we tell the truth we're going to jail." She raised her eyebrows. "We stole that money. We've spent a lot of it. We've lied to the police."

"Better that than face Jack Witkowski again." He pushed past, shouldering through her arm easily. Two steps took him to the intercom.

Her voice came from behind him. "How do you know his name?"

He froze, thumb on the button to open the door.

"Tom? He wouldn't have told you that."

He opened his mouth. Shut it again. There was no time to explain, to tell her that the things he had kept from her were different, that he had done it for the good of both of them, that he had only been trying to—

To protect her.

He felt the anger deflate. The buzzer sounded again. He turned to face her, then said, "Okay. We get through this. Then you and I need to talk."

The look she gave him was scared and wounded and sweet all at once. It was like watching something beautiful break.

He took a breath. Pushed the intercom and said, in as calm a voice as he could manage, "Yes? Who is it?"

* * *

ANNA WAS GETTING USED to lying to the police.

After Tom had buzzed them up, she'd barely had time to wipe away the blood in the hallway before opening the door and smoothing her expression as if she were icing a cake. Listened to the heavy tromp of their feet. One cop had his gun held at his side, which startled her. "Officer, I'm so sorry, this is all my fault." She shook her head ruefully. "We just got the alarm, and I'm not used to it yet."

"Is this your house, ma'am?" The first cop was a baby-faced blond; behind him stood a tall officer with a graying crewcut.

"Yes. We just came in, and I punched the wrong code." She gave him what she hoped was an embarrassed smile. "They taught us about the panic code, but I wasn't thinking and misdialed. The alarm shut off, so . . ."

The older cop relaxed, but the first said, "Do you mind if I look around?"

"Why?"

"The point of the panic code is that someone might force you to shut off your alarm."

"Officer, I promise, it's just my husband and me."

"Still, ma'am, I'm going to need to confirm that."

She hesitated, then shrugged, opened the door wide.

"Thank you." The blond officer moved with his gun out, playing at Serpico. Anna slid aside to make room as he swept down the hall. The older cop stepped in casually, hooked his thumbs in his belt and shrugged at her, as if to say, *Kids*. Anna forced a smile back. "I'm Anna Reed."

"Sergeant Peter Bradley." He glanced around the living room. "Nice place." It was at that moment that she remembered the bullet hole in the ceiling. She started to look up, caught herself, looked down instead, and saw a brass cylinder, shit, part of the bullet, that part that got ejected from the gun. It lay on the hardwood floor three inches from Bradley's left foot. She coughed, then said, "Thanks. Can I get you guys some coffee?"

"That's all right, ma'am." He rocked back on his heels, watery eyes calmly taking in the room. Anna found herself wondering about him, imagining his life: an ex-wife, two kids, child support that had him picking up extra shifts working security at a strip club. Strange, random thoughts. The cop shuffled his feet, and she said a silent prayer he wouldn't kick the bullet.

Tom came out of the bathroom. He'd washed his face and brushed his hair, and held his left hand behind his back, standing like a politician about to deliver a speech. He smiled, said, "Really sorry about this, Officer."

"Happens all the time."

They heard the younger cop from down the hall, barking that the bedroom was clear. Bradley shook his head, called down the hall, "Why don't we get out of here, let these folks get on about their day?"

"But, Sergeant, I'm supposed to check—"

"It's all right, son." Bradley keyed his radio, said, "It's a false. Dialed the wrong code."

Anna slipped her arm around Tom's waist. "You sure we can't get you anything?"

The blond cop, his gun now holstered, said, "Would you mind if I used your lavatory?"

She felt the muscles in her smile tighten. She wanted to scream, *Get out get out get Out!* Instead she said, "Of course, Officer."

She stood and willed herself to keep her eyes level, not to glance at either the ceiling or the floor. Reminded herself that these guys were just regular cops, not detectives, not people who knew what had happened in the last week. "I really do feel stupid. You guys must have better things to do."

"We were in the neighborhood." Bradley cleared his throat. "Your security company will bill you for the false alarm, though."

"Really?"

"Probably about two hundred." The cop shrugged. "It's steep, I know, but that's how they do it."

"That's okay, Officer," Anna said, remembering Jack sprinting out the back door. "I don't mind at all." She heard the toilet flush, the hiss of the sink, and then the other guy came down the hall, belt heavy with gear. As the two turned to go, the corner of the sergeant's boot caught the edge of the shell casing and set it spinning. She moved fast, stepping forward to silence it with a foot, her smile never wavering.

When the door closed behind them, Tom said, "Where's the money?"

"In the car."

His mouth fell open. "You left three hundred grand *in the car*?"

"I was going to put it at Sara's, but I thought . . . " She shrugged, feeling stupid. "I don't know. I didn't really think it through. I wasn't trying to steal it, like I said. But once I took it out, putting it back didn't make any sense. I was going to get a safe-deposit box, but with my job, everything." She shrugged again.

Tom closed his eyes, rubbed his forehead hard. "Okay." He held his left hand in his right. Winced.

"You should get that looked at."

"We'll hit a drugstore on our way."

"On our way where?"

THE W HOTEL ON LAKE SHORE was hipster heaven. Anna dug the décor, the mod chairs and muted colors, trip-hop playing over the lobby sound system. It made her feel cooler than she was.

When the woman behind the desk asked her name, Anna told the truth. Then she said, "I can give you a credit card. But could you put the room in a different name? My ex-husband . . ." She trailed off with a meaningful look.

"Of course," the woman said. "I understand. What name would you like?"

"Ummm . . . Anna Karenina?"

"You sure? Love didn't go well for her either."

"I suppose not."

"How about Annie Oakley? He shows up, you can shoot him, then ride into the sunset."

Anna laughed. "Thanks."

The room was all sleek planes and Asian light fixtures. Broad windows gave onto the lake and Navy Pier, the Ferris wheel burning bright against indigo skies. It made her want to take off her clothes and order champagne.

Tom set the duffel bag on the ground, then collapsed into the overstuffed chair beside it. His face was drawn and his lips pressed tight. He rested his left elbow on the arm of the chair so that his hand was above his head. It was swollen and crusted with blood.

"How is it?"

"It hurts." He said it simply. He wasn't much of one to complain, would always drive her crazy with his refusal to go to a doctor no matter how sick he was. *What's the doctor going to do?* he'd say. *I'll be better by the time I could get an appointment.*

She moved to the edge of the bed. Nervous again, not sure how to talk to him, what to say. "Want me to tape it up?"

"Let me have a couple of drinks and some pills first."

They'd bought a bottle of bourbon at the CVS, along with medical tape, gauze, antiseptic cream, antibacterial soap, Advil, and a splint. She shook out a couple of capsules and passed them to him, then dug the booze out of the bag. She knew you weren't supposed to mix ibuprofen and alcohol, but against the scale of their current concerns, that rule seemed laughable. She poured three inches into each glass. He took his wordlessly, eyes out the window.

"I'm sorry, Tom."

He nodded, still not looking at her.

"It was stupid. I should have trusted you. I *do* trust you. It was just . . . It was stupid."

He sipped his drink. Shrugged. Said, "Doesn't matter now."

"It matters to me."

"Yeah?"

"Yes."

"Okay. Then you want to know the worst moment?" He turned, hit her with an expression hard to read. "It wasn't when I saw the money was gone. It wasn't when he stomped on my fingers. It was after all that. I still didn't believe you'd taken it. Jack told me you had, but I refused to believe it. Until I looked in your eyes and realized he knew you better than I did."

"That's not true."

He raised his eyebrows. Took another swig.

"What about you?" She could feel herself on an emotional tightrope, self-loathing on one side, fury on the other. "How do you know who he is? What have you been doing that you haven't told me?"

"Trying to save our lives." His tone was level, uncombative, and it helped steady her on the rope. She said, "What does that mean?"

"Jack isn't our only problem." Tom drained the rest of his bourbon, leaned for the bottle. Anna beat him to it and poured into the glass he held. When she finished, he flashed a smile, nothing much, just a quick *thank you,* more habit and courtesy than anything, but still. "Someone else is after us as well."

"Who?"

"Genghis Khan."

"Huh?"

"Just listen," he said. She opened her mouth, then shut it, leaned back against the headboard, and nodded. He told her about his meeting with the man in the suit, about the threats against them both. About his conversation with the detective, his careful dance of exaggeration and obfuscation. Told her about talking real estate with Jack Witkowski while a knife burned in his pocket. She listened quietly, assembling the larger pattern: thieves that preyed on the Star buying drugs. A betrayal and a murder. Everyone scattering, one man left holding all the goods—a man who hid in a quiet rental apartment, the bottom floor of a two-flat in Lincoln Square. A grand epic had been playing out around them. "The guy in the suit, did he say how long we had?"

"No. But not long. He's probably looking for us now."

"Do you think he's dangerous?"

"Definitely."

"Worse than Jack?"

Tom shook his head. "I don't know. Does it matter?"

"I guess not." She rubbed at her temple. "What do we do?"

"We go to the cops," he said.

"We'd have to tell them everything."

"So?"

"Tom, we'd have to give up the money. Not just the cash we have left, but the stuff we've already paid too. We'd have to hire a lawyer." A thought struck her. "God, I don't even have a job now! How would we pay for it? We'd lose the house." She shook her head. "There has to be another way."

"I'm open to suggestions."

She hesitated. Even if everything went perfectly, if they somehow rode out the storm, if the police caught Jack and the drug dealer, if a lawyer kept them out of jail, they would lose their chance for a child. Time and debt would guarantee it. They wouldn't even be able to adopt. She'd researched the process, knew how stringent it was. People could be disqualified if the adoption agent just got a bad vibe. She imagined the interview: *Well, sure, we are nearly bankrupt. True, we stole money from our deceased tenant. Yes, we did have to sell our house to cover our legal defense against felony charges. But we're good housekeepers. You can overlook the rest, right?*

If they went to the police, they risked everything. If they didn't, they risked their lives. "I can't believe this. It's crazy."

"I know."

"I mean, it was just a coincidence. A nothing little thing. Our tenant deciding to make a cup of coffee. That's all. If he hadn't, there wouldn't have been a fire. We wouldn't have found the money. All of this would have been different."

"But there was, and we did. Now we have to deal with it."

The most crucial decision in her life could be traced to a cup of instant coffee. It hurt to think about. "We don't have to call the cops right now, do we?"

He shook his head. "Soon, though. The longer we drag it out, the less friendly they'll be."

"What do you think they'll do?"

"I don't know. Take the money, obviously. I can't imagine them locking us up or anything. We're not exactly murderers."

"Will they protect us?"

He didn't answer for a long time. Finally he said, "They'll do what they can."

She thought back to the apartment, Tom on his back, Jack kneeling over him, that big gun pointing at her beautiful husband's face. Remembered how loud the shot had been, how it had left her ears ringing for half an hour. An explosion, flame and fury. She had an image, quickly walled away, of what all that power could do to a human being. To Tom.

They had gotten lucky. Plain and simple. Lucky in the alarm, in the panic code, in the police response time. They hadn't beaten Jack, not by a long shot. They'd gotten lucky.

And even with that luck, all they'd done was get away. He was still out there. Smart and dangerous and now pissed off. Would the police protect them? *Could* they? For how long? "Maybe we should leave town. Hit the road."

"We'd have to come back sooner or later."

"I guess." She shook her head. "I'd just like to be farther

away from him. From both of them. I'd feel better if we were in Detroit."

He was sipping at his bourbon when she said that, and made a sound sort of like a laugh that quickly turned to a cough. He shook his head and swallowed hard, eyes watering.

"What?"

Tom beat at his chest, coughed. "What you said."

"What about it?"

"It's just"—he stared at her—"you *know* you're in bad shape if you'd rather be in Detroit."

Anna felt a smile burst out of her. Then a laugh. Then peals of it. It was freeing, a deep and cleansing silliness, and they kept at it, one triggering the other, the laughter far outstripping the joke.

When they finally stopped, Tom said, "Well, that's about as good as I'm likely to feel. Maybe we better . . . "

She nodded. Took him to the bathroom, ran the water until it was lukewarm, then held his hand under it. He gasped at the contact, but didn't fight her. She washed her own hands thoroughly, then, gently, washed each of his fingers. As the dried blood came off, she got a look at the damage. The knuckles were scraped and torn, and there was a nasty rip in the meat of his index finger. All of them were red and throbbing, sausage-thick and hot to the touch. His little finger was clearly broken, angled too far to one side.

She dried his hand and arm on a thick towel, then smeared antiseptic cream all over. "This is going to hurt."

He nodded, sat down on the toilet, his face pale. "Pass that washcloth." He spun it into a rope, then bit down. Huffed breath through his nose, one, two, three, then looked at her and nodded.

She steeled herself. Better to do it fast and only once. Anna took hold of his little finger and twisted hard. He yelled through clenched teeth and cotton.

"I'm sorry I'm sorry I'm sorry," she said, hating hurting him, feeling her own face contract. She bent over his hand. Worked the finger gently to make sure it was in position, terrified she would have to do it again. But it seemed reasonably well aligned. She fixed the splint to it, then taped it tight. "There. That should work." She began to bandage his other fingers. "I think you'll be okay. The others aren't broken. The little one probably isn't perfectly in line, though. We should get you to a doctor soon."

He spat out the cloth, let out a deep breath. "Promise me something." His voice throaty.

"Anything."

"No more lies. Okay? Never again."

She looked up at him, this man she'd known forever. "And no more trying to protect me. We get through this together."

His smile broke slow and sweet as a spring sunrise. "Partners in crime."

"Partners in crime." She leaned across his bandaged hand to kiss him, his rough lips and gentle tongue. Not a passionate kiss, not meant to lead to the bedroom. Just truer than words.

THE BOURBON WAS A FUZZY GLOW THROUGH HIM, sanding the edges off the pain and loosening his body. Tom lay on top of the bed, his left hand up on a pillow, his right enfolding Anna. Out the window, the Ferris wheel turned and turned and turned.

Tomorrow would be bad. But right now, this second, it seemed a million miles away. Maybe he was in shock. Maybe it was the liquor. But for now, mercifully, he felt warm and sheltered, a boat that had made it to safe harbor.

On the desk, his cell phone rang.

"Let it go," Anna whispered into his armpit.

"Can't," he said. Sat up slowly, untwining his arm from around her shoulder. Looked at the display, didn't recognize the number. "It's probably Halden. If we're going to turn ourselves in tomorrow, I should talk to him now."

"Are you going to tell him?"

"Not if I can help it." He stood, cracked his neck. "I'd rather do it in person. Besides, I want tonight. Things won't be calm again for a long time."

She smiled at him. "I love you."

"Back at you." He opened the phone and said, "Tom Reed."

"Hi, Tom. How's the W?" Jack Witkowski's voice was clear and cold. "They have those little bottles of booze in the room?"

15

HE NEARLY DROPPED THE PHONE. "How did you—"

"How did I find you?" Jack snorted. "This is what I do. You really think I wouldn't find you, douchebag?"

Tom's knees felt weak, and he sat on the edge of the table. Locked eyes with Anna, who had registered the tone of his voice and sat up alarmed.

"So, you haven't answered my question. The W. Nice place?"

"Yeah." He struggled for his cool. "Great view."

"I bet. What's it run, three hunny a night?"

Maybe it was the distance. Maybe it was shock or booze or exhaustion, but Tom just didn't feel like being cowed. "So what? On your money, we can stay here three years."

There was a pause, and then a short laugh. "I keep writing you off as a pussy, and you keep proving me wrong. That move with the knife was pretty good. Didn't work, but it was gutsy. And your wife too. Setting off the panic code anybody could do, but stalling, talking about the money in the heating vent? Pretty clever."

"Guess so."

"And now you're feeling safe in a luxury hotel room. Big windows, that romantic view you mentioned. Maybe got a couple of drinks under your belt. Am I right? You have a few?"

"Yeah."

"What's a guy like you drink?"

"Bourbon."

"Soda, rocks?"

"Neat."

"Huh. If I'd've known that, I'd've handled things differently at your house. Wouldn't have left you alone."

"I guess that wasn't in our mail. That's how you got my cell number too, right?"

"Sure." Jack paused. "By the way, what's the matter with your dick? There was a letter from a fertility clinic. You and Anna need a little help? I'd be happy to spot you some baby juice."

"Fuck you, you fucking psycho." The words came hard and fast, accompanied by a rush of blood to his face. After all they'd been through, he was surprised that Jack still had the power to violate them, to spread poison on something precious.

"Fuck me?" Jack laughed. "Maybe that's the problem. Not going to be any babies, you run around trying to cornhole middle-aged Polacks. That it, Tom? You queer?"

He stood, went to the window. Looked out at the Drive, headlights running in one direction, taillights in the other. The past here, the future there, and just a moment, a flickering blur, really, that marked the present. "We told the police everything."

"Now, I give you credit for balls. But it's your wife with the brains. I know you didn't tell the cops."

Tom had a sinking feeling, said nothing.

"That's right, tough guy. I was watching. I got balls too. I sat on your block and watched those two uniforms stroll in, then stroll back out maybe five minutes later. You didn't tell them shit. You're not going to, either. Because they'll make you give up the score. And if you do, I'll kill you and Anna both."

"Even if we haven't got the money."

"Quite a predicament, huh?" Jack's voice was merry. "You figured it was pennies from heaven, turns out you got bad men on your tail. Life's a bitch."

Tom opened his mouth, closed it. In the dark window he could see the reflection of the room, Anna ghostly behind him. Finally he said, "Why did you call? Just to say that?"

"I called to tell you it's your lucky day. I've got a way out for you."

"How?"

"Just give me my money, Tom. That's all."

"How do I know you—"

"Won't kill you? We'll do it in public, like on TV. See, I figure, you can't go to the cops without getting yourself in trouble, and besides, you don't really know anything that could hurt me. So just bring what's mine and get on with your lives."

Tom stood silent.

"I'm not going away. You won't go to sleep and find me gone in the morning. That money cost me a lot. So we can do this civilized, or I can show up again when you don't expect it. But if I do . . . well, I won't stop with your hand. Or hers."

Tom's fingers throbbed, hot against the tight tape.

"Which'll it be? Gonna bring me my money?"

"Yes," Tom said.

205

"Good boy. You know where Century Mall is?"

"Clark and Diversey."

"Be there tomorrow morning. Ten o'clock. Okay?"

"Okay."

"And, Tom?" Jack's voice hardened. "Don't fuck around. I'm smarter than you, I'm meaner than you, and this is what I do. You get me?"

"Yeah," Tom said. "I do."

THE STEAKHOUSE WAS HUMID, packed with men who wore cuff links and spoke in acronyms. Halden ordered a Bud, thought better of it, asked for a shot of Beam as well.

"Long day, hon?" The bartendress wore a shirt designed to push her breasts up and out in a pale spill.

"Long enough." After meeting Tom Reed at the coffee shop, Halden had hustled back to the station, feeling that tingle of excitement. If the drug dealer was everything Reed said, he could be the key to the whole case. He'd gone straight to the lieutenant's office, found Johnson with his feet on the desk, paging through a file folder. "Boss."

The guy raised one finger, but didn't look up from his pages. Just kept reading, his lips moving. Finally he closed the file. "Chris."

They'd made detective the same year, but Johnson cared more about politics than policing, and had put his effort into sucking up to the Irish Mafia, the system of favoritism that ran from Mayor Daley on down. He'd even learned to play the bagpipes so he could join the honor guard. It had worked, obviously, but it always made

Halden a little sick, the thought that if it would earn him rank, Johnson would probably put on a kilt and Riverdance.

Before Halden could get a word out, the man said, "We've got a body in a Dumpster at Sheridan and Buena. I need you to go out there."

"I can't. I'm on something else."

"What?"

"Will Tuttle."

"I thought he was an overdose."

"Yeah, triggered a heart condition. But there's more. His landlord, guy named Tom Reed—"

"You still calling it accidental death?"

"Yeah."

"Then that's all I need to know. Don't be digging in closed cases. Grab your gear and head for Sheridan. Victor's primary, you back him up." Johnson turned back to the folder in dismissal.

Frustration made Halden speak without thinking. "It's about the Shooting Star."

Johnson's eyes snapped back up. He straightened, then leaned forward. "What? Have you got something?"

And in that instant, the whole scenario played out in Halden's mind. A chance to close the Shooting Star? Forget it. The brass would get involved. The politicos would start angling for their close-up. They'd cut him out of it with a handshake and a pat on the head. He'd be a line item in the report. Meanwhile Johnson, or someone like him, would climb the ranks.

The same shit that had happened his whole career. Without letting himself think too hard about what he was doing, he said, "No. No, nothing like that."

The lieutenant squinted. "You sure?"

"Yeah." Halden coughed. "I just, you know, wanted to check in. See if there'd been any progress. Since I handled Tuttle."

Johnson stared for a moment, then shook his head. "If it comes to anything, I'll let you know." He leaned back. "Head out to Sheridan."

"Sure thing," Halden said. But he hadn't. Hell, he hadn't even called to ask Victor to cover for him. Instead he'd picked up the phone and dialed his old partner, Lawrence Tully, and invited him out for dinner.

The bartendress set up his whiskey and Halden knocked it down, then nodded for another.

Tully was twenty minutes late, but entered big, cracking jokes with the hostess, clapping Halden on the shoulder. Tully was a bear of a man, red-faced and balding; his chins had chins. "Chris Halden, you skinny prick. What does Marie see in you?"

"Jesus, Larry. Running your own company agrees with you, huh?"

"You betcha." The man turned sideways and slapped his belly. "I almost pity you for picking up the check."

The hostess led them to a table, dropped leather-bound menus. A guy in a vest plinked at a piano in the back corner. The air was buttery and dim. Halden ordered another round, Bud and Beam times two, and they each got a steak—Tully's a porterhouse with melted Gorgonzola, for Christ's sake—a baked potato, and a Caesar. Over the meal they caught up, bullshitting about their days riding a beat. It wasn't until Tully took the last bite, set his napkin on his plate, and leaned back with a satisfied sigh that

Halden got down to it, asked what he'd found out about the Reeds.

"They got a rich uncle recently died?"

"What do you mean?"

Tully sipped his beer, said, "You were right, they came into money."

Halden felt his pulse quicken, fought to keep a straight face. "Tell me."

"I called a friend of mine at Citibank. They just paid down a Visa to the tune of something like fifteen grand."

Fifteen grand. He remembered the innocent faces they'd both pulled when he'd come back to their house the second time, how they acted offended at the mere suggestion that they might steal something. People. Shit. "And there's no question about it? I mean, your source is solid?"

"Fuck you, Chris."

"Tully—"

The big man leaned forward. "I'm in the information business. That's what I do. I work for Michigan Avenue law firms. I work for the State's Attorney. Hell, Homeland Security too, not that that makes me unique, money they throw around these days. You call up a favor, now you ask if I know my business?"

Halden put his hands up in surrender. "You're right. I'm sorry. I'm on bended knee, okay?"

"All right." He leaned back, still sounding miffed. "You want the paperwork?"

"Anything you got."

The big man reached into his bag, took out a manila folder,

passed it across. "Not much else to see. They've got a mortgage runs a little higher than it should, some debt. A couple of parking tickets. They both work downtown." He shrugged. "Pretty normal, other than the Visa."

Halden thanked his old partner and made nice by ordering dessert and a round of single malt. But the whole time, his mind was racing and his fingers were tingling. When a theory came together, look out, man. Best feeling in the world.

I've got you, he thought. *I've got you now.*

Sure, he'd lied to the lieutenant. He'd need to get around that. Need to explain why he had worked alone, why he'd kept everything to himself. It wouldn't make him friends. But then, who gave a damn? Results spoke for themselves. Hell, once the papers started treating him as a hero, there wouldn't be much the department could do but follow suit.

He could see himself sitting on the porch of that cabin west of Minocqua, a cup of coffee in one hand, a dog beside him, Marie humming as she made breakfast. And all he had to do to get there was bring in a drug dealer from the Shooting Star, four hundred grand in stolen cash, and two civilians dumb enough to try to keep it.

It was almost too easy.

Anna watched Tom close the phone and set it on the lip of the window. He faced away from her, staring out at the city night. She put a hand on his shoulder, and he reached up to cover her fingers with his own.

"What did he say?"

"He wants his money. He says that if we give it to him, he'll leave us alone."

"He'll kill us anyway."

"Once he has the money, there's not much reason to."

"Yeah, but . . ." She paused, searching for words to capture the feeling she'd had as Jack fled their kitchen. The squirming certainty that he had planned to shoot them, maybe even wanted to. "I think this is personal for him. Like it would be revenge or something. Maybe revenge on Will." A thought struck her. "You know what else? He's probably expecting the whole thing. All the money."

"Shit. He talked about four hundred grand, before you came in." He rubbed at his forehead. "This is fucked."

She looked over at the gym bag, the sides sagging from the weight. She had an urge to upend it over the bed, let the money rain out. Stack and stacks of bundled bills. "Zucchini."

He raised an eyebrow.

"Remember that? When a party got boring, or one of us was trapped in conversation, we'd say 'zucchini,' figure out a way to work it in, and the other would know to rescue them. To find a way to get them out of there." She smiled at the memory. "You were always good at that."

He looked at his glass, at his taped hand. "I think we're a little past zucchini."

There was something in his voice so close to defeat that it broke her heart. "We're smart people," she said. "We can figure this out."

"You think?" He said it like he was trying for a joke, but it didn't play funny.

She started pacing. Short, tight little laps, the edge of the bed to the door, pivot, back again. "Okay. So what are our options? We can meet Jack tomorrow and give him the money, hope that he's okay with it being short."

"And that he's telling the truth about not killing us."

"Right. If he doesn't kill us, we're clear. We don't have to deal with cops and lawyers and all of that. And we're out of debt."

"Not my big concern right now."

"It's not greed, baby. I'm not picturing a mink coat. I just want—"

"I know," he said, sounding tired. "I know."

"We could go to the cops." She stopped, cocked her head. "What if we went to them right now? They could stake out the mall and arrest him there."

Tom shook his head. "We don't know for sure he'll be there personally. He's not alone. Someone sent him a text warning him you were coming into the apartment. Besides, even if he is there, he could probably spot cops."

"So what? Even if they don't catch him, if he sees the cops, he'll know that we don't have the money anymore."

"Yeah. Except that he just told me that if we give it to the police, he'll kill us."

She blew a breath, closed her eyes. Paced some more.

After a long moment, Tom said, "Still, I suppose that's the right thing to do. Go to the police, tell them everything. Stop pretending to be criminals, and just take our medicine."

The way he said it, it sounded like it was a matter of dinging someone's car in a parking lot. But it couldn't be that simple, could it? "The right thing to do is the one that leaves us safe."

"The cops would protect us."

"What if they don't catch Jack? What if he lays low for a year or two? Not like we'll be in Witness Protection."

He moved to the chair and sat, his legs crossed at the knee. "We're screwed if we go to the cops, and screwed if we don't. So what if we blow out of here? Go to Detroit, like you said?"

"What about the house? Your job?"

"I'll find a new one. We can sell long-distance. We could rent instead of buy, use fake names—"

"How do we get a fake ID? How do we get jobs or open a bank account without a social security number? I don't know how to do those things. Plus"—she shrugged—"this is our home. Sara lives here. Our friends."

He sighed. Nodded.

"There has to be a way," she said. "This is our life. This can't be the way it goes. It's not right."

"Not right?" He snorted. "Let's agree on one thing, okay? Let's stop playing the fucking victims. We took the money. That changed everything."

"Still. There has to be a way."

"I don't see it," he said. "And even if we get through this, we're not in the clear. We still have to deal with—" He went ramrod, eyes widening.

"What?" She looked at him, then over her shoulder, just to make sure someone hadn't come in. "What is it?"

Tom stared straight ahead for a long moment, eyes squinting the way they did when he was working something out. When he finally spoke, his voice was quiet, brooding.

He said, "I've got an idea."

16

WHAT CAME FIRST WAS EXHILARATION, a rush of energy. Like solving a brainteaser, that moment when something clicks, and you realize that the way two brothers could be identical and yet not be twins was if they were triplets. A new way of looking at a familiar problem.

He tested it, probed with his mind, thinking *What if* this and *What about* that. It seemed solid. Not bulletproof, but solid. Certainly a safer plan than anything they had on the table already.

Anna said, "What is it? Tell me."

He did. Speaking the words made it more real, not entirely a comfortable feeling. He watched Anna, saw her eyes narrow, the tiny crow's-feet appearing. When he was done, she said, "I think that would work."

"I don't know. Like Jack said, this isn't our world. Maybe we should just go to the police." Tom closed his eyes, pinched the bridge of his nose between thumb and forefinger. The darkness felt safe, like huddling under blankets on a snowy night. He made himself open his eyes. "Thing is, if we do this. I mean . . . What are we if we do this?"

"Alive." Anna spoke quietly. "Free." She cocked her head. "Rich."

"Oh, *forget* the money."

"Really, Tom? Forget the money?" An edge sliced her former softness to ribbons. "You don't care if we have to declare bankruptcy? Lose our house? If we can't have a child, a family? Have to hire a lawyer, go to court, see our pictures in the paper? If we have to spend the next ten *years* digging ourselves out? I'm getting a little tired of you making it sound like this was my idea. We decided together. Nobody talked you into it." She shook her head, blew a breath. When she spoke again, her voice was calmer. "If I knew then what I know now, I wouldn't take it either. I hate this situation. I'd give up the money in a second to get our old life back. *But that is not an option.* It's just not. So either we can be strong and come through this to a better place, or we can panic and lose everything."

"If we do this, a man is going to get killed."

"A bad man."

"How can you be so okay with it?"

She shrugged. "I'm just trying to be realistic. Jack isn't a nice guy. You tried to stab him this afternoon, and nobody would tell you that was wrong."

"I know. And believe me, I wouldn't shed tears if he died. It's just that planning it out ahead of time seems . . . evil."

She was silent for a long time. Finally she said, "We're not evil people, baby. We're just in over our head."

He could hear the buzz of traffic, faint through the double-paned glass. Cars heading north, cars heading south. Thousands of lives being lived, choices being made. No way to know which ones would end up meaning everything.

Tom said, "Pass me the phone."

He'd given the business card to the detective, but he remembered the number. Some things made an impression. One of them was having your life threatened by a drug dealer. He dialed, pressed Send. A bass voice rumbled through the phone, not the guy in the suit. "Yeah?"

"I need to talk to . . ." He hesitated, realizing he didn't even know the name. "This is Tom Reed. He—"

"Hold on."

There was the muffled sound of conversation blocked by someone's hand. Then a familiar voice came on the line. "Mr. Reed. Do you have what I asked for?"

"I tore my house apart. Top to bottom. What you're looking for isn't there. I'm sorry."

"That's disappointing."

"I know. But I have the answer to the question you asked," Tom said. "Yours. I'm on your side. And I can prove it."

"How?"

"By telling you where to find Jack Witkowski."

There was a long pause, and then the voice said, "Smart man."

ANNA SAT ON THE EDGE of the bed and watched her husband negotiate murder.

Tom's eyes were rimmed in black, but his voice was steady and his words carefully chosen. Despite everything, he was still strong. She felt a flush of love, and something else. Pride? Maybe it was wrong to feel pride in her husband's ability to hold his own against criminals. If so, she didn't care. It was the two of them against the world. Popcorn morality could wait. Perhaps one day she would agonize over what they were doing to Jack Witkowski. Perhaps it would haunt them both. But she doubted it.

Tom said, "I'm not going to tell you that."

He said, "I'm on your side, but I'm not an idiot."

Then, "That will work."

Finally, "Tomorrow morning."

He closed the phone, then opened it again long enough to stab the power. When it beeped off, he set it on the windowsill, then leaned back into the chair, a mod blue thing, boxy and too large. He put his arms on the armrests, then closed his eyes and rolled his head back. "He wants to meet for breakfast."

"He'll do it?"

"He was excited. I think he'd rather this than get his dope back."

"And you think he'll leave us alone afterwards?"

"I think so. He seems . . . professional. I'm sure he believes we don't have the drugs—I mean, why would we lie about that? Not like we can sell them on the street corner. Plus, we're white, educated, employed taxpayers. He kills us, it's going to be investigated. Can't see why he'd want that. Besides, after we help him . . ." He ran a tongue across his lips.

She finished his sentence in her head. Just to see. There was a twinge, definitely. A momentary regret. But most of the emotional turmoil she was swimming through had more to do with fear. Fear that it wouldn't work, that something would go wrong, that Tom would end up hurt. Measured against that, the twinge of morality was a trickle against a tidal wave. Who wouldn't put their loved ones ahead of everything else? "So what now?"

He rubbed at his forehead with his good hand. Shrugged. Said, "Want to see if there's anything good on TV?"

THEY'D LEFT THE CURTAINS OPEN, and the faint reflection of city lights swam on the darkened ceiling. Tom had looked at the clock two minutes ago, knew that it was just after three, but felt a powerful urge to look again. Didn't.

The pain in his hand synced to his heart, his fingers swelling and shrinking with every beat. He remembered one time talking to a doctor about stomach problems, the doc asking him to rate the pain on a scale of one to ten, which he'd found strange. How would you know what pain really was? Couldn't it always get worse? That was the way of life. You thought you understood things, had a grip on what was good and what was bad, and then wham, something came along that redefined your spectrum.

"Are we greedy?" He spoke to the darkness.

After a moment, she said, "For taking the money?"

"No. Yes." He stared upward. "Not just that. Are we greedy people?" A car horn sounded outside, muted by the glass into a faint and ghostly wail.

"I don't think so," she said. "Not more than anybody else."

"Six on a scale of ten."

"What?"

He shook his head. Said nothing. They lay on the bed, the comforter piled at their feet, only the sheet stretched over them. From the angle, he couldn't see the city outside the window, just an indigo glow creeping to midnight blue. Beneath that never-dark sky lay the depths of Lake Michigan, black ripples frosted white. He didn't know how to sail, but had always wanted a sailboat. He imagined being on one now, skimming over inky currents like the edge of a dream, just him and Anna and a cold wind and the hollow lap of water and the city's fevered light dwindling behind. Head east, sail all night, into a sunrise scrubbed clean by solitude.

"What are you thinking, baby?"

"Something Jack said." He flashed back to the moment, the twitch of adrenaline, the pressure of the knife in his pocket. The way Jack had gestured with one hand to encompass their living room, their marriage, their life. "He asked why we took the money. What we wanted that we didn't already have."

"Yeah?"

"I didn't know what to say. I mean, we aren't as well off as it must have looked to him. He didn't know about mortgage payments and fertility treatments and how badly we wanted a baby and how you hated your job. But . . ." He held his hands in the air, then folded them behind his head. "I don't know. Even with those things. He had a point."

In the quiet of the room, he could hear her breathing. "You know what I think? Everything finds a balance. An equilibrium." Her voice low. "I think rich people are fundamentally about as happy as poor people. It's the way we're wired. When things are good for any length of time, we take them for granted. When they're bad, we get used to them. Our heads level everything out."

"That's kind of convenient."

"What do you mean?"

"As an argument. It makes it easy not to worry about things or try to change them. It excuses us from concern."

"That doesn't mean it's not true. Give somebody a million dollars, they're going to live it up for a while. But eventually, the lifestyle will become normal. It won't thrill. They'll end up feeling more or less the same way they always did."

"So what's the point?"

"I don't know. Live a good life. Be nice to people. Have a family, and love them well."

He thought about it, staring at the liquid stir of light on the ceiling. "Maybe you're right. I look back at the problems we used to have, and I wonder what the hell was wrong with us. I mean, were we really sweating all that nonsense? Everything that mattered at the time, now it seems . . ." He pursed his lips and blew air like he was scattering the pods off a dandelion.

"I know," she said. "Worrying about advertising. House payments. Jesus. Even the baby thing."

They fell silent for a long spell, time marked in steady intervals by the slow throb of his hand. Finally he said, "We were greedy."

"Yeah," she said. "I guess we were."

AROUND SIX IN THE MORNING, he gave it up. His fingers ached, his head pounded, and it felt like someone had grabbed hold of his kidney and twisted. Tom rolled out of bed and tiptoed to the bathroom. He closed the door and started the shower, put one of the disposable packs in the coffeemaker. Thought better of it, and stuffed the second pack in as well.

In the shower he stood and let the water drench him, pounding off the top of his head in a soaking spray that hid the world and soothed some of the pain. It felt lovely, a quiet moment lost behind a curtain of water. The only thing that ruined it was having to hold his bandaged left hand up and away.

He reluctantly got out of the shower and awkwardly toweled off. At least there was a plan. He felt better for that. Maybe they had been greedy. Maybe they were in over their heads. But they were working together, sharing their strength, and they had a plan. It was something. He poured the coffee into two mugs and stepped into the room.

Anna lay nude atop sheets twisted like whipped egg whites. She smiled when he set a mug on the table. Tom picked up his cell phone and turned it on. The message indicator blinked, and he dialed his voice mail. A computerized voice told him he had four messages.

"This is Detective Halden. Give me a call back as soon as you can. We're ready to go ahead with setting up this man who threatened you." The cop rattled off his phone numbers. Tom sipped the coffee. Strong but lousy, which he supposed was better than weak but lousy. He punched a button to save the message and hear the next.

"Mr. Reed, Detective Halden. Please call me—we need to move."

The next. "This is Christopher Halden again. I need you to call me back ASAP. Day or night. I mean it, Tom—as soon as possible. I'll try your home line as well."

The next, from this morning. A hang-up.

Shit. Tom closed the phone, rubbed his jaw. They'd gotten so caught up in their plans last night he'd forgotten all about the cop. "I've got a couple of messages from Halden."

"Don't call him." Anna wriggled to a sitting position, stuffed a pillow behind her back. "We can't talk to him now. If you accidentally say something that tips him off about Jack or the mall . . ."

"I have to call him eventually."

"Once this is over. You can just tell him you changed your mind. That we talked it over, and you don't want to act as bait. He'll believe that. It must happen all the time, people backing out on identifying criminals."

He thought about it, nodded. Pulled his pants from the edge of the chair and stepped into them, then stretched with his arms above his head, first one side, then the other, wincing at the pain in his kidneys. "You have your cell phone?"

"Yes."

"Okay. I'll call you as soon as I'm done."

"Done?"

"Meeting the drug dealer." Tom buckled his belt. "He wants to talk first."

"I'm going with you."

"Like hell you are." He turned, stared at her. "You think I'm taking you into a meeting with a—"

"Jesus *Christ*." She sat up, grabbed a pillow, and whipped it at him.

Tom ducked sideways, surprised. "What?"

"There you go again. Trying to protect me."

"This isn't me being a hero. I just don't see any point in you being in this too."

"I'm already in it, you arrogant shit. You think Jack or your drug dealer friend are going to cut me slack because I have breasts?" She shook her head. "The only one doing that is you."

He opened his mouth, closed it. Stood with his hands spread. Finally he said, "I don't want you to get hurt."

"I don't want either of us hurt. And we went through this already. Last night."

Tom turned, stared. The horizon was draped in gray, fat-bellied clouds hanging low. The skyline was bleak and faded, the top third of the Aon Center lost in mist. The commuter rush wouldn't start in earnest for another hour, but the streets were already thick with taxis, the sidewalks dotted with tiny figures in skirts and suits. A spring morning like any other. Her voice came soft and low from behind. "Partners in crime. All or nothing."

"Better get dressed," he said. "We've got a long morning."

17

THEIR FIRST YEAR IN CHICAGO they'd rented a cookie-cutter apartment in a high-rise on Clark a couple of blocks south of Diversey. It had primer-white walls and carpet that smelled of cigarettes. The view was of the building opposite or, if they stood on the back of the couch and leaned all the way against the window, an inch-wide sliver of lake. But the neighborhood was great, full of bars and noodle shops and bookstores. There was a hot dog place across the street called the Weiner Circle, where the women behind the counter cursed at you. When he remembered that year, Tom usually found himself smiling.

Which made it all the stranger to be back in the neighborhood. He glanced in his rearview for the hundredth time. There was no sign of Jack, no car matching his turns, speeding to keep pace when he ran yellow lights. Best he could tell, they weren't being followed.

They followed Clark north another half mile, then he swung down a residential block and got lucky with a parking place. The morning was cool and alive with the promise of rain, not a pounding storm, but a steady drencher. He put his arm around Anna's back as they stepped onto the sidewalk, and she moved a half step closer, her shoulder nestling into the crook of his arm.

The restaurant wasn't what he'd expected. He'd anticipated a diner, faux wood and the smell of bacon grease. But the space was airy and bright, with colorful canvases over exposed brick. The water glasses had a slice of cucumber in them. As they'd discussed on the phone, Tom requested a four-top in the front, by the windows. A perky waitress passed them menus, set down a carafe of coffee, and asked if they wanted fresh-squeezed juice. Tom shook his head, his eyes on the other diners. At a table by the back wall, Andre sat with his hands on either side of an untouched plate of eggs. He smiled, predatory, wet lips parting to white teeth.

"That guy in the back. That's the bodyguard. The one with the gun." Tom kept his gaze on the man, saw no point in pretending. "I don't know where the dealer is."

As if in answer to his question, the front door opened in a jingle of bells. The man looked smaller than Tom remembered, slighter. A trim guy wearing an air of authority and a good suit. "Mr. and Mrs. Reed." He sat opposite them, crossed his legs and smoothed the crease of his pant leg. "Good of you to come."

Tom nodded.

"So. The situation. What time are you meeting him?"

"Ten."

"Where?"

"Century Mall."

The man tapped at his chin with one finger. His eyes were locked on Tom's, seemed like they'd hardly blinked. "Why?"

"Because the mall is public. He said that way—"

"No, Mr. Reed." The man leaned forward, spoke the syllable with great clarity and emphasis. "Why?"

"I don't understand. Why what?"

"Why does Jack Witkowski want to meet? Day before last, you said you'd never heard of him. Fact, as I recall, you *swore* it." A tiny tightening of the muscles around his eyes. "Were you lying to me, Mr. Reed?"

Tom felt a shiver of panic, but tried not to show it. "You know what? All this 'Mr. Reed' stuff is getting on my nerves. I feel like I'm in a Bond film. My name is Tom. This is Anna. What do we call you?"

The man cocked his head. Stared at Tom for a long moment. Then shrugged. "Don't suppose it makes much difference. Malachi. Ain't a name going to be of any use."

"I'm just tired of thinking of you as 'the man in the suit.' " Tom shook his head. "And no, I wasn't lying to you." He lifted his left hand from his lap, set it on the table. The exposed flesh was purple and hot. "Jack came to our house yesterday. He was looking for something, kept asking where *it* was, where had we put *it*. When I couldn't answer . . ."

"What was he looking for?" Malachi asked it like it was a casual thing, like he couldn't really care less.

"He never said. He just kept asking where 'it' was."

The perky waitress came back. "You folks ready to order?"

The drug dealer spoke without looking. "You know, honey, I think we'll just stick with the coffee. My friends here are a little off their stomach."

A lot of her perkiness vanished, but she nodded, walked away. Malachi said, "How'd you get away? I don't imagine Jack just let you be."

"No." Tom nodded sideways. "Anna set off our burglar alarm. After he ran, we left. Slept in a hotel."

"I see. So y'all are afraid he's coming back."

"Sure." Tom pushed his silverware around.

"Which does make me wonder." Malachi glanced over his shoulder at Andre, who'd been staring the whole time like a pit bull straining the end of his chain. "If Jack hadn't come at you, if y'all didn't need my help, would you still be saying you're on my side? Would we still be having this conversation?"

Anna said, "That would have been up to you."

He turned. "How's that?"

"If Jack hadn't come after us, we wouldn't have anything to offer." She shrugged. "You told Tom you'd be willing to kill us just for having a tenant. So whether we'd be having this conversation would depend on whether or not you were serious."

Malachi nodded slowly. "Fair answer. For the record, best you never doubt that. You hadn't come through . . ." He glanced over his shoulder again, then raised an eyebrow.

Tom fought to keep from clenching his right hand into a fist.

"So." Malachi turned back. "Jack wants something from you. Something he thinks you have."

"Yes."

"But you don't have it."

"Don't even know what it is."

"So then, if he was looking for something, and you don't have it"—the man spoke slowly—"why is he meeting you at ten o'clock?"

Tom fought to keep cool, forced a smile. "Well, I'll tell you the truth." He took a sip of coffee, set it down, moved his hand back to his lap, hoping the man hadn't caught the shake in his fingers. "I figured the only way was to get him somewhere I could tell you about. So . . ." He paused, shrugged. "I lied to him."

The man in the suit stared, eyes locked. The moment stretched thin and tense. Tom kept his gaze forward, a shit-eating grin on his lips. Thinking that this was it. Wondering if the guy would try anything here, whether he and Anna were about to get blasted right out of the breakfast nook.

Then Malachi slapped the table, threw back his head, and barked a laugh. Tom let himself breathe again. He felt Anna's fingers slide into his under the table. He laughed too.

"You lied to him." Malachi smiled, wiped at his mouth with one hand. "Well, good for you, Tom. You're turning into a regular gangster." He turned and inclined his head at Andre, who rose and walked over. For a moment Tom had a flash of panic, but the bodyguard only pulled out the fourth chair and sat down. "Now," Malachi said, "let's talk this thing out. He say where he wanted to meet specifically?"

"Just the mall."

"You got a cell phone?"

"Yes."

"Jack know the number?"

"Yes."

"Okay. Wherever you are, he's going to want you to go somewhere else."

"No way. We're doing this in the mall because it's public. We're not going to agree to—"

"Cool out. You don't have to leave the mall. Fact, he knows you won't. He'll just move you around some. You standing by one store, he's going to call, tell you to go to another. Simple good sense. What that means, though, I can't have my people just waiting around the corner. So you gonna have to stall."

Tom felt a faint sickness. Anna said, "How long?"

Malachi looked at Andre. The big man shrugged, said, "Minute or two."

"Wait. You want us to stall him for a couple of minutes while 'your people' sneak up on him?" Tom snorted. "No offense, but Century Mall is in the heart of Lincoln Park. A bunch of gangsters are going to stand out."

"You mean a bunch of niggers are going to stand out." Malachi smiled.

Tom felt his face go hot. "No, I—"

"I got a couple of white boys I use for situations like these. And I think even Lincoln Park can handle one black man wandering free," he said, inclining his head toward Andre. "Now, like I said, my people will be there. But Jack's got some savvy on him. So they going to have to be laying low. They won't come out till you give the signal."

"What's that?"

Andre rattled off a string of digits. Tom stared at him blankly.

"Program that shit into your phone," Andre said. "Once you got the dude distracted, you press Send."

"What if he sees me do it?"

"Make sure he don't."

"Also," Malachi said, "you need a bag."

"A bag? What for?" Anna's look of confusion was so perfect Tom fought an urge to kiss her right there. She hadn't given even a hint that she knew exactly why they'd need a bag.

"I have an idea what Jack is after," Malachi said. "You get yourself a decent size bag. Carry it like it's heavy."

"What if Jack wants to look inside?"

Malachi shrugged. Tom's stomachache grew worse.

"How are you going to grab him in the middle of a mall?" Anna asked.

"Now, that's a fine question. But I don't see you needing the answer."

"Here's one we do need the answer to." Tom looked the man in the eye. "After we do this, we're square, right? We're done with you?"

"You do this," the man said, "you prove what I need proved." He leaned back in his chair, shot his cuffs. "Long as everything goes the way you say, yeah, we square."

"And what about Jack? What are you going to do to him?"

Malachi shook his wrist to straighten the loose Rolex, then glanced at it. "I'm going to give him a history lesson. Genghis Khan style." He stood. "Now. You two best be on your way. You got a few details to attend before ten."

"Wait a second," Tom said. "Where are you going?"

The drug dealer laughed. "Son, I won't be inside five miles of that mall. And I'll have witnesses to back me. This thing, it's on you two. It goes wrong, you screwed it up." He raised his eyebrows. "We clear?"

"Clear that you're leaving us dangling." Tom was unable to stop himself from glaring, to keep the tone out of his voice.

Malachi just smiled again. "Pay to play, gangster. You got to pay to play."

*   *   *

"Well, that went great." Anna leaned back in the passenger seat, balanced the arch of her feet against the glove box. She had the window cracked to let cool spring air in. "Just great."

Tom shook his head. Pressed his lips together hard.

"What if Jack wants to look in the bag first thing? Not like there's a reason for us to chat. All he wants is the money. He's probably planning to just walk up, look in the bag, say something threatening, and then walk off."

"Assuming he doesn't plan to kill us anyway."

"Assuming that."

Tom sighed. "I don't know. We can stall him, I think. He'll feel safe. What scares me is that at the same time, we have to signal Andre. One thing we know about Jack, he's smart. He'll be watching for any sign something is wrong."

"He doesn't know about Malachi, does he?"

"No. He won't be expecting this. If he's expecting anything, it will probably be police. He'll have his eyes tuned for cops."

"That will work for us," she said. "He won't be looking for gangsters."

"Gangsters. Jesus." Tom shook his head. "What the hell are we doing?"

She looked over at him. His knuckles were white on the steering wheel, and his posture rigid. She could almost hear the whir and clank of his thoughts colliding. "Can I ask you something?"

"What?"

"Why did you ask what they were going to do to Jack?"

He was silent for a moment. "I don't know. I guess just to make it real."

"Is it going to bother you?"

He shook his head. "I wanted to see if it would. Whether planning something like this was going too far. But when Malachi said what he said, I didn't feel a thing. The truth is, I don't give a rat's ass what happens to Jack. After what he's done . . ." He shrugged. "Fuck him."

"So we're going ahead."

"I don't see any choice. You?"

She shook her head. They rode in silence, Anna looking at a familiar world gone strange. A guy on a bike, a woman walking a couple of dogs, a kid at the bus stop wearing a T-shirt that read "You looked better on MySpace." It felt like one of those ant farms, a pane of glass that let you stare into something that was supposed to be hidden. Only, the world was normal, and it was her eyes that had changed. "You sure about stowing the money?"

"Yes." His voice was firm. "We've been careless. What if the car got stolen or towed? What if Jack happened on it? What we're about to walk into, as exposed as we're going to be, that money may be our lifeline. We need to protect it."

"Things could go right too, you know." She turned to look at him. "Don't forget that. If we pull this off, it's all over. Malachi will be done with us, and Jack will be gone. No one will know we have the money. We'll be able to go back to our life. Only better."

He nodded, but didn't say anything.

They'd rented a space at the storage facility off Belmont years ago. In D.C. they'd kept separate apartments, so when they moved in together, they'd had twice as much furniture as space. Tom's had been garage-sale crap, but he'd been sentimental about it—or hedging his bets, something Anna had wondered at the time—and so they'd rented a ten-by-ten and piled stuff to the ceiling. Eventually they'd hauled most of it to the garbage and surrendered the lease, but when, leaving the restaurant, Tom had suggested that they needed to move the money, the place had jumped to Anna's mind.

He went inside to rent a unit while she walked to a *Sun-Times* machine. Dropped coins into the slot, then opened the front and pulled out the whole stack of papers, including the one in the display. By the time she'd returned to the car, he was waiting, the duffel bag in one hand, cell phone in the other. He shook his head, closed it. "Detective Halden again."

"You check the message?"

"No. I'm nervous enough. Let's get on with it."

He'd gotten the smallest available unit, a five-foot cube on the third floor. The hallway was fluorescent and concrete, marked by roll doors. Their footsteps echoed. Tom bent to fit the key into the lock and haul the door clattering upward.

The space was clean and blank. The two of them stepped inside, then dragged the door closed behind. Tom unzipped the bag and upended it. Bundles of ragged hundreds tumbled out, and Anna had the same surreal feeling as when they first found the money, that same breathless skipped heartbeat. All that freedom piled up on a concrete floor. In the confined space, she could smell it, a dank, unpleasant odor of humanity.

Tom shook the last straggling bundles from the bag, then set it on the floor and held it open. Anna piled the stack of newspapers inside. They bulged against the side much like the money had. Tom hefted it, testing the weight. "It's close enough."

Anna tore the band off one bundle, then dumped the money on top of the newspaper and smeared it around. At a glance—a quick glance—it might look like they had undone all the money and were carrying it loose. Thin, but better than nothing.

She looked up to find Tom staring at her, one side of his lips curled up in a smile. She could see a bead of sweat on his upper lip, and the weathered lines beginning to form around his eyes, and then he leaned in and kissed her, one hand going behind her head, and she went with it, her tongue sliding into his mouth, his beard stubble rough against her lips, the two of them bending across a pile of money to breathlessly neck like high school kids. When they finally parted, she put a hand against his cheek. "What was that for?"

"Luck," he said. "And gratitude."

"Gratitude?"

"Not everybody has a partner in crime like you."

"We're doing okay, aren't we? For a couple of regular people, I mean?" She could feel the pounding of her pulse. For just a second, she had a flash of what they were up to, how crazy it was, like the moment on a roller coaster just before the plummet when it was way too late to get off.

"We're going to be okay," he said. "I promise."

She forced a smile. "Cross your heart?"

THE CAB REEKED OF APPLE from the air freshener hanging over the mirror. Tom wrinkled his nose, watched the blocks crawl. Anna had suggested parking the Pontiac away from the mall and taking a cab, a good idea.

He remembered that kiss, in the cramped unit, his knees propped on three hundred thousand dollars as he tasted her. The whiff of desperation they'd both tried not to acknowledge. He looked over, squeezed her hand, got a thin-lipped smile in return.

The rain had started, fat gentle drops that stole color, reducing the streets to a tapestry of grays. People crab-walked under umbrellas, and shopkeepers sniffed the air from the safety of their awnings. The cab passed a discount electronics store, a rug mart, a couple of artsy boutiques, a falafel joint. There was a toxic lightness in his chest. He'd gone skydiving once, back in college, and remembered most the staticky panic as the plane circled upward, the sense that he was moving closer and closer to something irrevocable.

The driver pulled to the side and tapped the meter. Windshield wipers slip-slopped back and forth. Outside was the block-long gray bulk of Century Mall, baroque columns rising above the movie marquee, shimmering display windows and glass doors below. Tom passed the driver a twenty, waved off the change. They needed all the good karma they could get right now.

"I know what you're going to say, but please, would you consider letting me do this—"

"We're in it together." Her face shone pale, but her shoulders were set. "Let's just get through it."

He nodded, blew a breath, and they walked to the entrance, Anna stepping ahead of him to open the door. The duffel was unwieldy, kept banging against his knee, but he found himself grateful to have something to hang on to. Inside, the hum of the rain and the whir of tires was replaced by pop music and a jumble of chemical smells from the bath shop. The woman behind the information desk didn't look up from her novel as they passed.

Century Mall was a squared spiral rising four stories around a center courtyard. It had always reminded Tom of the Guggenheim, only instead of paintings, the walls gave way to two dozen shops: clothing and laser hair removal and lingerie and a tanning place. A ramped walkway ran all the way around, and from where he stood, he could look up at a cross section of commercialism rising to a broad glass ceiling spotted with rain. In the middle and down a level was a gourmet grocery store, one of those places that sold prepackaged sushi and elaborate salads. "Where do you think is best?"

"We'll want to end up around the second floor, so no matter where they are, Malachi's people aren't too far away."

"So we can't start there. Up top, then?"

They waited at the glass elevator. Tom rocked on his toes, looking around, trying not to seem nervous. Anna stiffened. She turned to face him, then whispered, "There's a cop here."

He glanced as nonchalantly as he could. The policeman leaned against the railing above the grocery, looking down at display cases of imported meats and upscale potato salad. He seemed calm, casual, two-finger-spinning an unlit cigarette.

"Shit," Tom said. "I figured on a security guard, not a cop. Jack sees him, that could screw everything." He pressed his lips tight. "Nothing we can do."

The elevator dinged open, and they stepped on. He thumbed the button for four, turned to look out the glass rear. It was early yet, and he wondered who all these people wandering around the mall were. Didn't they have jobs? Brass doors slid closed, and the elevator rose slowly. He kept his eye on the cop. The motion of the elevator had apparently caught his attention, and for a moment they locked eyes. Then the officer turned away and strolled off.

When the doors parted, Tom could smell popcorn. The air-conditioning kept the place icy, but sweat soaked his armpits anyway. They moved to the left, away from the movie theater, to a quiet corner. Anna leaned over the railing, looking in all directions. "I get why he chose this place. You can see everywhere. If we brought the police, he'd probably be able to tell."

"Let's hope Malachi's people are more subtle."

"Only a little." Anna gestured with her head. "Over there, a level down. The luggage store."

He looked where she indicated, saw Andre standing inside, pretending to examine a matched set of suitcases. The man nodded slightly.

"Jesus." Tom's stomach was watery. His head understood all the advantages to meeting in a public place, that these people around him should keep them safe, but he felt exposed, open air and shops on all sides. What were they doing? Selling out a killer to a group of drug dealers, bluffing that a bag of newspapers could pass as a fortune, a cop wandering below and Jack coming from who knew where?

Easy. Take it easy. Just get through this. Get through this, and get her through this.

His watch read five till ten. In fifteen minutes, they'd either be clear or dead. Tom took a deep breath and squared his shoulders.

FIVE TILL TEN. Jack laced his fingers and stretched his arms up to crack the knuckles over his head. The movement pulled at the gash on his forearm, and he winced. He'd cleaned and bandaged it, knew it wasn't deep enough to do much more than leave a nasty scar, but still, the thing stung like a motherfucker.

He adjusted the bandage gingerly and leaned back against the concrete of the parking deck. They'd spent three hours last night walking every inch of the mall and its surroundings. It was a good spot, plenty of escape routes, stairwells on three corners with connections to the parking deck, the grocery in the bottom, even the loading docks out back. Plus, security was a joke. Jack unzipped the navy jumpsuit, fingered the pistol slung against his T-shirt. The rain smelled good, even layered over the exhaust and oil smell of cars.

On his belt, the cell phone vibrated once. He opened it, saw the text message from Marshall:

theyre here

Jack took a deep breath, then slipped through the break in the chain-link fence, rounded the corner, and stepped into the loading dock, a wide concrete bay, dingy and smelling of trash. A guy unloading a panel truck looked over, and Jack tossed a salute. The man nodded and went back to work. As Jack opened the door into the mall, he felt that old tightness in his stomach. It felt like home.

ANNA'S SKIN WAS STRETCHED TOO FAR, like she might split at the seams. All around them, people shopped and ate and chatted as though everything were normal. Two men laughed at a downstairs table. A couple of hairstylists from the salon wandered into Victoria's Secret. They were easy to spot, black clothes and fried bangs. Why did stylists always have the worst hair? A woman pushed a stroller, the boy in it wearing that slightly stupefied expression like the world was a hell of a show.

This had seemed like a good idea last night, clean and easy. Just a thought experiment, a move they were contemplating in a game. But now that she stood here, it wasn't rational thought that filled her. It was dread and nerves and a child's desperate fear of punishment.

A muscular man in a Cubs jersey rounded the corner to their right. He moved swiftly, not running, but with fast, long strides. His eyes were on them.

"Tom." She nudged him. He turned to look, saw where she was staring. His fingers went white on the handle of the bag.

The guy kept moving, staring straight at them. He had short-cropped hair and broad shoulders. She remembered Tom saying yesterday that they didn't know if Jack would come himself. The guy was thirty feet away. Twenty. She heard a woman talking in a singsong voice, saying, "Isn't this fun, baby?" The mother pushing the stroller, coming from the opposite direction. The man in the jersey sped up, one hand moving to his waist.

"Tom." Her voice breaking. He took a half step in front of her.

Fingers lifted the edge of the jersey.

The woman said, "Don't you like shopping with Mommy?"

Ten feet.

Anna wanted to scream, to run, but found herself locked in place. Watching the man pull up his shirt and reach for his waist.

Grabbing at something. Panic pounded in her temples, panic clenched her fingers. Jesus, it was all going wrong, this guy was going to just shoot them, right here, in the middle of the mall, right in front of this mother pushing a child, believing herself safe, borne up by belief in a world that followed immutable rules, the same ones Anna used to believe in.

The hand came out. Clutching a cell phone.

"Nah, nothing. Just shopping," said the guy in the jersey, moving right past them, one hand pushing at the door to the stairwell. "When you want to—" The slamming door cut off the rest of what he had to say.

She didn't realize she'd been holding her breath until she let it out in a long, hard whistle. The world spun, and she put a hand on the railing. Tom slumped too, dropped the bag to the ground, reached up to rub at his forehead. The stroller reached them, one wheel creaking a little. The mother smiled at Anna as she passed. The railing was cool. She put both hands on it. Watched people move. "I can't do this."

Tom turned, touched her upper arm. "We're almost done. Just a few more minutes."

"I can't. I can't. What if someone gets hurt?" She gulped air. "I thought . . . that guy—"

"I know." He spoke soothingly. "We're both jumpy. But it'll be okay. Nothing's going to go wrong."

"Are you *kidding*? Where have you been for the last few days? Let's get *out* of here. Go to the police." She stared over the edge of the railing, to the levels below. "Wait, better. There's a cop here. Let's go get him, tell him—"

"Tell him what?" Tom's voice a slap. "Tell him we set up a thief to get kidnapped and tortured to death by a drug dealer so that we could keep our stolen money? He'd think we were crazy." He shook his head. "Worse, he might believe us." He put his good hand on her shoulder. "If we screw this up, Malachi will kill us. That's if Jack doesn't. We have to get through. Just a few more minutes. Okay?"

She stared at him, at the tension in his jaw, the wide eyes. He was scared too. She could see that. But he was beating it. She straightened. Tried to breathe like yoga class, in through the nose, steady exhale through the mouth, picturing the air filling her with pale blue light. In, hold, out. *I am the center of calm.*

I am pale blue light.

THICK PIPES RAN UP THE CORNER. A sign beside the door marked this as the west stairwell, ground floor. Jack stepped to the door, looked out the window in the center. Beyond he could see the mall, the ramps spiraling upward. A brunette with a shirt that read "Porn Star" strolled past, oblivious to him three feet away. Jack smiled. Put on work clothes, stand in a stairwell, he could have been invisible. He could have been Mexican.

He was reaching for the door when his phone buzzed. "Yeah."

"Hold on." Marshall's voice quiet.

"What's up?"

"I'm not sure. I think something's wrong. I'm going to get closer."

"Where are they?"

"Fourth floor, northwest corner. Near the movie theater. They're carrying a bag," Marshall said. "You want me to just go get—"

"No. Stick to the plan." He hung up, peered out again. *What are you doing, Tom?*

Jack unzipped the jumpsuit halfway, then took his phone from his pocket and dialed.

TOM'S PHONE RANG. He didn't recognize the number. Taking a deep breath, he flipped it open. "Hello."

"Mr. Reed? This is Detective Halden. Where have you been? After our last conversation—"

Shit, shit, shit! "Detective, now isn't a good time."

There was a pause. "Are you in danger? Is the drug dealer there?"

He snuck a glance at his watch. 10:02. "No, no, it's not that. It's just"—he looked around, sure he would see Jack coming toward him at any moment, that big gun in his hand—"I can't talk right now."

"Listen, whatever you're doing, this is more important. That guy, he's going to be looking for you, and you won't see him coming. Just tell me where you are, and I'll be there in ten minutes. I can keep you safe."

Tom hesitated. The window of the luggage store was empty. Where had Andre gone? Everything was happening so fast. He thought of the guy with the jersey, how he'd realized in that moment that they were in way over their heads. Maybe he should tell Halden everything. Get the cops here. The idea was tempting: Give up control, let the professionals handle it.

"Mr. Reed?"

Tom opened his mouth. There was a beep in his ear, and he

pulled the phone away to look at it. Another number he didn't recognize.

"Tom, I know you're scared. Let me help."

His pulse was heavy enough to shake his vision. "I'm sorry. I'll call you back soon. I promise."

"Wait—"

He hung up, clicked to the new call. A familiar voice said, "Who were you talking to, Tom?"

ANNA SAW THE WINCE, saw Tom look around wildly. He mouthed the word *Jack,* then said, "No one." Paused, and said, "It was my mother, all right? I got her off the phone as quick as I could."

Her heart throbbed in her chest, and her fingers tightened on the railing. *I am pale blue light.*

Tom said, "Yeah, well, you don't know my mother."

She looked left, toward the theater. A bored college kid behind the ticket counter, posters for indie films, a bench with an old lady sitting on it. If things started to go bad, they could make for that. Motion caught her eye, a level down, the cop strolling past a display window. There was a stairwell to the right, where the guy in the Cubs jersey had gone.

Tom said, "We're not leaving the mall. No way."

Pop music still played from overhead, inane and insistent, that stupid boy band song that went "Bye-bye, baby, bye-bye." She could smell stale popcorn.

Tom said, "Okay." He hung up. "He wants to meet on the ground floor, in front of the salon. He said to not take the elevator." He glanced over his shoulder, then passed his phone to her. "You'll have to page Andre. I can't and still hold the bag."

"I'll—"

"Jack would never believe I'd have you carry it."

She bit her lip, knew he was right. Slipped the phone into her pocket and her hand in after it, one finger on the Send button. *I am pale blue light.* "We should go."

They started down, Tom slightly ahead. The fourth floor slowly gave way to the third. Her eyes scanned fast, looking for Jack, for Andre, for any of them. Overhead, the boy band's singer said that he didn't want to be a player in a game for two, and Anna wondered what the hell that meant. Three floors to go. There was no sign of Jack, but there were a whole lot of people around: a cluster of teenagers at the elevator, women fingering clothing in the Express, a clerk on break reading a book. Two and a half floors to go. She found herself thinking of that mother with the stroller. Wondering if she knew how lucky she was. Wondering if anyone did, until they didn't. Life could fall apart so fast.

Which was what she was thinking at the exact moment Jack Witkowski stepped out of the stairwell door in front of them.

To Jack, the pair of them looked ragged, stretched thin with panic. Something in Anna seemed particularly off, her hands in her pockets and her eyes wild. Perfect.

He smiled, gestured to the gym bag in Tom's hand. "That for me?"

Tom's eyes darted like a rabbit looking for cover. He took a step back. "I thought you wanted—"

"Never mind what you thought, dipshit," Jack said. "Open the bag."

Tom Reed stood still.

"Tom," Jack said, and unzipped his jumpsuit so that the holster was visible. "Open the bag."

"You're not going to use that. We're in a public place." The guy said it like it was a contract, like a kid on the playground whining about the rules.

Jack laughed. "Are you kidding?" He shook his head. "You've passed a dozen people in the last few minutes. Can you tell me what any of them looked like?" He cocked his head, smiled. "What makes you think any of them saw what *I* look like?"

TOM FELT LIKE his face had grown apart from him, like it was a separate entity. He could feel the blood banging in his forehead, could feel the heat in his cheeks. "We had a deal."

Jack shrugged, the motion rippling the blue jumpsuit and revealing more of the big pistol. "We still do. It starts with you opening that bag and showing me what's mine."

"You just said you were going to kill us." Trying to keep conversation going. Praying that Anna had been able to page Andre.

"Actually, Tom, I said that I *could* kill you." Jack was smug, obviously enjoying himself. "If I do decide to kill you, I probably won't tell you about it in advance. Now open the goddamn bag."

"No," Tom said, as steadily as he could. He had to hold out.

Another few seconds, a minute. His life, their lives, it came down to a minute. Sixty endless seconds. Where the hell was Andre? "Not until you tell me, straight up, that once you have this money you'll leave us alone."

Jack smiled. "My word."

Something went cold inside Tom, and he realized that one way or another, today or tomorrow, Jack meant to kill them. Had simply decided that it would happen.

Then, over Jack's shoulder, he saw someone coming up the escalator that bisected the mall. A bulky guy with a boxer's moves. Wet lips and white teeth. Andre was walking, his jacket open. Anna had done it.

"All right." Tom took a deep breath, trying to draw things out, feeling a rush of adrenaline and a surge of wild hope. He rolled his shoulder and then set the bag on the ground.

Behind Jack, two white guys came around the corner to fall into step with Andre, the three of them moving steady and easy. One wore a maroon tracksuit and a gold ID bracelet. The other had on a broad-cut suit. The one in the suit slid his hand into the pocket and pulled out something plastic. A blue spark arced along it. A stun gun.

Tom squatted beside the bag, put his hand on the zipper. Timing would be everything. He hesitated, said, "Remember, you promised."

Jack's eyes narrowed, and he said, "Quit stalling."

No way around it. If he went any further, he risked Jack looking around, things going south. He had to pray that the money on top would fool Jack, or at least hold his attention long enough for Malachi's people. Twenty feet now.

He drew the zipper down as slowly as he dared, then reached for the sides of the bag, planning to open it just enough to flash Jack. Ten feet.

The cop stepped from a store that sold games and toys, coming out behind Andre and his soldiers. His hand was at his belt, and he was moving fast. Did he know something? Had Halden somehow figured out where they were and called him? As Tom watched, kneeling beside the bag, the cop drew his gun. Jesus. He was going to stop it from happening.

Except the officer didn't say, "Police, freeze!" He didn't say, "Stop or I'll shoot!"

What he said was "Jack, get down."

And then fire blasted from his pistol, and the head of the man holding the stun gun exploded.

WHEN JACK HEARD Marshall's voice telling him to get down, his first urge was to look back. But he'd long ago learned that in the moment, you trusted your partners or things went south, so instead he got the hell to one knee.

Even braced for it, the roar of the first shot hit like a thousand volts, kicking every cell into life, adrenaline pounding fast and hard. People didn't realize how loud the things were, like God clapping his hands. There was a bare half heartbeat of silence, and then more explosions. Jack reached into the jumpsuit and jerked his pistol, thumbing the safety as he crab-spun, his other hand on the floor.

Marshall stood thirty feet back in his fake cop uniform. Between him and Jack, a shuffling horror staggered forward on momentum alone, his head a mass of gore. Beside him, a chubby guy in a tracksuit was fumbling to draw an enormous pistol. A third man, black and built, was charging Marshall, body low and arms pumping.

Jack didn't take time to think. He just raised the Colt, centered it on the back of that hideous tracksuit, lined up the bars, and squeezed the trigger. The .45 kicked in his hand, and he took the time to aim again before firing a second time, the second bullet punching in right next to the first, ninety calibers' worth of violence that blew the man's chest out.

The screaming began. Jack tried to ignore it, to filter out the shrieks and the gunfire and the rain of sparkling glass from the front windows of a store. To find his calm in the center of the hurricane. Everything was messed up again, just like the night they'd taken the cash from the Star. It wasn't the way he liked to work. But just like that night, he had to get control of the situation. The world belonged to people who bent it to their will.

He swept his arm sideways, trying to line up on the black guy. The angle was no good, Marshall just beyond him. Too risky. Marshall was a big boy. Focus on priorities. He turned back.

Tom Reed squatted like he'd been turned to stone. His mouth hung open and one hand was on the zipper of the duffel. The bag was partly open, and inside it, Jack could see faded green piled almost to the top. The money Bobby had died for.

*OhJesusohJesusoh*Jesus.

Anna had two fingers to her mouth and the other hand at her

forehead, where something wet had slapped her, wet and warm like spit, like someone had cleared their throat and hawked up something thick and nasty on her forehead, only it wasn't spit, it was blood from the man the cop had just shot, Jesus, the one the *cop* had just shot, which meant that Jack owned cops, Jesus *Christ,* Jack owned *cops,* and now everything was unraveling, more gunshots, loud, so incredibly loud, her ears humming, and the warmth on her forehead was running into her eyebrows, a stranger's blood was spattered on her forehead and running into her fucking eyebrows and this simply couldn't be happening. They were good people, and good people won out, good people worried about bills and mortgage payments and having children and how hard it could be to love each other sometimes, but that was as far as their worries went, and yet here she was one step from losing it, she could feel something rising inside her, something dark and winged and frayed, and she wanted to open her mouth to let it out but didn't, afraid that once she started she wouldn't be able to stop, would just stand there and scream and scream and scream, and she had to be stronger than that, she was stronger than that, and then Jack stood up and started for Tom.

TOM WAS SURPRISED by how quiet his mind was. He could see everything. He admired the way Jack drew his pistol, the careful way he aimed and fired and then aimed and fired again. Methodical. The cop who had warned Jack was trying to bring his gun to bear as Andre charged him. Tom wondered if there were any other cops here, and whether they were with Jack too, and whether Andre had a contingency plan and more guys waiting, and whether—

Jack was staring at him, and at the money.

Tom could sense his own panic. It had a tug, like an undertow. Only he realized he didn't have to give in to it. Maybe this was shock. Maybe this was what shock felt like. If so, he'd take it over panic any day.

Jack started forward. He wore a blue jumpsuit unzipped to the waist. The gun was in his hand. Rising slow. Tom's thoughts were still running apart from the world. Out of the corner of his eye, he could see Anna frozen in place, her hands to her head, blood between her fingers.

Oh God.

It all snapped, everything coming back into focus like a record tracking to speed. Panic wasn't a tug. It was a wave. It crashed into him fast and hard and nearly swept him off his feet. She was hurt and Jack was still coming, and somehow he had to get her out of here.

Jack raised the gun, finger moving inside the trigger guard. Tom grabbed the handles of the bag, stood fast, and hoisted it to rest on the railing, a little more than halfway off. Let it lean, holding it lightly, just two fingers.

Down below, people were scrambling in all directions, shoppers streaming for exits, screams and chaos. At the other end of the hallway, Andre had driven into the cop like a linebacker, bowled him right off his feet. Everyone was yelling, and behind all of it, that same insipid pop song was still playing, some spoiled brat saying bye-bye-bye to some teen queen, neither of them knowing the first goddamn thing about the first goddamn thing.

The bag wobbled on the railing, three stories above the sunken courtyard with the gourmet grocery. Jack looked at it. Then he turned his head and looked Tom in the eyes. Stared. "Okay," he said. "Okay." Jack slipped the gun back in the holster and held his hands out at chest height. "It's not too late."

Tom wanted to laugh. Instead, he let go of the straps.

Jack yelled, "No," and lunged forward, his arms scrabbling, fingers stretching. Tom got a half-second flash of wide eyes, and then he was running past, not caring one way or the other if the bag went over.

Anna had taken a step forward, lowered her left arm, but her right was still covering her mouth. There was blood on her forehead, and spattered across the bridge of her nose. This couldn't be, he couldn't lose her, not now, not ever. "Anna, baby, no, no, are you hurt?" Thinking that if she was, then he was done too, he was just going to . . . just going to . . .

She stared at him with pupils like black holes. Her lips twitched. Then she said, "It's blood. I mean, not my blood."

"You're okay?"

She nodded.

Thank God, thank God, thank you, if I didn't believe in you before, I do now. He threw an arm around her shoulder and pulled her toward the stairwell.

As Jack flung himself forward, he had the strangest moment, a weird flash of something like déjà vu. It was like he was living a memory: lunging for Bobby as he fell, his kid brother with arms up and reaching, Jack his only hope. Problem was, best Jack could remember, it hadn't actually happened, that moment. When would it have?

Regardless, as his hands fumbled forward and he saw the bag start to go backward, as he felt the strain of muscles, the rush of air against his cheeks, as he begged his body to go faster, just a little faster, please, his limbs stretched to their max, as the duffel sagged and drooped and finally slipped, as his fingertips traced the texture of the fabric, scrabbling for anything, a handle, a zipper, a pocket, and especially as he realized he wasn't going to get hold of it, that the thing was going to fall, through all of it some part of him was seeing Bobby. Bobby falling backward, Bobby lit in panic, Bobby scared, reaching out for his brother to save him.

Then gravity claimed it. Loose hundreds confettied out the open flap, and the whole thing turned a slow half spin before landing with a crash of glass and a splat in a tray of gourmet potato salad three stories below. He stared. Unbelievable. Four hundred grand soaking in mayonnaise. He tried to picture himself vaulting the railing and dropping the distance. Leaned over to check. Jackie Chan, maybe. A forty-three-year-old Polack, no.

Fine. The stairs. They'd scoped the whole place yesterday. The stairwell nearest him stopped at the ground floor, but the far one went all the way down. He started running, taking in the scene as he did. Marshall was flat on his ass, one hand behind, the other trying to bring the gun to bear. The black guy had bowled him over. Jack raised his Colt and fired as he ran, lousy snap shots that shattered glass windows and prompted another round of shrieks. The black guy looked at him, then at Marshall, then turned and ran. Jack reached his partner, ducked down to haul him upward.

Marshall tried to sight in on the guy who'd knocked him over, but Jack shoved him into motion, yelling, "Come on!" The money was the only priority.

The two of them hit the stairwell door, started thundering down. No telling exactly how long before the cops got here, but this was Lincoln Park, a nice, white doctor-and-lawyer neighborhood. It wouldn't be long. He squeezed the grip of the pistol.

The stairs were clean and smelled of paint. Bare bulbs flooded each flight. He had a hand on the railing and was hauling himself around, more jumping than running. When he reached the bottom, he didn't even slow, just spun, raised a foot, and kicked the emergency exit door. An alarm screeched as they burst into the grocery store. A Mexican in an apron huddled behind the sushi counter. Wine to the left, imported cheese to the right. Jack charged through, knocking over a display of salsa, jars spilling and smashing. A server stood in the center of a broad octagon of cases filled with precooked entrées and sides. The duffel bag had broken through the glass to spatter potatoes and couscous and sautéed broccolini in all directions. A dozen hundred-dollar bills had settled amid the food like garnish. The server was staring at the bag, one hand half out like he was trying to work up the courage to touch it. Jack pistol-whipped the base of his neck, then pushed past the falling body to claim what was his. "Let's go."

"Which way?"

"The back."

Marshall spun. An employee's-only tunnel led out to the rear of the mall, into a dingy concrete space littered with cigarette butts and broken glass, loud with the buzz of generators. They burst into the rain, hearing sirens now, close. Jack slung the bag over his shoulder, then hit a low wall moving, grabbing the top with his free hand and hoisting himself up. The move opened up the slash on his arm, but the pain felt far away.

There was a cop on the other side, hurrying down a short alley from a group of three-flat apartments. For a moment, they looked at each other. Then the cop reached for his gun and started yelling to freeze.

Jack had been in before, wasn't going back. Without removing his left hand from the wall, he brought his right up.

The gun was quieter out in the open space. The cop staggered. His legs gave, and he fell to his knees in a puddle. Water splashed murky and silver.

"Jesus," Marshall said from beside him. "Jack."

The cop rocked back and forth. He looked at his hands, bloody and shaking. Jack raised his pistol again. Took time to aim.

18

EAST WAS AS GOOD AS WEST. It didn't seem to much matter. Moving was the point, staying mobile. Driving minute after minute, mile after mile, with no goal but keeping away from everyone, from the whole world, while they figured out what to do. How to make this right.

The thought almost made Tom laugh. *Make it right? What would that look like, Einstein?*

He shook his head, filled with a terror and loneliness he'd never known. The world he used to believe in had imploded, and the new one was a horror show inhabited by monsters. Everything he loved was at stake. And there was no one they could trust. They were all alone.

Anna shivered in the passenger seat, arms clutching her chest, and Tom leaned forward to turn up the heat. He punched back and forth between AM 720 and 780. A commercial for volunteer teachers, an overdubbed voice saying that positive role models could dramatically lower drug usage amid blah blah blah.

Nothing so far. It wouldn't be long now, though. It couldn't be. Your average shooting didn't make the news in a city like Chicago, but a firefight in a Lincoln Park mall would. How had things gone so *wrong*? He still couldn't understand it, couldn't wrap his head around what had happened.

An announcer came on and they both held their breath. Waited to hear their own names, that they were fugitives. Prayed that they might hear about a known criminal, Jack Witkowski, gunned down by police while fleeing the mall. Instead, the announcer started in on the economy, the expected fall in the real estate market. People had been talking about how Chicago was overbuilt for a year or two, and coupled with a shaky mortgage industry, it seemed a recipe for imminent disaster. Once, that had really worried them.

From up ahead, Tom heard sirens. His fingers tightened on the wheel. In a blur of red noise, an ambulance blew past.

"Do you think—"

"I don't know."

There was a gap, dead air, and then the anchor came back on, his voice different, harried. Tom leaned forward to turn up the volume.

"—early reports of a shoot-out in a Lincoln Park mall. According to our information, at approximately ten o'clock this morning, shots were reported at Century Mall. Witnesses say that perhaps as many as ten people were involved, with gunfire wounding several and possibly killing others, including, it is currently believed, at least one police officer. We, ahh . . ." He stalled, and Tom could picture the host trying frantically to read. "We understand that police have evacuated the mall and may be in a standoff with the shooters. The identities of the men involved are currently unknown, as is whether they have been captured. There are only preliminary details at this time, but we will obviously be keeping you posted as more information becomes available on this story. Again, this took place at the Century Mall, an upscale center in Lincoln Park, not an area known for . . ."

Tom turned the volume down.

"Do you think they know we were there?" Anna clicked her thumbnail against her teeth.

He blew a breath, shrugged. His cheek itched, and he went to scratch it with his left hand, caught himself, reached around awkwardly with his right. "If they do, they'll be after us."

"Along with Malachi, and Jack, and the cops that work for him."

"Yeah."

They rode in silence. Lightning blew the sky like a bulb. Eventually she said, "What are we going to do?"

A light turned red ahead of them. He braked. Sat with the rain bouncing off the roof, the radio announcer muffled in the background. After a moment, he turned sideways. "Baby," he said, "I don't have the first clue."

HALDEN HAD BEEN turning down Tom and Anna's street when the reports started coming over his radio. Like most detectives, he let the thing run when he was in the car, just kept the volume low and listened subconsciously. Chicago was a big city, with plenty of badness. You got used to the rhythm, the steady call and response of mayhem and tragedy.

This had sounded different. The calls were faster, the voices strained. He'd coasted to a stop outside the brick two-flat and turned up the volume.

"—10-1, all available units, shots fired at Century Mall . . ."

"—ambulance, we need another ambulance . . ."

"—Jesus, it's a war zone . . ."

"—officer down, repeat, officer down . . ."

He didn't understand the situation, but it was clear what he should do. The mall was in his area, which made it his problem. What he was supposed to do was hit flashers and haul ass.

Instead he parked and got out of the car. Climbed the steps to Tom and Anna's. He rang the bell, leaning on it, holding it down. Banged on the door. Nothing.

Halden walked around back, to a small yard with a picnic table and untended flower gardens. He looked up at the window, cupped his hands around his mouth, and yelled. "Tom! Anna! This is Detective Halden. I need to talk to you right now."

Nothing.

He yelled louder for the benefit of the neighbors, hoping embarrassment might drive them out. "Mr. and Mrs. Reed, this is the police. Come out right now."

Nothing.

Damn it. Where were they? The house had been a long shot, but worth a try. Had they spooked somehow? Could they have talked to another cop, found out that he hadn't told the lieutenant after all? He chewed on his lip, fought the urge for a cigarette. Finally he turned and walked back to the car. Until they turned up, may as well do his job.

It took him ten minutes to get to the mall, and he barely recognized the place once he did. The front glass was broken out onto the concrete. An ambulance and at least a dozen squad cars blocked the street and sidewalks, light bars spinning blue. Sirens wailed from every point of the compass. As he watched, EMTs raced out with a gurney, a tech running alongside to keep pressure on a chest blooming red. Two hundred citizens clustered behind yellow tape, watching the show. A reporter screamed obscenities at a cop trying to hold her back.

Halden left his car on the sidewalk, badged the guys at the door. "Who's the detective in charge?"

"Detective? You kidding?" The cop shook his head. "Half the brass is here. The security office."

Inside, the mall had a surreal quality, chairs and benches overturned, glass broken from store windows, pop music playing over the sound system, but instead of shoppers, there were crime techs and tactical officers and photographers. Most of the action seemed to be concentrated a couple floors up, but Halden wanted to find out what had happened before looking at the scene itself.

The mall security office was small, a windowless room with a couple of grainy monitors and too many people huddled around them. He gave up hope of pushing inside when he saw how much his rank would bring down the average. Instead, he wandered until he saw a detective he recognized from a raid the year before, an Uptown meth house. "What's the story?"

"Some sort of a meet gone wrong," the man said. "A couple of bodies. Six or eight bad guys. They shot a cop on the way out."

"He okay?"

The detective shook his head. "Took one to the head."

Somebody was fucked, then. You didn't shoot police in Chicago. Halden gestured to the security office. "What's the big attraction?"

"They pulled a security feed from one of the stores."

"Anything useful?"

"Yeah. One of them looks like Jack Witkowski."

"The Shooting Star suspect?" Surprise came first. Then Halden felt his stomach tighten. Yesterday, Tom Reed had said the drug dealer had mentioned Witkowski. Then Reed had gone AWOL. When Halden had finally gotten hold of him, the guy had sounded scared. And behind his voice, there had been the random sounds of a public place, and a persistent beat, like music.

Maybe the same music that was playing over the speakers right now. Shit. Shit, shit, oh shit. The other detective started to walk away, but Halden grabbed his arm. "Wait. Did you see the tape?"

"Yeah."

"Who else was there?"

"Nobody anybody recognized. The angle is lousy. They're looking at cameras from other stores now."

"Could you see anybody else?" He couldn't keep the panic from his voice. "Anybody at all?"

The detective looked at him strangely. "Yeah. Witkowski, if it was him, he was talking to two people. A man and a woman, looked like taxpayers. Had a bag that they started to show just before everything went crazy. They ended up running."

Halden let go of the guy's shoulder. Forced a nod.

"You okay?"

"Yeah. Thanks." He turned away. The other detective stared for a moment, then shrugged and headed for the doors.

Tom and Anna Reed. It had to be. Which meant that since yesterday, he'd had information that might have prevented this from happening. In all the messages he'd left, he'd never said anything about the money because he hadn't wanted to spook them into running. He'd pretended he was going to set up the drug dealer, when really he just wanted to lure Tom and Anna somewhere. Wanted to grab them himself and make the big arrest. Be a hero, get his name in the paper, jump clear of his lieutenant and the rest of the politicians.

Which made this his fault. At least partly. If he'd told the truth, things might have gone differently. A dead cop might still be alive.

He'd screwed up before, but never like this.

Halden took a deep breath and started toward the security office, trying to figure out how to share what he knew in a way that didn't make him the scapegoat for the whole mess.

Eight men were crammed inside the tiny room, talking in low voices. Among them the deputy chief of D's, his boss's boss. Halden had caught his eye, started to gesture him over, when a thought hit.

Maybe there was still a way to save this. To come out on top, a hero.

Being a detective was about asking the right question. Right now he was focusing on his own mistake. But that wasn't what Tom and Anna would be thinking about. Their plan had just backfired horribly. So the real question was, what would they do now?

With the question reframed that way, the answer was obvious. After they knew they were safe, they'd remember that they weren't criminals. Not in the real meaning of the word. So they'd call the police. And not just any cop—they'd call one who knew them, who would understand their circumstances.

They would call *him*.

Halden spun on his heel, went back down the corridor. It was a dangerous game, sure. But he could pull it off. Go to the bosses not with hat in hand, but with two people from the incident, a bag full of money, and a complete explanation for what had happened and why. Lemonade from lemons. Instead of being a scapegoat, get a promotion and a pay bump and a hell of a lot closer to that cabin up west of Minocqua. And all he had to do was wait. And pray.

"WELL, that didn't go quite how you planned." Marshall sounded like he might have been trying for a joke, but didn't quite hit it, his voice tight and shoulders tense.

Jack said, "We got out, didn't we?" The handles of the duffel bag were heavy against his palms, the bulk bumping his knee as they walked through the rain. The heft of the thing felt good, right. He'd worked hard for it. He knew it wouldn't bring Bobby back—he wasn't a fucking idiot—but it was something.

Sirens screamed toward them, but Jack held himself steady. The car blew past in a spray of water and flashing light, heading east toward the mall three blocks away. After he'd killed the cop, they'd hit the apartments across the parking lot. A simple matter of jimmying a window lock and they were off the street. Marshall had snagged a black tee from the owner's dresser and balled the shirt of the fake uniform deep in the kitchen trash. Then they strolled out the front door and down the steps like they owned the place, right past a prowler car coming up to blockade the back of the mall.

"We did get out," Marshall said. "And we do have the money. But I just feel like there was something that didn't go quite right. What was it?" He paused theatrically, then put a finger up in a eureka gesture. "Oh yeah—you shot a *cop*."

"What did you want me to do? Ask nice if he'd let us walk?" The bag was getting heavy, but his other arm throbbed from the reopened cut. The bandage on his left arm was staining a slow scarlet. "Cop's just a guy in a funny hat."

"Chicago PD, man, they're brutal when one of theirs goes down. They'll never stop looking for us."

"They'd never have stopped anyway. Besides, it's done."

They turned into the drugstore parking lot. The truck was a beater, an old Ford F150 they'd bought off a Western Avenue lot for a grand in cash. They'd left the stolen Honda parked on a pleasant neighborhood street, where it would likely sit for months before anybody noticed it. No sense pulling off a deal and then getting nabbed if the highway patrol happened to punch their plates. He swung the door open with a creak, tossed the money behind the driver's seat, then leaned over to unlock Marshall's side. Fired the engine, turning the heat on full blast to battle the chill from his wet clothes. "Just one more thing to do."

"What's that?"

"See to my favorite couple." They'd been a pain in the ass, almost gotten him killed twice. And while he recognized that it didn't make strict logical sense, some part of him held them responsible for Bobby's death. It had something to do with Will Tuttle being dead, because the guy he'd looked forward to getting revenge on had shuffled off swift and sweet instead of slow and painful. There was a word for the thing he was doing, something he'd seen on daytime TV, one of those psychology words. Projection? Transference? Whatever. Since he couldn't get Will, he wanted Tom and Anna.

"Huh?" Marshall looked over sharply. "The cops'll have them."

"Maybe." Last he'd seen, they'd been running down a back stairwell. "Maybe they walked out the same door we did."

"Even if that's true, we have the money. We don't need them."

"They saw us. They can ID us."

"Come on, man, they're doing that right now. You really want to be in town once our faces start flashing on TV?" He shook his head. "You shot a *cop*. Chicago just got way too small for us."

"But—"

"You do this, you're on your own."

The line fell heavy. Jack looked sideways at his partner. Saw the stare, the sincerity. Not like Marshall to back away from a fight. It made Jack pause.

Truth was, the guy had a point. They had the money, and their freedom, and there really wasn't anything they could do about what Tom and Anna knew, not now. It irked, the idea those two yahoos might walk away unscathed, might not have to pay for stealing from him, for trying to game him. But he'd learn to live with it. Jack sighed. "All right. Forget it," he said. "Let's go."

Marshall blew a breath. "Amen."

Jack put the clutch to the floor and forced the stick into reverse. The truck coughed and shook, but moved. Marshall pulled the pistol from his holster and popped the clip. "You recognize that black dude?" He squinted, counting rounds. "He was with the drug dealer. The night we took down the Star."

"No shit?"

"I'm pretty sure. Didn't recognize the other two, though."

"What the hell were they doing there?"

"Dunno. One more reason to get clear."

Jack nodded. He hated leaving all this shit undone, all these loose ends, too many of them personal. But they'd won. That would have to be enough.

"Now," Marshall said, slamming home the clip and holstering the pistol, "let's see how we did, eh?" He fumbled behind the seat, dragged the duffel bag up to his lap. Jack turned the truck south. They could take Halsted down, pick up the freeway at Lake. Be in Saint Louis by afternoon. From there they could flip for the truck, split the take, shake hands, and part ways. Marshall wanted to go south, to Florida, but Miami was no kind of place for a middle-aged Polack. No, forget Miami, forget Chicago. Forget Tom and Anna Reed, forget the Star and the police and the drug dealer. The time had come to head west and hang up his spurs.

Then he heard a sound from Marshall, a kind of choking inhale. "Jack?" He had the bag in his lap, the top held wide, money bunched up in his fists, hundred-dollar bills green and crumpled, and beneath that, revealed now, the front page of the *Chicago Sun-Times,* and the edge of one beneath that, and beneath that. For a second, Jack just stared, trying to understand what he was seeing, how his money had turned into newsprint.

Then he jammed the gas and spun the wheel, tires squealing, engine roaring up to the red as he popped a U, missing an oncoming car only because the other driver jerked onto the sidewalk. He held his right foot down and worked the clutch to jump from second to fourth.

Motherfucker. Tom and Anna Reed. They wanted to play? Fine. Time to play rough.

"MAYBE WE SHOULD RUN," Tom said, watching the rain arc off the tires of the cab in front of them.

"Where?

"Anywhere. Get out of town. Now that Jack has killed a cop, the police are going to go crazy finding him. We could just get out of the way, come back once they have."

"What if they don't?"

He shrugged, didn't know what to say.

"Tom?" Her voice husky.

"What is it, baby?"

"I was wrong."

"When?"

"Before. I said we could still win." She was drenched and solemn, hair flattened to her cheeks. She shook her head. "But it's like a fairy tale."

"Huh?" He looked over, wondered if she was starting to lose it.

"An old one, I mean. Brothers Grimm, that kind of thing." She rubbed her eyes. "The violent ones, before they were Disney-fied. Rub the lamp, you get three wishes, but none of them go the way you planned. Like, you wish for riches, and your father dies. So you've inherited his fortune but lost your dad."

"*The Twilight Zone.*"

She nodded. "I remember, when we found the money, thinking

it was like a magic lamp. It was going to turn everything around for us, dig us out of the hole we were in, the stupid concerns of our old life. And it was going to give us the thing we most wanted."

Tom sighed slowly. The world felt heavy, something that could bear down, crush you slow and complete. "Well, I'm definitely not worried about the devaluation of Chicago real estate anymore." He didn't know if he was making a joke or not. Didn't know what he was saying. His head hurt, and his fingers throbbed in his lap.

She continued as if he hadn't spoken. "When I was a kid, I had this illustrated book of myths. I read them over and over. There was one with this dog, not cute, sort of menacing, with a bird he's caught in his mouth. And he's taking it home to eat. But before he gets there, he crosses a river and sees a dog with a bird in *his* mouth. And he wants that bird too, so he opens his mouth to attack the other dog. Only it was his reflection, of course, and he ends up with nothing. I always felt sorry for him, even though he was kind of a stupid dog." She shook her head. "Or that Greek one, the kid with the wings that melted?"

"Icarus."

"Right, Icarus. He and his dad were locked up somewhere, and his dad made the wings with wax and feathers. He told Icarus not to fly too high. But first chance the kid gets . . ." She whistled through her teeth, skimmed a hand upward. "The illustration was all orange and red and yellow, and just a silhouette shooting upwards, feathers falling away. I always wanted to warn him. But of course you turn the page, and . . ." She sighed, rubbed her face.

Tom said nothing, just nodded, waited.

"Back at the hotel, I was talking about how fate was funny, how everything came down to a cup of instant coffee. Like the fire in our kitchen was what started everything. But that's bullshit, isn't it? You can't blame life on a cup of coffee." She shook her head. "Everything I needed to know was in those books. But I kept going. I just . . . kept going."

"You weren't alone."

"I pushed you, though," she said, her voice small. "I wanted it more. I always wanted it more. I know you'd love to have a child. But I was the one who pushed. After we tried the shots, the hormones, you were ready to adopt. But I wanted to have one of my own. So I kept pushing, and we got deeper into debt, and you and I, we lost track of each other."

"Stop," he said. "None of that matters now."

She looked over at him, held the gaze for a long time. Finally she said, "You would have been a great father."

Something in him broke, some tenuous, fragile connection deep in his chest, it just gave. He felt a rush of emotions, too many and mixed to name. His fingers tightened on the steering wheel. He knew what she was saying. What it cost her, cost them both.

"It's time, isn't it?"

He nodded. "Yeah. It's time." He flipped on the turn signal, pulled into the lot of a Jewel, and parked.

"The police are going to be tough on us." She wiped her hands on her pants. "We don't have much of a story to tell, not with a cop dead."

"I know," he said. "But every time we try to get out of this, we only make it worse."

"Should we tell them about the deal we made with Malachi?"

"We should tell them everything. Every detail."

"We'll go to jail."

"Probably," he said.

She nodded. Reached over and put a hand on his thigh. "I love you."

"I love you too," he said, and for the first time since this whole thing started, since the moment, Christ, it seemed like years ago, when they'd looked at each other across the pile of money and each realized the other wanted to take it, for the first time since then he felt right. No more running. No more playing angles or choosing convenient truths. No more pretending to be criminals. He leaned across the parking brake, and she met him halfway, the kiss passionate, her hand snaking around his neck to pull him close. The rain pattered on the roof, less urgently than before, and it seemed safe somehow, a childhood sound, a rainy day home from school.

When they finally broke, he stayed near, their eyes inches apart and staring. "I'm sorry," she said.

He shook his head. "Me too." Then he took his phone from his pocket and dialed.

"THIS IS STUPID, MAN." His partner rubbed his chin, the stubble grating. "The cops could be here any minute."

"Why? If Tom and Anna are talking to them, why would they send someone to the house?" Jack sniffed hard, popped his knuckles. "No one's coming."

"Even if you're right, you don't really think the money is here, do you?" Marshall stood in front of the door. "They probably turned it in already. And if they're running, it's going with them."

"Only one way to be sure."

"Look—"

"Move." Jack stared hard. With a sigh, Marshall stepped aside.

He didn't bother with picks this time. Just wound up and booted the door at the handle. The wood cracked and snapped. A second kick, and the thing flew open, the lock mounting tearing out of the frame, splinters flying. He was through before the door banged against the opposite wall.

Beep.

"Oh, for Christ's sake," Marshall said. "The alarm."

"Yeah," Jack said. He stepped over to the control box and punched a six-digit string. The beeping died.

"How—"

"I watched Anna."

"You said she hit the panic code."

"Panic code is one digit higher than the regular code. Alarm companies do it so people remember when they've got a gun pointed at their head." He made a slow turn, surveying the space. "All right. Tear this place apart."

"Listen to me, this is a waste of time—"

"Would you just fucking *do* it?" Jack grabbed the back of a knockoff Eames chair and yanked the thing over. It flipped and slammed loud. His head hurt, and inside his chest he could feel something crackling like a downed power wire.

His partner stared. For a moment, Jack wondered if he was going to make a play. But Marshall shook his head, turned, and went down the hall to the kitchen, started looking through cabinets.

Good enough. Jack turned back to the room. There was a lock-back knife sitting on the coffee table. He opened it, saw that the blade was crusted with dried blood. Jack smiled, then dug the point into a sofa cushion and yanked, feeling the tearing shiver up his arm, the rich physical pleasure of it. He yanked out a handful of foam, then tossed the cushion and eviscerated the next. Slashed at the back, then reached for the bottom and flipped the sofa up on its ass.

He went to the bookcase and began shoving novels to the ground by the armload. Opened the cabinets below and scattered DVDs and board games. Went to the entertainment center, took hold of the TV, a big Zenith, forty inches easy, and yanked it forward. The thing hung for a moment on edge, wavering like a beast on the lip of a cliff, and then it plummeted. The picture tube exploded with a high-pitched pop, and glass crunched against the hardwood. He could feel his heart starting to go, his breath coming a little faster. It felt good.

In the bedroom he slashed the mattress in a dozen places, tore the pillows to clouds of wobbling feathers. Yanked the drawers from the dresser and upended them, then tossed them on the mauled bed, leaving the dresser to gape. He tore clothes from the rack in the closet, striped yuppie shirts and fancy sweaters. Ripped down a shoe rack, a dozen varieties of what looked like the same black heel clattering. Jerked the medicine cabinet off the bathroom wall. Ripped down the shower curtain. Used the lid of the toilet to shatter the tank, porcelain ringing loud, water pouring out to drench his pant legs, drown his shoes. A migraine had been forming behind his eyes, but the destruction seemed to keep it at a distance.

The spare room was stacked with banker boxes, no furniture, like they'd had other plans for the room that never came together. One by one Jack tossed the lids and shook the contents out, bills and letters and tax returns flipping and fluttering like crazed birds. Yanked a bookcase off the wall. Found a box of photos and up-ended them, a dozen years of weddings and Christmases and quiet Sunday mornings spilling across the ruin of the den. He unzipped his pants and pissed all over them. Fuck Anna and Tom Reed. Fuck them eternal.

From the doorway he heard Marshall speak. "Unless that thing in your hand is a magic wand, I don't think it's going to help us."

Jack shook himself dry, zipped up. His breath coming hard, steady and strong, even as his head throbbed. He wanted to spit in the eye of God. "Nothing in the kitchen?"

"There's nothing anywhere, man. The money's not here." Marshall paused. "But you knew that, didn't you?"

Jack didn't answer. He stepped into the hallway, looked around. The floors of every room were covered with broken glass and piled fabric, spills of paper and upended furniture.

"Let's go." Marshall spoke calm, steady.

"One more thing," Jack said.

The pillar candle in the bedroom would do. He walked back to the kitchen, where pans and broken dishes lay strewn among multigrain waffles and Tupperware and butcher packages of steak. Every kitchen in America had a junk drawer. He found where Marshall had dumped it, rubber bands and batteries and take-out menus, and kicked through to find a pack of matches. Lit the candle and set it on the kitchen table.

"What are you doing?"

It made sense. For the Reeds, this was the way the whole thing had started. There was a nice sense of circularity. Jack gripped the edges of the big Viking range and yanked. The base squealed against the tiles, and a metal flex-hose stretched out to the wall. He hoisted himself up onto the counter, maneuvered a foot around, then stomped the point where the hose met the stove. Again and again, the coupling bending, then, one more good hit, snapping free, the sweet fart stink of gas rising fast.

"Jack—"

"Let's go," he said.

Marshall looked at him, then at the stove. He shook his head and started down the hall. Jack followed, closing the front door behind him. They walked down the stairs, stepped out onto the porch. Jack felt better than he had in days. Destruction had, at least temporarily, transmuted the anger and frustration and grief into an almost sexual tingle. They started down the block.

After a moment, Marshall said, "It's easier running together."

Jack nodded.

"Somebody to watch your back, no worries about the other guy having been caught, making a deal. I'd rather we stuck together. But you need to understand something." Marshall's voice formal, like he was picking his words carefully. "I'm sorry about Bobby, but you need to let it go."

"He wasn't your brother."

"That's right. He wasn't my brother."

"You have a point?"

"Yeah." Marshall stopped, and Jack turned to face him. "I'm done. I'm not disrespecting you or Bobby. But I'm done here."

"We can't run without the money."

"Bullshit." Marshall shook his head. "If we knew where it was, nothing would stop me getting it. You know that. But we don't. So I'm going. You want to come, great. If not, you're on your own."

Jack narrowed his eyes. He and Marshall had known each other a long time, done a lot of work together. But in the end, everybody stood alone. "Might be that's best."

They stared for a long moment. Then Marshall shook his head, started walking again. Jack followed.

There was a bright orange ticket under the windshield wiper of the Ford. Parking without a neighborhood sticker. This town. Everybody playing an angle, even the government. Especially them. Jack dropped the ticket on the street, then pulled himself into the cab. Marshall got in the other side.

They could run without the money. But the thought of Tom and Anna winning? He'd rather pull out what was left of his hair than let that happen.

Yeah? Rather spend the rest of your life in a SuperMax? Twenty-three hours a day in solitary?

The thought came from a quieter part of him, and came cold. It chilled the destruction high right out of him. Had he climbed so far into his own head? He'd shot a cop earlier this morning. If he got caught, that was that. Everything else they'd done, he might have gotten away with for lack of evidence and witnesses. With a good lawyer, call it ten, out in four. But nobody walked after murdering a cop.

If only he knew where Tom and Anna were, knew whether

they'd given up the money. Somewhere in this city, the two of them sat safe. He punched the steering wheel, hitting it hard. An image of Bobby popped into his head, ten years old and beaming as he rode wobbling down an alley on the bike Jack had stolen for him.

"How much was in the bag?"

Marshall looked up, his gaze quick. "Maybe ten grand."

Ten grand. Plus they had the briefcase of drugs. They'd have to unload that wholesale. Call it another ten, twenty in all. Not something to retire on. Not money that would let him buy into a bar in Arizona. Not money that was worth his brother's life.

But it was enough to get them the hell out of here, and to lie low for a while. Plan the next move. Get back to work. He sighed, said, "Count it, would you?"

"Sure. Sure thing." Marshall's voice sounding relieved. He reached behind the seat, pulled the bag into his lap. Jack sat and watched. Every time Marshall dipped into the black duffel bag, he came out with a handful of hundred-dollar bills. But soon the handfuls dwindled to pairs, and finally to single bills. Finally he zipped the bag and hoisted it by the handles, turning to put it away. The image reminded Jack of something. Something he'd seen recently. What was it?

It hit. "Wait."

"What?"

He felt a smile beginning somewhere deep. Could it be? "The bag."

"What about it?"

"It look familiar to you?" The smile pushed upward, bubbling from inside of him, and as it did, from behind came a sudden roar and the sound of a dozen windows shattering at once. They both turned to look as flame punched out the glass in a shimmering arc, the wash of heat physical even at this distance. Photographs and loose paper rolled in front of the blast of fire, twisting and looping like they were surfing the inferno. Even as the explosion faded and reversed, sucking air back in, yellow-orange tongues began to lick up the curtains. Jack could imagine the cashmere sweaters and Egyptian-cotton towels and high-thread-count sheets smoldering and twisting. Trickles of gray began to ooze out the broken windows, darkening with every moment as the house caught. A smoke alarm shrieked senselessly.

And as he watched Tom and Anna Reed's pretty little world begin to burn, the smile broke free and bloomed on Jack's lips, and he leaned forward to start the truck.

19

THE SAND WAS PITTED and scarred from rain. Beneath swollen skies, Lake Michigan rolled in steady slate curls. Anna wrapped her arms around herself against the wind. They'd been waiting in the tree line north of Foster Avenue Beach for twenty minutes, and the whole time, she'd been trying to figure out what to say, how to explain the simple mistake that had led them here, to a meeting where they turned themselves in to the police. She knew it wouldn't matter, not in a legal sense, but she wanted the cop to understand. That seemed important.

It had been something in the touch of the money itself. The heaviness against her palm. Not greed, exactly. More like fantasy. A selective blindness to consequence. Holding that much money, it wasn't part of life. It was the definition of surreal. So when it actually happened, she had already fallen down the rabbit hole. Everything else was just their attempts to deal with the twisted Wonderland they'd found themselves in.

"There he is," Tom said. He nodded toward the low bulk of the shuttered concession stand, not yet open for the season. This had been their beach, a million years ago. Less crowded than most of the others, and without the meat-market factor. They used to bike over, set up folding chairs right in the edge of the surf, where the water frothed and tugged at their ankles. Read and nap in the sun, watch kids make sand castles. Now Detective Christopher Halden strode in front of the concession stand where they'd once bought hot dogs and Popsicles. He wore a dark gray suit and an expression she read as pissed from a hundred yards away. "Looks like he's alone."

Tom shrugged. "Not like he isn't going to take us in anyway."

She felt an icy shiver, wrote it off to the wind. Having finally overcome her money blindness, she wasn't going to let a little fear stop her. "Let's go."

Halden saw them coming, turned to watch. Anna's eyes were drawn to the big black gun, the way his right hand rested on it. She imagined what it must feel like to carry death on your hip, to walk around like it was no big deal. The air had that worm-and-dirt smell of a spring rain, coupled with a faint odor of rotting lake weeds. When they were ten feet away, Halden said, "You want to give me one reason not to arrest you both right now?"

"Actually, no," Tom said. "We're here so you will."

The cop squinted at that, thrown off his game, eyes drawing to slits, lines furrowing in his cheeks. He looked like he was about to speak, hesitated, then said, "Go on."

"You once tried to warn us about getting in over our heads." Anna took a deep breath. "Well, that's where we are." Halden said nothing. She got the feeling that she was telling him something he already knew, that he was the sort to stay quiet until he saw the advantage in speaking. It made her nervous, made her want to watch her own words. "Everything has gone wrong. We're in a lot of danger."

"Yeah?" He stared. "So why have you been dodging me? The runaround is not generating fuzzy thoughts toward you."

"I know."

"You know, huh? Did you know that a cop got killed this morning at the mall?"

Anna put a hand to her mouth. Tom cut his eyes over to look at her.

"Maybe," Halden said, "instead of talking in riddles, you better start with the part where you found four hundred thousand dollars." He watched their eyes. "Yeah," he said. "I know about that. I know a lot of things. You two have been lying to me."

"We're done with that now," Tom said quietly. "We'll tell you everything."

The detective nodded, dug in his pocket, came out with his keys. "Good. Come on, you can ride with me."

"Wait," Anna said. "The reason we met out here. At the mall, Jack Witkowski, he had a cop working for him."

The detective cocked an eyebrow.

"I know how that sounds," she continued, "believe me, I do. But it's true. That's why we wanted to meet here, why we wanted you to come alone. You we trust, but there's at least one cop working with Jack, and maybe more."

Halden looked from her to Tom and back, eyes appraising. He put his keys back in his pocket, then reached inside his suit, came out with a pack of Winstons and tapped it against his palm to pop one.

Tom said, "You mind?"

Halden held the pack out, then produced a gold Zippo and fired both cigarettes. He snapped the lighter closed. "I didn't know you smoked."

"I don't." Tom inhaled, then blew a stream of gray. "Quit last February." The cop nodded. Stared, content to wait them out.

Anna took a deep breath. "We found the money when we came down for the fire," she said. "It was hidden in the flour, in all the food boxes." She told how it had been a game at first, strange and wonderful. How they hadn't exactly planned to take it, but one thing led to another. She told him about hiding it, about paying down their debt. The drug dealer. Jack coming to their house. Their flight to the motel. The arrangement with Malachi.

"It was my idea," Tom said, cutting in. "Setting Jack up."

Anna said, "We did it together."

Her husband looked at her, his lips tight. Slowly he nodded. "We didn't want anybody to get hurt. Anybody but him, I mean. But then that cop started shooting, and . . ."

"We never meant for anyone to get hurt," Anna said.

The cop dropped the cigarette to the concrete, rested the toe of his dress shoe on it, swiveled once left, once right. "Nobody ever means for someone to get hurt. But it's what happens when you're over your head."

"We know that now," Tom said. "That's why we're here."

Halden scratched at his chin. "You'll make this same statement officially? You'll sign it?"

Tom looked at Anna. She felt the weight of the moment, the formality of it. She put her hand behind his back, drew closer to him, the two of them standing like a couple before a priest. "We will."

"All right." Halden nodded. "Right now, the only person who knows you have the money is me. Let's keep it that way. I'll bring you in personally. You'll talk only to me. Once you've made your statement and given me the money, even if you're right and there are police involved, they won't have a reason to come after you."

"What about Jack?"

"Jack shot a cop." Halden said the words clear and level, and she heard the meaning beneath them.

"And Malachi?"

"We'll deal with him too."

They stood in silence for a moment. Finally Anna said, "What will happen to us?"

"I'm not going to lie to you." Halden rubbed his hands together against the chill. "What you did, it was wrong. Worse, it was dumb. But if you do exactly what I tell you, help me close the Shooting Star, bring in Jack Witkowski and the drug dealer?" He shrugged. "That will matter. A lot."

Relief flowed through her. She felt like a little girl escaping a spanking. They could get out of this. They'd done the right thing, finally, and could have their life back. It was the best she'd felt in days.

There was a sound of music, muffled. It took her a minute to recognize the theme from *Hawaii Five-0,* her ring tone. She dug out her phone. The caller ID read "Sara." Anna glanced at Halden apologetically, said, "My sister. Let me get rid of her." He nodded, turned to Tom, who said, "How does this work?"

"Hey," she said, speaking as soon as she stabbed the button, "I can't talk right now."

"Anna! Oh God, he—" There was a burst of noise, like someone grabbing the phone, and then a rough male voice came on. "Do you know who this is?"

The world wobbled, the closed concession stand and wet sand

and gray skies swirling and bleeding. She fought an urge to scream the breath from her lungs. "Don't you—" She caught herself, realized the detective was looking at her. She had to tell him, get cops racing toward her sister's house, oh Jesus, her nephew's house—

Stop. This is the most important moment of your life.

"Don't I what, Anna?" It seemed a terrible obscenity that Jack's voice could hang in her ear while the real man stood in her sister's home miles away. "Hurt her?"

Halden turned back to Tom, said, "Simple enough. You two come in with me, I'll take you into an interview room, we'll go through the story again."

"Who was that?" Jack's voice came quick.

If Halden realizes who you're talking to, he has to act on it.

If Jack realizes who you're standing with, Sara dies.

"No one," she said. "I'm outside." She wanted to step away, but was afraid it might make the cop suspicious. "What do you want?"

"Do we need a lawyer?" Tom asked.

"What do I want?" Jack laughed. "Your aunt's secret recipe for chocolate chip cookies. What do you think?"

"I thought you were just going to come clean," Halden said. "Why would you need a lawyer for that?"

Her stomach felt greasy. Her thighs trembled. Choosing her words carefully, she said, "I'll get it for you."

"Don't jerk me around, Anna. I know it's here."

"What?" Her mind raced. Why would he think the money was at her sister's house? Unless . . . Oh God.

"It's just, on TV, they always say you should have a lawyer present for something like this."

"I saw you bring it here," Jack said. "The other day. You

walked in with this duffel bag, the one I'm looking at right now. Your sister, she says she doesn't know anything about it, but I'm wondering if I just haven't asked her the right way." He paused. "What do you think, Anna? Should I ask her again?"

"No," she said quickly. "Please."

"Look, it's up to you," Halden said, his voice growing colder. "But you should know that the more you delay, the more trouble you're going to be in."

"Then tell me where it is."

"It's not there."

Jack said, "I want you to listen to something." A brief silence, and then she heard the scariest sound of her life.

Julian crying into the phone.

She wanted to beg, to plead, to shriek. Instead, she said, "It's not there. I swear. You're right, I was going to leave it. But then I thought of you. Of this."

"You've got a chance to help bring in a cop killer. But time is a factor. If a lawyer dicks us around long enough for him to get away? All that leaves us with is you."

"I don't believe you," Jack said.

"Yes, you do," she said. "You're"—she struggled for safe words—"with my nephew. Do you really think I would mess around? Now?"

There was a long pause. "Then where is it?"

"We'll bring it."

"Besides, you really want to risk letting him get away? The guy who beat you, broke your fingers, threatened your wife?"

"You'll bring it, huh?" Jack clicked his tongue. "I don't know. That sounds like stalling. Are you stalling?"

"No. I'm not."

"You'd better not. Because this morning I shot a cop. Do you know what that means?" His voice terrible. "It means that it doesn't matter what I do now. I could set this baby on fire, and it wouldn't matter, because I've already done something they will never, ever let me go for. Do you get it? I'm beyond consequences."

"All right," Tom said. "It doesn't matter anyway. We'd say the same thing either way."

Her legs nearly gave. "I understand."

"Good," Jack said. "Smart choice."

"Good," Halden said. "Smart choice."

The line went dead, but she stood still, holding the phone to her ear. Thinking of Sara and Julian, trapped and confused and very, very scared. The helplessness nearly brought tears to her eyes. To have to listen to him threaten her sister, her nephew, and be unable to do anything about it . . .

Forget the police, forget her and Tom walking away, forget that sweet half second of safety. There was no safety. Not for them. She knew that now.

They had to get away from Halden. But how? No way he was going to let them go now. They had to find a clever way to slip him. Some circumstance where he would leave them alone for a minute or two.

It came to her all of a sudden, and the irony was bitter enough to burn. To be really convincing, it would need them both. She closed her phone and put one hand on her stomach, praying Tom would understand.

*　　*　　*

HE WANTED ANOTHER CIGARETTE. Funny, fifteen months had been enough to reset his nicotine tolerance so that he had the tingling fingertips and pleasant light-headedness he hadn't known since his first smokes a decade ago. But it hadn't done a damn thing to quell his body's desire.

Halden put his hands in his pockets. "Where's the money?"

Tom hesitated. It was their last secret. "In a storage locker. Not far from the mall."

"Okay. We'll get it on the way into the station."

Anna hung up the phone, turned to step back into the conversation. Her eyes raked his, and he thought he saw something there, but couldn't make out what before she turned to Halden. She had a hand on her stomach, said, "Sorry about that. My sister. She's got a little boy she's starting to feed solid food. Apparently her kitchen is now coated in creamed zucchini."

"Zucchini, huh?" Halden laughed. "Why do they make baby food out of the worst-tasting crap? I'd throw it too."

Had he made a mistake telling the cop where the money was? Once it was in police custody, they had nothing to bargain with. Maybe they could—

Zucchini?

He looked at Anna again, saw her looking back. She was pale. Paler than the cold explained. Could it have been something from the phone call? She put the other hand on her stomach, winced.

"You okay, baby?"

"I'm feeling a little queasy."

Halden turned to study her. "Nerves, probably. But you're doing the right thing."

She shook her head. "No, it's not that. It's—" She looked at Tom again.

Could it have been coincidence, her using their old code word, the one that signaled she needed a rescue? He stared at her. Something in her demeanor seemed almost to be pleading. Her hands moved on her belly again, and all of a sudden he knew what she needed.

"It's morning sickness," he said. The words strange on his tongue. Words he'd once looked forward to saying. The kind of phrase that marked a whole new phase of life.

"You're pregnant?" The detective seemed surprised.

"Yes," she said, trembling. Something terrible was happening.

"I don't know why they call it morning sickness," Tom said, remembering one of the half-dozen books they'd read. "Happens all day long." He stepped forward, put a hand on her shoulder. "The bathrooms might be open." Turned to Halden. "Do you mind? It'll just be a minute."

Halden shook his head. "Of course not."

"Thanks," Anna said, her face contorting again. She started walking, and Tom moved with her, his hands supporting her weight. They passed the food counter, metal shutters drawn, and turned the corner to the back, toward the bathroom. His thoughts pounded and tumbled, trying to imagine what could possibly have made her tell this particular lie.

HALDEN WATCHED THEM GO, Tom supporting her as they hurried past the concession building. When they rounded the corner, he turned and stared out at the lake. Smelled the air, listened to the rush of water, watched waves roll in. Savored the slow smile.

*God*damn, but he was one hell of a detective.

This would make him. Closing the Shooting Star case single-handed? He'd get the works: the press, the commendation, the immunity from shit work, the patrons up the ladder, the pay-grade jump. Be able to retire with a fat pension. Buy that cabin and spend the rest of his life reading and walking through the woods, far from the city and the shitheads that lived here.

He reached into his pocket, took out the cigarettes. Normally he limited himself to two a day, but a victory cigarette didn't count. He fired it, dragged hard. The sound of gulls merged with a car engine heading away.

Anna being pregnant explained some things. He'd wondered why they'd taken the money, been a little pissed about it, in fact. It was dumb, tempting or not. He'd tried to tell them that, the day they'd sat drinking coffee at the kitchen table. But people did crazy things for their children. Funny, though, that she hadn't mentioned being pregnant before, not even when she was talking about Jack breaking into their house, slapping her around. You'd have thought that would have been the first thing she'd think of, the health of her baby. And wasn't coffee one of the things you were supposed to avoid when you were pregnant?

On the other hand, shitty parenting wasn't something he was exactly unfamiliar with, his line of work. He'd seen many a mother suck the grocery money through a crack pipe.

Still. He turned away from the waterline. The bathroom entrances were on the other side of the concession building. And past that, a hundred yards or so, was the parking lot.

Halden threw the half-smoked cigarette in the sand, started forward, a walk that grew quicker with each step, dress shoes ringing off the concrete. He rounded the corner of the building, headed for the bathroom.

The door was closed. A heavy padlock dangled from the latch.

"No, no, no," Halden said, turning fast, staring at the parking lot, remembering the sound of the engine driving away.

He felt a terrible heaviness settle on him. It was over. Forget bringing them in himself. Forget being the guy with all the answers, the hero cop that saved the day. They were on the run now, probably on their way out of town. It was time to call in the cavalry. And suffer all the consequences that came with that. He sighed, rubbed at his forehead.

What had happened to spook the two of them? Tom had been nervous about the lawyer question, but Halden couldn't imagine them running for that. And Anna, she'd been on the phone with her—

Wait.

He sprinted for the car, thinking of the folder Lawrence Tully had given him at the steakhouse, all the personal information he'd collected on the Reeds. Bank statements, bills, credit history. Addresses and family members.

Fuck the cavalry. He could still pull this off.

"PLEASE," the sister said. "Please, he's scared." Even by the murky light filtering through the closed blinds, he could see her eyes, wide as a girl in those Japanese comics.

Jack felt for her, he really did. No way he was going to hurt a baby, but she didn't know that, and he couldn't imagine what was going on in her head, the raw-veined panic of it. Still, this was the job, and sometimes the job was ugly. He set the phone down. "That was good," he said. "You did good."

There was a clatter from the other room, a crash like pans falling to the floor. He heard Marshall curse.

The woman winced. "Please," she said, and took a step forward. Raised an arm, the fingers shaking. Her skin was pale, and he could smell her from here, the fear sweat. "Please."

"Please what?"

"He's only. He's. Please. My son."

Jack looked down at the baby cradled in his left arm. A cute kid, all cheeks and wide, curious eyes. "Don't worry," he said. "This will all be over soon." He looked back up at her. "I promise."

20

TOM HAD BEEN DOWN THIS STREET more times than he could count, but everything looked different now. Brighter and in sharper focus. He could see the detail in every leaf as though each was on a distinct and brilliant plane. It was almost overwhelming, all that clarity.

"You have the key?" Anna clenched the steering wheel at ten and two. Tom patted his pocket, stopped his knee from rocking.

They'd fled south on Lake Shore, and every moment he'd expected blue lights behind. He had seen the effort it cost her not to put the gas to the floor, to stay at the same five-miles-over everyone else was maintaining.

"I'll do it," he'd said. "I'll bring it to him."

"No. Both of us."

He knew that tone, hadn't argued. Instead, he'd just quietly made a plan: After they picked up the money, he'd hop in the car, lock the doors, and leave her behind. No point both of them strolling up like sheep.

But then Anna came up with a better idea. It was simple, it was elegant, and it protected Sara and Julian. Downside, it left the two of them screwed. But there were things worth fighting for. Worth dying for, if need be. It was funny, though. With everything else stripped away, life came down to just the two of them. They would make it through together or they would go down together. Not long ago, all he'd wanted was for them to get back to the place where they stood two against the world.

Careful what you wish for. "There's a spot," he said.

She nodded, pulled the Pontiac to the side, threw it in reverse, and parallel parked. The location was good, halfway down the block from Sara's house, far enough for their purposes.

Anna turned off the engine, and it was like that triggered some gland in his head, got the chemicals flowing. His fingers tingled and his armpits were suddenly swamped. He took steady breaths, wanting to be ready but not so deep in fight-or-flight that he was nothing but jangling nerves. Anna opened her cell, then closed it again. She set it in the cup holder, then looked at the clock. The shrubs outside. A Cubs flag fluttering from a porch. Everywhere but at him.

"We're going to be okay," he said, not believing it. "Once he has his money, there's no reason to kill us."

She turned, lips quivering. For a moment she hesitated; then she threw herself across the seat, wrapping her arms around his neck, his back, ratcheting against him like she would never let go. "I love you so goddamn much."

He smiled into her neck, ran his fingers through her hair. "Shhh."

For a moment they held each other, and then she leaned back. "If we make it through, I'm going to—I'll never—"

"I know," he said. "Me too." He glanced at the clock. Thirty minutes since they'd left the beach. He wanted more than anything to stay right here. "It's time."

Anna wiped at her cheeks with the back of her hand. Drew a trembling breath, then a stronger one. Opened the cell phone and pressed three keys. "I'm ready."

He nodded, feeling a sick heat through his bowels. He opened the car door with a squeak, swiveled to get a foot out.

"Tom." Her voice a levee holding back too much. He turned, and for her sake made himself smile. She managed a thin smile back, eyes shining. "Be careful."

He winked. Then he shut the door and started down the sidewalk before his nerve collapsed. Wolfram was a quiet street, trees and brick apartment complexes and the odd town house. He remembered helping Sara move in, angling her futon through the front door, hauling an armoire that had to weigh ten thousand pounds. Afterward, they'd headed to a nearby bar she knew, place called Delilah's. Great music. The three of them had pounded Old Style and Jim Beam, sweaty and laughing and singing along.

He pushed the thoughts out of his mind. Too much at stake to be any less than a hundred percent. The clouds had begun to break, patches of scattered sun spilling through the trees. His mouth was dry, and his legs felt light. Tom dug in his pocket, came out with the brass key clutched in his good hand. Sara's blinds were all closed, but he thought he saw movement at one of them. His heart felt like it might smash through his ribs.

He stepped onto the porch.

*   *   *

ANNA WATCHED HIM WALK AWAY, and every step cranked barbed wire around her heart. All this time they had been so caught up in chasing the things they thought they wanted, they had forgotten the things they already had. *Never again.* She thought it repeatedly, a mantra that would keep him safe and bring him back to her. That was all she wanted now.

And all she wouldn't get. No matter what lies they had told each other, Jack wouldn't let them live. No chance. But at least they'd save Sara and Julian.

With the phone in hand, she slid low in her seat until she could just barely see Tom climb the steps to Sara's porch. As he reached the door, it swung inward. She couldn't see inside, but she saw her beautiful husband hold up the key. He stood calm, strong, like trading his life for his family's was the simplest choice in the world, and in the moment she most risked losing him she loved him more than she ever had.

A STRANGE SORT OF CALM settled on him. Facing the monster, the fear was still there, as much a part of the moment as the air he breathed. But it felt like something apart. He held the key in front of him, willing his hand not to shake.

Jack stood in the door frame with his arms crossed. White gauze stained with blood wrapped his left forearm. All the blinds were closed, and the light inside the house was dim, but not so dark that Tom couldn't make out the shoulder holster, the way Jack's fingers fell lightly, almost accidentally, on the handle of his gun. The moment stretched like a power line, so taut and charged it hummed.

Finally Jack said, "Where's the missus?"

"Watching from somewhere safe, with 911 dialed into her cell phone and her thumb on the Send button."

"Somewhere safe, huh?" Jack gave a bemused sort of smile. He leaned out the door, glancing left and right down the block. "You couldn't just bring my money, could you? You people, always complicating things."

"Nope. Simplifying them." He took a breath, could taste the air. "You don't want Sara or Julian. You're willing to use them, but all you're really after is the money, right?" He shrugged. "So swap us for them, and we'll take you to the storage locker where we stowed it."

"Let me get this straight. I walk out with you, hop in your car, and you take me to my money. And if I don't, Anna calls 911. Is that it?"

Tom nodded.

"It can take ten, fifteen minutes for cops to respond to a 911 call," Jack said. "You know how long that could feel?"

Tom's mouth went dry, but he didn't flinch. "That won't get you what you want." His hands were shaking, and he put them against his legs to hide it. This was the anchor everything hung on, the assumption that no matter how angry Jack might be, what he wanted more than anything was the cash. If that calculation turned out to be wrong, this would get uglier than he dared imagine. "Just let me make sure that Sara and Julian are okay, and then let's go get your money."

For a long moment, Jack just stared. Then he shrugged, stepped back inside the house. "Come on in."

Stale light filtered through the closed blinds, making the familiar seem sinister. The air was thick with the smell of baby powder and something else, a faintly burned tang he couldn't identify. Jack gestured toward the closed bedroom door. "In there."

Tom walked ahead, back tingling with the knowledge that Jack was behind him. *Easy. It's working. There's no reason for him to jump you. He knows Anna will call the police if he does, knows they'll respond fast if she tells them who he is. So just do this and get out. Every step forward is one away from this house.*

He put his hand on the bedroom door and pushed it open. The light was faint and dusty, and the smells stronger. He stood for a moment to let his eyes adjust, vague shapes resolving into a bed, the armoire he remembered hauling, the crib in the corner. He could see the outline of Julian lying within it.

A pair of legs stuck out from beside the bed.

Tom took the three steps to them without realizing he was moving. Sara lay facedown amid a pile of junk, postcards and books from the night table drawer yanked out of the frame. In the dim light, the mess of blood and tissue that used to be her back looked almost black.

Behind him, he heard the snick of metal against leather, the gun coming out, and then Jack said, "It was a nice plan, Tom. But I've got a different one in mind."

ANNA HATED being helpless.

Sunlight danced on the dashboard. She watched Tom on the porch, saw Jack lean out the door, look in her direction. Fought the urge to duck lower, knowing the motion would catch his eye.

When she was a child, she'd pretended her eyes were laser beams, that they could cut and shear everything she saw. Now, pressed against the seat, powerless to do anything but wait and watch, she wished for those laser eyes. Imagined them blasting through the window, spearing into Jack, a beam of light that tore him open, cut him in half.

Her mind raced, thinking of all the ways this could fail. She had the windows half-open, but the porch was too far away for her to hear what Tom was saying. She stared, watched him rest his good hand against his thigh. After a long pause, he walked forward into the house.

She let herself breathe again. Good. They had agreed that if Jack pulled the gun, Tom would signal. The fact that he was walking in on his own meant it was working.

Still, this would be the worst part. Her palms were sweaty and her heart banged and her head hurt. A moment passed, then another. Tom wouldn't dally, but he might have to calm Sara down, make sure she understood not to call the police. It could be a couple of minutes. On the other hand, if things were going wrong, every second she didn't call was one more he might be getting hurt. She counted breaths, her thumb on the button.

She was just about to press it when there was a knock on her window, and she turned to stare down the barrel of a gun.

For a moment, the world was just visual, nothing but images flashing against his eyes. The slippery ruin of Sara's body, wet tissue exposed, the smell rising, an animal smell, copper and worse, and then he remembered the way she used to laugh, throwing her head back, and how she gave the best hugs, her arms tight around his back, and thought of what that would feel like now, and his stomach seized up. Something awful and bitter slid up his throat, in his mouth and nostrils, and he fought the urge to vomit. His eyes cataloged details he didn't want: the pool of blood spilled across the cheap carpet, the wood of the drawer splintered and torn, a flash of metal, something shiny he couldn't make out just beneath the bed.

"It's hard, isn't?" Jack spoke from behind. "To see what we really are. You can go your whole life knowing somebody, and then." He sucked air through his teeth. "I'd say I'm sorry, but then, it's not my fault, is it?"

Sara. Oh God, poor Sara. Then another thought hit, and he whirled, took a step toward the crib. Julian lay on his back. His eyes were open. Tom's whole being shook, something inside him gathering itself into a howl that made no sound.

And then the boy blinked and gurgled, staring up at Tom.

"The kid is fine," Jack said. "Your sister-in-law, well, she tried to run. Chose the wrong direction."

Tom turned, started forward. He was going to beat this fucker to death with his bare hands if he had to, for what he'd done to Sara, to their lives.

Jack raised the gun faster than Tom would have thought possible, leveling it square on his forehead. Against his will, he froze. His good hand balled into a trembling fist. When he spoke, his voice came in tatters. "Anna is calling 911 right now."

Jack shook his head, smiled. "I'm afraid not."

* * *

ADRENALINE LIT HER UP, and she yelped, not quite a scream, more startled than anything else.

Halden stood outside the car door with his gun pointed at her, the same gun that had caught her eye every time she'd seen him, the one she'd wondered what it would be like to lift and hold and point, only now it was aimed at her.

"Set down the phone and get out of the car," he said.

She stared, swallowed, blinked. "You don't—"

"*Get the fuck out of the car.*" His voice was commanding, and she found herself reaching for the door handle. He stepped back, the gun level. "Slowly."

"Detective, this. Tom, he's inside that house, with—you have to get out of sight. If he sees you—"

"Get out of the car, turn around, and put your hands on your head."

"But—"

"*Now.*"

She stared into eyes gone cold and professional, realized that all he saw was a criminal, someone tied up in the death of a cop. Worse, a woman who had lied to him, embarrassed him. The thought made her heart sink in her chest. There was nothing more stubborn than a man humiliated. Somehow she had to calm him down, explain what was going on in the house. Tom could be bringing Jack out any minute. If he saw a cop here, everything would fall apart.

The best thing would be to go along, put him at ease. She opened the door, stepped out, keeping her hands at chest height. "I'm not going to do anything. You don't need the gun."

"Turn around and put your hands on your head."

Her mind raced. Tom was depending on her. "Listen to me. Jack

Witkowski is in that house"—she nodded with her head—"that was him that called me. I'm sorry we ran, but he has my sister."

He shook his head. "Here's what's going to happen. I'm going to cuff you, and then I'm going to cuff Tom. Then you two are going to tell me where the money is. I'm going to walk into the station with you in one arm, Tom in the other, and that cash slung on my back."

"Didn't you *hear* me?" She stared at Halden, realizing that it wasn't just a professional distance in his eyes. He had the same fixity of vision she'd only recently overthrown. For her the blindness had centered on the money; for him it was something else, maybe, but the intensity was the same. She had to reach him. "Listen to me. Jack is here. He's here *now*."

The cop said, "Turn around and put your hands on your head."

Then there was a sound, a strangely familiar *shhk-chhk* sound, loud and to her left.

That got Halden's attention, his eyes widening as he spun fast, the gun leading the way, and she turned in the same direction, saw a figure, a man, *oh Jesus,* the other guy from the mall, a shotgun pointing right at her.

The blast was louder than she would ever have imagined.

A ROAR CAME FROM OUTSIDE, loud and sharp and close. A gunshot, and then another.

Anna. She was out there alone. And she didn't have a gun.

Tom knew right then that she was gone, and nothing else mattered. The howl that had been building inside broke in a terrible roar, and he threw himself forward. The rage was stronger and crueler than anything he had ever known, and he lowered his head and charged, slamming his shoulder into the man's gut, straining forward with every muscle and sinew, the breath whistling out of Jack's lungs, and something falling, the gun, shaken loose, and Tom kept pushing, slamming him up against the door frame. He hammered a punch into Jack's stomach, then wound up and did it again. This close he could smell sweat and aftershave, could see the texture of his shirt, the perfect straps of the empty shoulder holster. He would tear him apart, yank his arms from their sockets and twist his head off his body. Jack brought his elbows down on Tom's back, the impact like lightning, but he wasn't letting go, he would never let go, he'd take everything this fucker could dish out. He threw another furious blow into the man's side and was rewarded with a sharp gasp, and knew that he was going to win.

Then Jack's right hand squirmed between their bodies to find Tom's left. He gripped the bandaged fingers and jerked them back, and Tom's legs gave in a flash of white agony.

THE WAY HALDEN stepped backward into a shaft of sun, it looked like the light had speared him, like the sun had turned him red and wet and yanked his insides out. His mouth was open as if surprised. Anna stared, one hand reaching, like if she could catch him, she could somehow put him back together, and then there was another roar and his body spun and splashed and the pistol fell from his hand and she turned back to see the man from the mall with a shotgun raised to his shoulder, turning now toward her.

She ran.

There was another roar, and the windshield exploded in a rain of sparkling prisms. Her foot hit the edge of the curb and she stumbled, nearly fell, but got her balance and lunged forward, aiming for a narrow path that ran between two buildings. Her brain was on automatic, an animal desire to get away, she was every hunted thing that had ever run through the forest, and the corner of the building blew up, brick chunks flying, one of them touching her face with razor edges, red dust like sand, and then she was down the path, her arms pumping. Behind her she heard a curse, and the sound of heavy footfalls.

THERE WAS NOTHING but the roar of blood in his ears and the pain shivering up his nerves, the agony so sharp and hot it seemed to blend senses, to be something he could taste and smell and hear. Tom told himself to get up, that he'd been winning, but Jack got hold of his little finger, the broken one, and wrenched it sideways, and the air sucked out of his lungs.

A fist smacked into his nose, the blunt intimacy stunning, stars popping behind his retinas. He felt Jack let go of his hand, and rocked forward, hugging it to his chest, fighting for breath. His head was inches from Sara's body, and he imagined what the bullet would feel like, how he would fall across her, and he welcomed it.

He told himself to move, but his body didn't respond. Darkness beckoned, and from it, Anna.

IN HIS HURRY, Marshall hadn't seated the shotgun properly, and the stock had twice punched his shoulder like a giant's fist. Adrenaline muted the pain, but the mistake had caused him to miss two easy shots on the woman.

It didn't matter. When he'd played ball, he could clock a sprint to first faster than anybody. He raced after her, holding the Remington one-handed.

The path between the buildings was narrow, maybe three feet, and by the time he'd hit it, she was rounding the corner. He leaned into his run. There was a rattle of wood and metal, and he burst into a back patio just in time to see her drop to the other side of a wooden privacy fence. He charged it dead-on, planted a foot and let the momentum carry him enough to grab the top one-handed, then rocked over and down to the concrete of an alley. He raised the Remington, but she was already spinning down another path, heading back the way they'd come.

A mistake. As long as she'd zigzagged and used the cover, he would have had to run her down. But now she was heading back toward the street. Jack had said she was the smart one, but the silly cooze wasn't thinking, because the street was wide and clear, and a magnum slug was accurate to a hundred yards.

Marshall took the corner with his left hand against the edge to keep his velocity, and then poured it on for the length of the path.

Rehearsed the moves in his head: break clear, stop, spread his feet, seat the shotgun properly.

Anna Reed had maybe ten seconds to live.

A FIST HIT HIM AGAIN, this time in the cheek, and Tom's head snapped sideways. The world was wobbly and wet.

"Fucker," Jack said above him, his voice guttural. "Mother-fucker."

A boot cracked one of his ribs. In his crib, Julian cried, his voice thin.

"I bet you wish you were back in your safe little life now," Jack said. "I just bet you do."

A strange calm had settled over him. Everything hurt, but the pain, like the fear, was too large to grasp. He almost welcomed the blows. Anna was gone. The harder Jack beat him, the sooner he would be with her again. That was all that mattered. His vision was screened by cotton, but when he looked at Sara's face, he thought he saw a strange peace in it. Idly, he wondered why she had run in here, where she would be trapped. Trying for the phone on the night table, maybe.

He saw Jack bend over, push through the junk on the ground, then come up with the key. "It doesn't matter anyway," Jack said. "There aren't that many storage lockers in Chicago. I'll find it eventually."

The thought of Jack winning brought anger, and a keener pain than his injuries. But it wasn't enough. Not without her.

*   *   *

ANNA'S FEET HURT, and her face where it was cut. She could hear the man behind her. She didn't think he was any closer, but he hadn't fallen behind, either.

Almost there. You have to make it. Tom needs you.

She tore down the path, one hand tracing the edge of the building. The street lay just ahead. Safety. The man's footfalls grew louder as she burst into sunlight. She'd ended up right where she'd hoped to.

Funny, the way the thing had drawn her eye from the first moment she'd seen it, weeks ago. Like she'd known even then. It was heavier than she'd expected, and felt wonderful.

She turned around and leaned across the hood of her car, arms braced on broken safety glass, hating the seconds passing, the time she wasn't able to help Tom. The fear for him and the frustration and the hatred all boiled up in her like a scream.

When Marshall came into sight, she let it go, and yelling words she didn't hear, Anna pointed the gun she had taken from Halden and pulled the trigger again and again, until his chest was pocked with red, until he fell backward and slid down the wall with an expression of disbelief frozen on his features, until the pistol stopped kicking in her hand.

THE PUNCH SHUT HIS LEFT EYE with a sick feeling. The end was coming soon. Tom knew it, could see by the look on Jack's face as the man squatted in front of him.

"Okay, Tom. Save me the trouble. Tell me where that storage locker is, and this will all stop."

What difference did it make? Jack would find it sooner or later. And a bullet was all that stood between him and Anna.

Then he remembered that Jack had killed her, had killed Sara, had torn their life apart. Had taken everything that mattered to them. All for money. Bits of colored paper. He straightened as much as he could, his body barely under his control. Forced a smile, tasting blood from the broken nose. He coughed and then said, "Fuck you."

The man stiffened, and Tom braced for a blow. But Jack chuckled, said, "You know, it's funny. I kind of like you. You and her both. You've got spunk." He laughed again, then reached out to pat Tom's cheek in a soft slap. "It's good that you're being a man about this. Taking responsibility." He stood up, stepped back. "Took you long enough."

And as Jack moved out of the way, Tom saw what Sara had been going for. The flash of metal he'd seen earlier. A gun. A snub-nose pistol inches from her hand, just under the bed.

He blinked, shook his head. The gun was still there. He willed himself forward.

His limbs hung heavy. His body throbbed. He couldn't move. Jack walked back to the wall Tom had driven him into earlier. Where he had dropped his own gun.

Tom stared. Knew he wouldn't make it. He'd taken too much, been hurt too badly. And Anna. If he did kill Jack, he wouldn't get to her. His sweet girl, gone.

Then came a series of cracks, gunshots, one tumbling after the other. They were loud and fast and obscene. But he barely noticed them. Because above them, he heard Anna. Shouting his name, over and over, like a prayer. She was still alive. His wife was alive.

Tom crawled forward, his ribs stabbing, world wobbling, but none of that mattered, he put it all aside, and then he had the pistol and was turning, spinning on his knees, just as Jack came up with his own gun.

WHEN SHE HEARD THE SHOTS from inside the house, Anna screamed. Her legs seized up. The empty pistol fell to clatter against the concrete.

Too late. She was too late. Nothing mattered now.

Later, lying awake at night, listening to the steady rhythm of Julian's breathing, she would remember this moment, unspool it like thread. The moment everything changed. The impossible sunlight against her back, the shifting sounds of leaves, all of it going on as though nothing had happened. The way the world didn't notice that it had ended.

Time lost its grip. She stood still, wanting to disappear, wanting to run into the house, but not moving. She could hear sirens growing closer, police responding to gunfire on this quiet residential street. A bird sang above.

None of it mattered.

A sound from inside drew her attention. Something was moving. A figure, a shadow in the dim light. A man with a pistol in his hand. Moving slow. Coming her way. She decided to stand right there and let Jack kill her.

And then she saw that it was Tom.

It was like being born again, the two of them newly made by the heat of a terrible fire. For a moment, they just stared at each other. Then, as police cars swooped down the block, all force and fury, she ran to him, and they came together, gripping each other to keep from falling, and she swore, in that moment, that she would never let go again.

Ever.

21

"... ACCORDING TO POLICE SPOKESMAN Patrick Camden, investigation into last week's fatal shootings in a Lincoln Park mall has been closed. The two men responsible have been identified as Jack Witkowski, age forty-three, and Marshall Richards, thirty-nine, both killed in a shoot-out later that day that left several others dead, including a decorated police officer. After leaving the mall, Witkowski and Richards allegedly killed Sara Hughes, a single mother living nearby, and hid in her home for several hours.

"Both Witkowski and Richards have extensive criminal records, and are considered prime suspects in what has become known as the Shooting Star robbery. That incident, which took place on April 24, left two men dead. While rumors abounded that a large sum of money was also stolen, police have released no information on that, and no money has been recovered—"

Malachi leaned forward and shut the radio off. Always interesting, hearing what was reported versus what actually happened. The media had spun Tom and Anna Reed as civilian heroes who helped bring down a pair of cop killers, but the police weren't sharing many details as to exactly what that meant. Malachi had friends on the force, and from what he'd heard, there were plenty of people who wanted to hang the Reeds, but the thing had turned political. A decision to close the books had come from on high. With no fresh information, the news reports were already getting shorter. Soon something else would happen, and the story would be forgotten. The world was a play of shadows.

"That's it," Andre said, nodding toward a blocky building with a big orange sign.

Malachi nodded, said nothing. He wasn't sure what this was, the game at work here, and over the years he'd found that when he didn't know what was going on, it was better to think than to speak. Andre parked the Mercedes half a block away. Outside, blue sky burned from horizon to horizon. A short white girl walked three dogs trying to go three different directions.

Strange situation. A lot to weigh, and not enough information to do it. Just a cryptic telephone call and his instincts. Still. Risk nothing, get nothing.

Malachi leaned forward, slid off his jacket, then slipped out of the shoulder holster and passed the Sig to Andre. "Put that in the case in the trunk. Yours too."

The big man got out. Malachi waited till the trunk was closed before he stepped out himself. The police needed probable cause to search a vehicle, and permission or a warrant to open a locked case found in the trunk. He didn't see that as the play, but always best to be safe.

The front desk was manned by a bored brother with a scraggly mustache. Malachi nodded as he approached, said, "Think you're holding a key for me?" The dude passed him a small manila envelope.

"Elevator?"

"Back and to your right."

They rode to the fifth floor in silence, then exited into a bare hall lit by fluorescents. Malachi passed the key, and Andre bent down to fit it into the lock and haul the door up. "Moth-er-fucker."

On the floor in the center of the small locker was a pile of bundled hundreds. An envelope sat atop. Malachi stepped inside and shut the door, then eyeballed the pile, figured it about three. Andre looked at him, eyebrows raised.

"Grab me that envelope. Don't touch nothing else."

It was a standard number ten, unsealed. Malachi opened it, took out the folded paper, shook it open.

No more choosing sides.
This is poison.
We don't want it.

That was it, just three lines, typed on plain white paper and unsigned. Malachi read it twice, then folded the letter and tucked it into his jacket pocket. "Huh." The fluorescents buzzed overhead.

"What you want to do?"

Malachi looked over at his man, shook his head. "You kidding? Pack that shit up."

Poison he knew.

JULY
2007

22

THE SMELL OF FADING LILACS mingled with the faint salt tang of the sea. Tom sat on the wooden bench. He'd read somewhere that lilac was good for headaches, but it never helped his. Dr. Carney said the migraines were something he'd have to live with. "What," she'd said and shrugged, "broken nose, fractured cheekbone, teeth knocked out, concussion, you expect your body to throw a party?"

It didn't matter. He leaned back, pinched the bridge of his nose between two fingers, ignored the wobbly necked feeling of needles in his eyeballs. When he thought about that night, a year gone now, two thoughts warred. The first was the memory of Anna shouting his name, and how, in that moment, he came back to life, resurrected by her. He liked that part.

The other was the memory of pointing the gun at Jack Witkowski and pulling the trigger. That he didn't like. Not because he regretted it; on the contrary, he hoped there was a hell so Jack could burn in it. But Tom was afraid that that moment would be the one that would define his life, would outweigh every precious thing. That on the day he died, what he would remember was not

Anna's eyes or Julian's smile, but Jack Witkowski, still leering as half his head was torn away.

The sky was fading orange to purple, the moment of dusk that seemed darker than night. He liked the quiet here, in the garden behind their little house near the shore. It was a good place to think. For a while the world he'd believed in had turned to smoke, and it took effort to rebuild.

The poor police, he'd almost felt sorry for them. Between the Shooting Star and Century Mall, they had had two major incidents in less than a month, both in upscale, politically connected areas. Dead cops and dead citizens and an orphaned child. Two dangerous bad guys who had escaped, only to be killed by two completely normal people—completely normal people they suspected had stolen a lot of money. A mess.

At first he and Anna had started to tell the whole truth. The detective had stopped them, left them in the interview room for a long time. When the door opened again, a different kind of cop came through. He still wore a star on his hip, but the suit that covered it cost a lot more, and he talked like a lawyer.

It took twenty minutes of his careful leading before Tom realized that the police wanted nothing to do with the whole truth. Not on this case. Because with Jack and Marshall dead, all they could hope to do was recover the money for a millionaire who wouldn't admit it had been stolen, who would happily pay the same amount again to keep things quiet. In trade, they'd convict two civilians who had avenged the death of several of their own, and land a one-year-old in foster care. All of which was secondary to their real concern, of course—that the whole affair would play out on the front pages and the five o'clock news.

So solid ground had turned to smoke, and suddenly he and Anna were free to go, taking with them an unsubtle suggestion to keep their mouths shut. The truth was that sometimes the truth wasn't enough.

Afterward, things had gotten worse. There was Sara's funeral, the agony of coming face-to-face with what they'd done. Anna, shaking and pale as milk, staring at her sister's waxy, too-pink face against the casket pillow. Reporters waiting at the cemetery. Pictures in the paper, people recognizing them on the streets, staring with vampire eyes. The discovery of what Jack had done to their home, burning the last connection to the people they used to be. And worst of all, the lonely midnight hours when the demons whispered that they weren't done paying. That there was more to come.

But there were also the quiet spaces when they held each other, talking and crying and making love. And there was Julian. He was a joy, and he was a duty, and he was maybe all that kept them going. The demons whispered most about him, about what would happen, someday, when they— It didn't matter. If there was one thing he and Anna could promise, even in this world, it was that Julian would be loved intensely. That was all that mattered.

Overhead, the stars were coming out. A backward way to think, of course. They'd been there all the time. He just hadn't been able to see them.

JULIAN SAID, "Momma, gobba la," and smiled.

"That's right," Anna said. "Mommy gobba la." She buttoned

his onesie, bright green with an orange monkey, and pulled the cotton blanket up to his belly. Sometimes when he cried there was nothing she could do to console him, no matter that she held him and whispered and swayed, and in those moments, she couldn't help but wonder if he was crying for his real mother. If there was some smell or sense of safety that she would never be able to duplicate, not quite. Tonight, though, he was happy.

Anna flipped on his night-light and turned off the lamp, then got his favorite stuffed animal, a one-eyed, tentacled thing worn and spotted with drool. He reached as soon as he saw it, little hands opening and closing. She touched his cheek, felt the smoothness of it. Every day he seemed more perfect than the one before. Softly she began to sing, going with the last thing she'd been listening to, Kevin Tihista, sweet and sad, "Do-o-n't worry baby, I'll keep an eye on you, till you know what to do." Julian stared, eyes sparkling and then, slowly, closing.

She sat by the crib and listened to him, and to the sounds of a South Carolina night drifting in the open window. After a while she heard the screen door creak and bang, and she tiptoed out of the bedroom. She found Tom in the kitchen, one cabinet open, shaking Advil into his palm. "Headache?"

"It's nothing."

She pressed herself to his back, arms around his chest, rising and falling with his breath. He leaned into her, put a hand up to cover hers. For a moment they stood silent, just the buzz of the fridge and their thoughts.

"Are you okay?"

She shook her head against his shoulders.

"What is it?" He turned to face her.

"I was giving Julian his bath. He was slapping the water with both hands, and he started smiling, this huge thing that stretched to about his knees. It . . ." She trailed off, glanced away.

"What?"

"He looked just like—it was the way she used to smile."

Tom stared for a moment, then pulled her into his arms. He stroked her hair and pressed her to him, and she took the comfort he offered. It was a thing they passed back and forth, that stock of comfort, each sharing it when the other needed it, nurturing and tending it and helping it slowly grow. She let the warmth flow through her, let it ease the pressure of memory.

Then he said, "I finished."

"YOU DID?" Anna let go, stepped back. Her T-shirt was damp from the bath. The crow's-feet he'd first spotted last year had deepened to lines. Tom gave a half smile, put a hand to her face. "Yeah," he said.

"Can I see?"

He nodded, led her through the house to his office. The lamp on the desk spilled golden light. He opened a drawer and took out a thick sheaf of paper, maybe three hundred pages, then gestured to a chair and sat in the one opposite. "It's rough."

"Did you tell the truth?"

"I tried."

She held out her hand. He passed her the manuscript, leaned back to watch her read the first page, the letter. Her face ran a gamut, first a smile, then a tightening of the lips, then a wetness to the eyes. Finally she finished, set the page down on top of the others.

"It's perfect," she said.

"Are you going to read the rest?"

"Not yet."

He nodded. There was so much between them now, they hardly needed to speak sometimes. He could see her wrestling the same things he fought, trying to find her way to a happiness that didn't forget the cost. A joy that was built on sadness.

"We're going to be all right, aren't we? Someday?"

Tom rubbed at his cheek. "I've been thinking about what you said, about this being like an old fairy tale?"

She nodded.

"The thing is, stories end, but life keeps going. All we can do is try to take what we learned and do better." He hesitated. "We just have to find our way through the part that comes after the story."

Anna looked at him with an expression no one had named. She said, "I love you."

"Come here." He leaned back in the chair.

She set down the thick bundle of pages, the book he'd always said he'd write, then crawled into his lap. He wrapped his arms around her and squeezed. Took one last look at the manuscript, and then closed his eyes and concentrated on the moment.

It was what they had. It was enough.

Dear Julian,

As I write this, you're a baby; when you read it, you'll be a young man. I don't know how to prepare you for what you'll find here. When you're done, you won't think of us the same way. You might even hate us.

That scares us more than anything in the world. Your mother and I considered keeping this a secret, and some part of me wants to. I want to tell myself that so long as we raise you to be better than us, it will make amends for what we've done. But that's a lie. We won't have paid in full until you know the truth.

That's what these pages are, the truth, as best as we can tell it. It's the story of how we became who we are now, and of how you became our son. There were parts I had to guess at, things we couldn't know. But I tried to tell you everything— even the things that might drive you away.

As you read, remember that we were greedy, yes, but only when it came to love.

Your mother and I had a conversation once about what the point was. About what there was to believe in if the world can change so quickly, if there aren't any absolute guidelines, or anything you can trust completely. And she said that maybe it was just this: Live a good life. Be nice to people.

Have a family, and love them well.

We love you, son. Always.

Chapter One

The smile was famous. Jack Witkowski wasn't particularly a fan, but he'd seen those teeth plenty of times . . .

ACKNOWLEDGMENTS

This book wouldn't exist without a whole passel of other people. My sincerest thanks to:

My friend and exceptional agent Scott Miller, who always gets it done; his assistant, the ever-cheerful Stephanie Sun; and Sarah Self, who rocks Hollywood. When people ask if I have any advice regarding agents, it comes down to this—get mine.

My editor Ben Sevier, a man on his way to living-legend status. It's amazing how much improved a book is once he's done with it.

All the other folks at Dutton, especially Brian Tart, Trena Keating, Lisa Johnson, Rachel Ekstrom, Rich Hasselberger, Carrie Swetonic, Aline Akelis, Erika Imranyi, and Susan Schwartz.

Over coffee and beer, during panic breakfasts and late-night brainstorms, Sean Chercover, Joe Konrath, and Michael Cook repeatedly saved my butt.

Thanks to my early readers: Brad Boivin, Peter Boivin, Jenny Carney, Darwyn Jones, and Dana Litoff. A special thanks to Blake Crouch for a particularly thorough and accomplished read.

The crime fiction community in general, especially Jon and

Acknowledgments

Ruth Jordan, Judy Bobalik, Ken Bruen, Lee Child, Ali Karim, Dennis Lehane, Laura Lippman, David Morrell, T. Jefferson Parker, Patricia Pinianski, Sarah Weinman, and all the folks in Killer Year and The Outfit Collective. Thanks also to Brett and Kiri Carlson, artists extraordinaire.

The booksellers and librarians—without you, we got nothing.

All the friends who keep me sane, and the ones who undo their work.

My brother Matt and my parents, Sally and Anthony Sakey, whose support never blinks, much less wavers.

And finally, my wife g.g., who has all the good parts of Anna and none of the bad. I love you, babe.

ABOUT THE AUTHOR

Marcus Sakey is the acclaimed author of *The Blade Itself* and *At the City's Edge*. His books have been translated into numerous languages, and the film rights have been sold to major studios. Born in Flint, Michigan, he now lives in Chicago with his wife.